A SEAL'S HONOR

CAYCE POPONEA

D1715255

Edited by ELIZABETH SIMONSON
Cover by JADA D'LEE
Cover Model RYAN HARMON
Photography by ERIC BATTERSHELL

WRITE HAND PUBLICATIONS

A SEAL'S HONOR

CHAPTER ONE

RYAN

"I'm sorry, Sir, but you must turn off your mobile device before we taxi away from the gate."

My attention is robbed from the latest email to hit my inbox, to the friendly face of the flight attendant. "My apologies, Ma'am." Selecting airplane mode, I hold it up for her inspection, sharing my signature grin to lighten the mood. "Got to love electronic leashes."

"Thank you," she smiles, her perusal of my upper body doesn't go unnoticed. I wonder how shocked she would be if she knew how many times I've flown halfway across the world, a cell phone to my ear, no harm ever coming to any of our instruments or inhibiting our ability to take off?

"Enjoy the flight."

Glancing out the window, I relax into the marginally comfortable seating first-class affords. With my long legs and broad shoulders, the more economical seats in the safer part of the plane would have me twisted like a pretzel. With the stewardess checking on the couple behind me, I open the photos on my phone, admiring the smiling faces of my teammates and their wives from the wedding. Everyone looks so relaxed and happy, even Zach, who's lost more sleep than the rest of us, worried something would happen to his wife and unborn child before we captured the last member of the Konar family.

While I didn't have as much to lose, not a single threat was ever made to a member of my family, this mission had changed me. Somehow, somewhere, along the way my ideas of what matters in life shifted. I want to be happy, to have the type of joy I see in the faces on my screen. Feel the kind of love Kennedy has for Zach by giving him a child. Know the level of forgiveness Rayne extended to Matt. Live the dream with your one true love like Jordan and Aiden. Experience deep-rooted love at first sight like Eleni and Alex. Most of all, I want the level of devotion Logan has for Harper, willing to give up everything to be with her.

When the tone for the fasten seatbelt sign sounds overhead, the gentleman beside me opens his laptop, logs onto the airlines free WIFI and settles in as the headlines of the day fill his screen. I'm about to close my eyes to sleep the duration of the flight when I see a familiar name spelled out in block letters.

CNN reporter Lindsey Jennings on Senator Green and his plans to run for President.

Turning back to the window, my heart crashes from seeing her name. We'd been happy once, unable to keep our hands off each other, but it's been months since we shared a bed or exchanged a kind word. Each of us blaming the other for the distance, her with a budding career and me with my military obligations. I foolishly assumed the moment I look off the uniform and moved to DC things between us would return to what they once were. I'd been

2

wrong, in my absence, Lindsey had created a life, one I didn't exactly fit into.

We met when she was filming a documentary around the military and its treatment of refugees. Some idiot thought it would be a great idea to allow a civilian camera crew in the middle of a turf war on the Syrian border.

My team had been on a training mission in Tajikistan, testing out a new explosive the government was considering, when the powers at be became nervous. My team was the closest to the camp, so we were ordered to pack up and go babysit. Grabbing an available helo, we collectively decided to give them something to film by rappelling from the side of the helicopter into the rendezvous point.

Once on the ground, we met up with the crew, where I got my first glimpse of Lindsey Jennings. She was straight out of Hollywood with her inches of makeup, perfect hair, high-heeled designer boots and clothes which wouldn't last a day out in the field. She shamelessly flirted with my Lieutenant, who returned the favor by tossing a pack of baby wipes at her, telling her to wipe the makeup off her face. She argued when we made them show us everything in their bags, forcing them to leave behind cell phones and anything that would identify them, including photos.

Less than an hour into the journey to the refugee camp, Doc, our medic, broke the heel off her boots and wrapped her foot with gauze to help with the blisters. She threw a fit when he pulled a shemagh out of his pack and wrapped it around her head to camouflage her blonde hair. She argued it clashed with her jacket, but Doc pointed out the men behind the guns pointed at us in the surrounding hills didn't care if she was color coordinated or not, her blonde hair would bring a hefty reward.

Once we reached camp, she jumped into journalist mode, interviewing women and children about how they were treated. She ignored the rules of what not to do when approaching, so Chief snatched her up, tossed her in the tent they gave us to sleep in that night and threatened to gift her to the Syrians outside the gates.

After she calmed down, Viper asked me to escort her to the mess hall and make sure she behaved. We hadn't made it ten steps in the yard before bullets flew. I pushed her to the ground and covered her with my body. I expected her to scream and beg not to be killed, instead, she tried to look around to see where the bullets were coming from.

That night, as I lay in my cot to sleep, Lindsey was curled up naked in my bedroll. I tried to argue, but she'd slipped her wet fingers between my lips, the taste of her pussy reminded me how long it'd been since the last time I'd had sex. We fucked every chance we got during the filming, it didn't matter the surroundings, Lindsey was always ready to go.

The documentary was a success, earning her a huge promotion and establishing our relationship. After a while, critics wanted to hear more about the love story with a SEAL than people suffering at the hands of terrorists. She gave them what they demanded, a love story played out from thousands of miles apart. I've lost track of how many 'surprise' video chats I'd been involved in, the fake tears from a girl who played it up for the camera. Lindsey was branded America's Sweetheart, and I was the SEAL with Honor. I had loved every minute of it until the uniform came off and she landed her dream job as co-anchor of a national news organization. Now, nothing about me is good enough, not even the million-dollar condo I purchased as a surprise for her, and especially not my honor.

The second the plane touches down, I pull my phone out and move it out of airplane mode. Dozens of messages fill up my inbox before the door to the aircraft can be opened. I shuffle past the handful from my boss, Judson Cane, a know-it-all asshole who suffers from delusions of grandeur. His sole purpose in life is to out-do any tragedy or illness those around him suffer from. I would have loved to have been a fly on the wall when news of my promotion hits his ears, the last few months of sedentary work would have been worth it to watch the steam billow from his ears.

Tipping my head at the pilot as I exit the aircraft, opening the first of five messages from Congressman Howard as I run up the jetway. My steps slow as I read his apology for dragging me from my weekend away in Florida. The urgency from before postponed until further notice, but he requests me to meet him first thing in the morning for a private meeting.

Slipping into my car, I send Lindsey a text message, asking if she's free for lunch tomorrow. I dread driving home, and I wish I'd invested in a helicopter, like Aiden in order to avoid the traffic, instead of an overpriced condo. As expected, my invitation goes unnoticed, an hour later as I sit in gridlock, she hasn't taken a moment to read it.

Pulling up to the garage for my condo, the security guard scans the barcode on my key card and checks the photo on his screen matches my face. Pennsylvania Towers, the place Lindsey labeled as the building where the 'in crowd' lives. I fell for the dreamy eyes she gave me as she spoke of the luxury condo in the middle of everything during a video chat shortly before I got out of the military. I contacted the building manager the next day, wiring him the asking price two weeks later. I even had one of DC's top interior designers go nuts and make the place somewhere Lindsey would never want to leave. The joke was on me when I surprised her, showing up to her work three days before I was supposed to. She took one look at the condo, assumed I was mortgaged to the hilt and could never do anything fun since in her eyes I was now in the poor house. The furniture was too this or that, and clearly, a knock-off as a poor ex-SEAL could never afford the real thing. At the time, I had half a mind to show her my bank balance, but she made some excuse about dinner with her boss, leaving me to spend the first real night in the condo I hate by myself.

Tossing my keys on the entry table, a card sits on top of a stack of mail the concierge delivers, brings a smile to my face. My mother's familiar handwriting scrawls across the front, her signature return address label complete with a galloping horse in the corner.

Hope Biggs is the quintessential housewife and mother to six rowdy boys, with the ability to make us each feel special even when she's laying into one of us. She works right alongside my father on our horse ranch back in Montana, and volunteers with the local school, even though she hasn't had a child attending since my youngest brother, Cooper, graduated. She has her hands deep in every church event and community need. When I chose the military over mending fence posts, she was my biggest supporter. Even after I left the military and didn't return to Montana, she still sends me a home-made card complete with news clippings from the local paper and tidbits of the circulating gossip. She, like most of the people in my life, hates Lindsey.

Pointing the remote at the television, the woman in question fills my screen, her birthday present to herself by way of a boob job, on display for the nation to see. I've never been a fan of cosmetic surgery, enjoying the natural feel of a woman in my hands. Not that I've so as much as breathed on Lindsey in months. There's always an excuse: her period, a new cream she's trying, or too tired from running her mouth.

Opening the card, a slip of paper falls to my lap, an obituary for Jon Perkins, a retired Air Force pilot, and my grandfather's best friend. Those two would spend hours together, talking about the old times when life was so much simpler. They shared a love of HAM radio, each owing an impressive setup, and shared a piece of that antiquated communication system with me. Jon taught me about listening to Mother Earth, using her beauty and wonder to convey a message across the street or around the world. They both stood proud the day I held up my hand and pledged to defend the constitution, entering the Air Force as a communications specialist. When my grandfather died, Mr. Perkins got on his radio, making sure I heard the news from him and not some guy behind a desk who'd never met him or myself for that matter.

When the opportunity presented itself for me to become a SEAL, I called Mr. Perkins on the radio, asking advice on the decision. I'll never forget how he said any decision that big needed a full night's sleep before giving my word. He'd been right, I took a few days of leave, drove until I ran out of road and made the decision to end my time with the Air Force and enlist in the Navy to become a SEAL.

I gained the respect of my superiors when I could still accomplish my job when networks went down. My coworkers labeled me MacGyver due to my ability to splice pieces of equipment together and get us back online. Sadly, the name was more of a kick in the teeth than friendly banter as one of my teammates, Joe Snider, accused me of being a sellout, tossing my wings for a trident shield.

Taking the clipping in hand, I make my way down the hall to the room I use as my office. While I don't have the ability to build a bunker like Matt, I do have means to create a false wall in the event Lindsey ever decides I'm good enough to visit with again.

Closing the door to my office, a stupid habit I've had forever, I cross the room to the bookshelf on the far wall, entering my code and stepping back as the fake wall opens toward me. The space is small, originally a closet, but enough to hide my current projects and the computer I use to scan the web for chatter. To the left of my computer is a small cork board filled with all the things I missed during my time away. Removing a pin from the bottom, I add Mr. Perkins to the collage of memories.

Standing back, my hands hooked on my hips, I survey the notes and equipment that has occupied my time for years. Countless nights I've sat here listening to conversations, tracking every move the Konar brothers made. Waiting and planning for the day we would rid the world of the evil those three men stood for.

Reality hits me, buckling my knees and forcing me into my chair. It's like the day after Christmas when all the surprises are over and all that's left are the decorations you haven't got the energy to take down.

In what feels like the blink of an eye, the alarm on my phone signals it's time to get up hit the gym and get to my meeting on time. I've managed once again to zone out and become lost in the chatter which means nothing to most people. Reaching in my pocket, I see a message from Congressman Howard.

Capitol Building gym, four-thirty. Code for the door: the date you had me under surveillance.

CHAPTER TWO

ELLI

The brakes on my car squeak as I pull into an empty spot outside Tripp Brothers Plastics Plant. Jupiter, Virginia is a small town with only two places to work, the plastic plant and a tire factory on the edge of town.

The faded blue letters on the white background show the age and disrepair of the company. I've worked in the front office since the law in Virginia allowed. My father wasn't too keen on the idea of me working but relented when my mother said it would give me an appreciation for how hard a man's job is.

I started off answering phones until Myrtle's, the office managers husband suffered a stroke, forcing her to cut back her hours. She showed me how to do everything in the office, assuring me and Mr. Tripp, it would be temporary for as soon as her husband was better, she'd be back. Unfortunately, a month later, Myrtle died in her sleep. That had been six years ago, and I've been running the place ever since.

Once I graduated from high school, I noticed the company

slowly sliding into the red. When I mentioned it to Cliff, one of the owners, he brushed me off saying not to worry, business would pick up and we would be fine. When business continued to decline, and he refused to see the writing on the wall, I had to do something to protect myself.

Growing up in my father's home, there were expectations in place for me. Be a good and honest person, attend church regularly, keep your legs shut, and marry the man he chooses. For me the first few were easy, honesty was something that felt right, as remembering a lie is too much work. Going to church meant working with the kids in Sunday school, there are few things I love more than little children, their innocence and honesty is refreshing. Keeping my legs shut was the easiest of all, as most of the men my age made me ill.

However, it was the man my father chose for me to marry, Wesley Owens, who inspired me more than the likelihood of losing my job to go against my father's expectations. Wesley was the third of five brothers, his aspirations for the future didn't exactly correspond with mine. He was content to purchase a run-down mobile home from the repo lot across from the church, slap it on the freshly poured concrete slab on my father's land and live not-so-happily-after with me, cooking and cleaning, and tending to his every need.

I, on the other hand, want to travel the world; see the Pyramids of Egypt, the Tower of London, and take a gondola ride in Venice. I want to meet new people, getting a taste of other cultures. Most of all, I want a love so deep, we share the same breath.

Hidden in my closet, behind the dresses I ironed at my mother's instruction, is a map of the world, push-pins in every city I read about, dreaming of the day I could board a plane and set off to those places, replacing the pins with photos and memories I would have forever.

Sadly, even though I'd saved almost every dime I've ever made, it won't be enough to get me far, not with the closing of the plant and my only source of income hovering overhead. Wesley made it abundantly clear the day we went to the Justice of the Peace, I would no longer be allowed to work, as feeding him would be my top priority. Cooking and cleaning for a man you don't particularly like may be appealing to some girls, I'm not one of them.

My salvation came one morning as I helped my mother clean the living room. My father kept a stack of newspapers beside his chair and every Saturday, my mother would clear them out to make room for next week. As I hauled them to the trash pile for burning, an article on the top page caught my eye.

The University of Virginia offered an online business program with special rates for residents of the state. Enrollment was easy and my acceptance came in an email, not to the house. The guidance counselor I was assigned sent me a list of scholarships I qualified for, including a first-generation college student. Spending very little of my own money, I finished my degree using the Wi-Fi in the office. My diploma arriving in a post office box I rented in the next county, away from the prying eyes who would run their mouths to my father.

My search for a new job came the minute I had the credentials in hand, purposely seeking work in other states. I sent my resumé to hundreds of job openings, receiving immediate offers from three companies. The first, an adult video production company out of Miami, one I quickly and politely declined. The second, a chicken farm in Arkansas. This one I considered until I researched the company and found litigation against them for consumer fraud.

The third, a railroad company in Tennessee, but the money they offered was less than what I made at the plant.

With a heavy heart, I aimlessly surf the internet, filling the time I have left of my shift. Nothing seems to capture my attention until I notice an ad on the side of the screen for government jobs. Clicking the link, I spent the rest of the day and most of the next answering question after question building my resumé on the site.

Six weeks later, I receive a notification my resumé was sent for review for a personal assistant position. My nerves skyrocket and several times a day I check my email for any word on the status of the review. Another six weeks pass before a notice comes they want to conduct a telephone interview. I eagerly respond back a date and time I will be available.

On the morning of my interview, I make sure the phone I'd purchased behind my father's back was charged and ready. Every Wednesday, it's my job to take the checks we received in the mail to the bank and deposit them for Mr. Tripp. As I climb into the rusted out truck my boss makes me use, Wesley pulls his old Ford in behind me, blocking me from going anywhere.

"You going somewhere?" With his signature ball cap, and sleeves ripped off his shirt, exposing the ample flesh hanging over the metal door. Wesley Owens, like the rest of his family, is on the larger side. He, being the smallest of his brothers, stands at five-nine and weighed-in, well above four hundred pounds. He loves to hunt and fish, fix old junk cars and play some crazy video game on the television in his room. Add his favorite food in the mix and he's occupied for days.

"It's Wednesday, Wesley. You know I go to the bank for Mr. Tripp."

Moving his head further out the window, "Why do you call me

Wesley, not Wes or honey or darlin' like your momma does your daddy?"

I know I should be honest with him and tell him I'll never be like my mother, a servant to a man who dictates everything from what to eat to how many children to have. But I can't risk running late for my interview, so I settle instead for a partial truth.

"Because it would be inappropriate at this stage in our relationship to give you a term of endearment."

Wesley turns up his lip, "Ain't no man want a smart woman, Elli. Best you 'member that, cause after next Friday, I'll have enough to put a deposit on that trailer I like."

His truck putters and stalls until it kicks into gear, spraying gravel as he fish-tails down the drive. Swallowing thick, I jump in the truck, sending a prayer to baby Jesus himself to help me land this job.

I choose the tallest point on this mountain, gaining me four bars of service on my cell phone. Two minutes after I settle on the hood of the truck, the hardly used phone rings, the caller ID listing DC as the source.

"Hello?"

"*Good afternoon, may I speak with Ms. York.*" My heart races at the sound of my name falling from the lips of who I imagine is a sophisticated woman sitting behind a large desk in a business suit.

"This is Ms. York. How can I help you?" I tried with all my might to hide the southern drawl in my words, having recently read an article depicting intelligence is based on locality.

"*Ms. York, my name is Olivia Wesson, personal assistant to Congressman Joseph Howard. Your resumé was forwarded to my office and I'd like to ask you a few questions.*"

My upbringing emphasizes I respond with a 'yes, ma'am', giving respect to a person of authority. As I look out over the tops of the trees growing alongside the mountain, their bright orange, gold, and red leaves point my attention to the endless horizon, the places far beyond where my eyes can see. I need to see what is beyond this mountain, see what life is like for people like Olivia Wesson. All I need is a chance to prove myself, a foot in the door to show the world how bright I can shine.

"Of course, what would you like to know?"

The interview lasts for nearly an hour and by the time the call ends, I knew Olivia was a native of DC, her late father a reporter for a national newspaper. She never married, choosing instead to have a career in politics, never once regretting her decision.

Three days later, I receive an email offering me a tentative position of being Ms. Wesson's second assistant. The salary makes my eyes widen, but my research explains the number of zeros. I immediately begin the hunt for an apartment in the area, my heart dipping as I realized it would take every dime in my savings to land even the tiniest room. Unwilling to let this deter me, I accepted the position and signed the paperwork for my background check.

Yesterday, when I was about to leave work, I received an email from Human Resources explaining my security clearance has been granted and the job is mine.

Climbing the same steps I have taken for years, a gentle breeze lifts my hair as I pull open the office door. I barely slept last night as I made mental lists of everything I have to do, at the very top was a discussion with a pair of brothers in denial.

Not bothering to stop at my desk, I made my way to the back of the building, knocking politely before entering the room. "Mr. Tripp? I need to speak with you, it's important."

CHAPTER THREE

RYAN

Nerves grip me as I park my car in the mostly empty lot of the Capitol building. My swipe badge and CAC card enough to gain entry into the monitored area. As directed by the Congressman, I enter the date I sat in the woods outside his cabin, watching as he read the paper and made a few calls. Slipping into the building, I make my way down the marble halls until I come to the fourth door on the right. Inside is an executive looking locker room, complete with mahogany shelves and cushioned benches. The man I know to be Joseph Howard sits with his phone in his hand and two men I recognize as Capitol police standing sentry behind him. I wait until I'm two feet away before clearing my throat and announcing my arrival.

"Jesus..." Congressman Howard jumps, his phone clattering to the floor. The two police officers reach for their guns.

"It's all right, gentleman." Howard raises his hands to stop them. "This is the man I've been waiting for." Standing to his full height, he holds out his hand for me to shake. "My new personal trainer." His grip is impressive for a man his age, his smile, one I'm sure comes with the job. "Or do you prefer Life Coach?"

Shifting my eyes to the men behind him, "Trainer is fine for now. Although, once we're finished today, you may have a more colorful title for me."

Howard laughs, as do the two cops behind him, "Of that, I have no doubt."

"Shall we get started?" I offer, pointing to the door labeled gym.

Howard keeps his eyes locked with mine, "Gentlemen, you can wait for me in the hall. I chose this ungodly hour for a reason, no need to give you additional laughs this morning."

The pair walks slowly passed us, cataloging what I'm wearing and how deep blue my eyes are. The Congressman waits until the door thuds shut before sitting on the bench and inviting me to do the same. "I apologize for the cloak and dagger routine, but I've found it necessary as of late."

Ignoring his invitation, I stand with my feet apart, hands clasped at my hips." Still trusting Capitol police after what happened in Alaska?"

Howard takes a breath, glancing around to the closed door behind me. "I'm assuming, based on our previous encounter, you possess the means to make this conversation completely confidential?"

Needing to know why in the hell he called me, I pull my phone from my pocket, open an app and place the phone face up on the bench. "Go ahead, no one can listen."

Picking his phone off the floor, he taps the screen bringing a photo of his wife and dog to life. "No service," he muses, tossing his phone to the bag propped up against the leg of the bench. "Impressive. Although, I don't know why I'm surprised."

Congressman shifts his body on the bench, his hands gripping the edge as he raises his head toward me. "Trust isn't the word I would use, Ryan. Knowing I have to play the game a little longer in order to finish what I've started is why those two have been my constant companions of late."

Joining him on the bench, "Which is why you called me."

"That, and I gave you my word after the last time you helped me, I would return the favor. Although, your superior was none too happy in agreeing to release you."

"Cane's an idiot who couldn't find his way out of a paper sack if it was torn in half and came with a map."

Howard tips his head back in laughter, "Oh, my boy. You are not one to mince words."

Crossing my arms over my chest, "Which is not why you brought me here. Care to explain what's going on?"

Standing to his full height, the light from above casts shimmers on his silver hair. "In the near future, I will call upon you to accompany me to a meeting. I can't give you a time or day, so I need you ready at a moment's notice. You are to blend-in, take on the role of one of my staff members. I'll need you fully packed and ready for any situation. Can you do this, Ghost?"

THE DOOR to my condo is unlocked as I stand outside in the hall, pulling my gun from its hiding place, I push the door the rest of the way open and creep down the entry. I'm ten steps in before I hear her voice, demanding someone get her an appointment for today. Holstering my gun, I make my way into the main room, finding Lindsey sprawled out on the fake-as-fuck couch as she calls it.

When her eyes shift to mine, she unceremoniously ends the call, jumping from the couch, a fire burning in her eyes.

"Why were you at the Capitol Building today, and why did I have to hear about it from someone else? What's going on, Ryan? I thought you loved me, you don't keep secrets from someone you love."

Something in her questions sparks anger in my chest. Ignoring her for the moment, I step to the side and make my way to the kitchen, desperate for a cup of coffee.

"Don't you walk away from me, Ryan Biggs. I asked you a question, why were you at the Capitol Building this morning?"

Collecting my thoughts as I pour water in the machine, the anger she ignited now a full-blown blaze.

"Let me ask you something, Lindsey. Why is it I can leave a million messages for you to call me and you ignore every single one, but when one of your spy's whispers in your ear they allegedly saw me do something, you break your neck to get here?"

Rolling her eyes, "Don't be dramatic, I didn't break my neck."

Slamming the coffee pot on the counter, the glass shatters in a million pieces. "Goddamn it, Lindsey. I begged you to go to Florida with me and you refused."

Not affected in the least by my outburst, Lindsey appraises her fingernails, her attention shifts to me a split-second before she responds. "And spend a weekend in some tiny-ass town no one has heard of? What was I supposed to do for fun?"

"Oh, I don't know? How about spending time with your boyfriend? Have crazy-wild hotel sex, or here's a thought, actually talk to me for more than a few seconds. Who the fuck cares?"

"You know I have this interview coming up."

"No." I roar. "Actually, I don't. Because you can't take the time

18

to call or come to see me, I know nothing about what you're up to."

Grabbing a broom and dustpan from the closet, I clean up the broken glass littering the floor. "I got out of the military for you, took this fucking desk job for you, bought this ridiculous condo because you said you wanted to live here, only you didn't want to live here with me. Now, when you need something from me, I'm tapped out. Go ask your boss for answers, show him your pussy, it's always worked for you in the past."

Lindsey looks at me with shocked eyes. Pulling her hand back, she slaps me across the face, the pain nothing compared to what she's done to my heart.

"I'm not happy, Ryan, not with you, not anymore. Can't you see that? I'm not the same girl you met on the battlefield. I've grown and matured, maybe you should do the same."

The sound of Lindsey's heels clicking against the marble tile fades as she steps onto the carpet in the hall, not bothering to look back as she closes the door, effectively walking out of my life. Dumping the dustpan into the trash, I toss the broom in the closet before slamming the door and heading to my office. I'd told Eleni I wanted Lindsey to listen to me, hear for herself how much I loved her. But I was wrong, it was I who needed to listen, as she never loved me.

Scrolling through the contacts on my phone, I select the number for my building manager, sending him a text I'd like him to list this condo for sale. I don't give a shit how much I lose, as all I can think about is getting the fuck out of DC.

Less than five minutes later, he responds he would do his best, but there are several other units available. Tossing my phone to my desk, I do what I always do when life turns to shit, burying myself into the world of the dark web.

19

Hours later as my eyelids grow heavy, the latest information I've uncovered on my computer screen. Picking up my phone, I stare at the words on the screen as the phone rings twice in my ear before anyone picks up.

"You've got yourself a deal."

CHAPTER FOUR

ELLI

Wesley's truck is parked outside one of the trailers on my father's land when I pull up. He and my oldest brother, Elijah, are pulling a trap with a raccoon in it out the front door. My mother, Bettie, beats a worn-out rug tossed over a clothesline strung between two oak trees, dust and debris falling from it like summer rain.

She waves to me as I amble over the dirt road, my father, Ervin, too cheap to have the dang thing paved. Pulling my car to the left, I roll down my window to see what she wants.

"Look what we found for your new living room?"

The rug has seen better days, the threads around the edge are so frayed they're begging to be put out of their misery. "It needs a good scrubbing, but we'll have it looking brand new in no time."

While I love my mother's optimism about basically everything, the last thing I want my bare feet to touch is that nasty rug.

"Head on up to the house, Elli, dinner needs starting and Wesley has something he wants to talk to you about."

"Yes, ma'am." The words are out of my mouth before I can think them. From the time any of us could talk, my mother instilled the importance of manners. She believes, being poor doesn't dictate being rude, too bad she has zero influence over my father.

Heading toward the house, I pretend to pay attention to avoiding the washed-out areas of the road, instead of the nod of Wesley's head as I pass. I've no doubt he'll have something to say about it when he's granted his time alone with me by my father. While Wesley has never laid a hand on me, his words are cruel.

Twenty minutes later, as I stand loading two pans of biscuits into the oven, my father and brother, Earl, come in through the front door, kicking off boots and leaving them where they fall. Less than a second later, Wesley and Elijah come tumbling in, their fight for dominance to enter the door has nothing to do with bragging rights, and everything to do with their size. Wesley's mother, like mine, believes it's a wife and mother's responsibility to keep the men in the house fed and happy. I don't necessarily agree. However, she succeeded, as all of my brothers are of a good size.

Wesley sits hard on the well-used sofa, not bothering to remove his muddy boots, propping them on the coffee table in front of him. "There's two raccoons out there ready for you to clean, Elli."

Stirring the simmering pot of beans, I keep my attention to the chicken coop just past the small garden we used for growing herbs. All my life, the majority of what we ate came from the land around us. I'd hunted my fair share of deer and rabbits, able to skin and dress a full-grown buck in half the time as most of my brothers. My problem isn't in touching a dead animal, it's the tone Wesley uses, giving me orders when he has no right to.

My mother comes in, saving me from saying something I'll regret later. "Look at this," pride coats her words as she picks up a piece of fried chicken from the plate. "Elli you have a gift for cooking, it will keep Wesley coming home to you at night."

Bile fills my throat at the thought of being with him. Like most of the boys in town, Wesley parties over in Blacksmith Hollow, drinking, smoking, and messing around with some of the looser girls in town.

As we sit down to eat, my mother and I take our places at the end of the table closest to the kitchen, making refilling plates much quicker. I've never known my father to lift a hand other than to shovel food in his mouth. It's expected in his eyes for my mother and I to do everything.

"Elli," my father calls from the opposite end of the table, a fork full of corn posed at his mouth. "I gave Elijah's old trailer to Wes today, best you make a list of what you need."

Had this conversation occurred a few weeks ago, my reaction would have been different. "Oh? What happened to the trailer from the lot by the church?"

"Elli," my mother clips under breath.

"What, Momma? He said not even a week ago, come this Friday he would have enough to put a deposit on one."

The skin on my father brow furrows, his fork clanging to his plate below. "Ain't none of your concern where the man's money goes, young lady. Get a list of what you need."

Before I can open my mouth to argue. "Don't worry about furniture. We'll put the word out at church, besides you have a little saved from your job I 'spect."

"They will need that to fix the floor, Bettie." My father argues.

"Don't we have some old plywood left over from the chicken coop, Ervin?"

I watch the conversation center around the funds in my bank

account as if I'm not in the room. By the Wesley is shoving food in his mouth, he could care less as long as there are seconds.

"Ain't enough," he spits back, pushing his plate away. "Damn foods cold now woman."

My mother springs from her seat, her own food, and the conversation quickly forgotten as she takes the plate from him, replacing it with another. Wesley stops her mid-retreat, swiping the biscuits and untouched chicken off the plate, taking a huge bite before waving her off.

I'm excused from clean up as Wesley wants to take a walk. My father allows it, but only after Wesley agrees to stay where he can see us.

"I'm going over to Doverville, pickin' up an engine a guy is holding for me." Wesley uses a closed fist to pound into the center of his chest, dislodging an ear-shattering burp in the process. "I want this trailer clean when I get back, do you hear me?"

Checking over my shoulder to make sure my father is still sitting on the porch. "I suppose that's where the deposit money is going."

Wesley turns on me. "I don't know where you got this smart mouth, but you best return it. The minute that judge makes you my wife, things are gonna change."

Unable to resist, "Like what, you gonna join Jenny Craig?"

Grabbing me by the shoulders, he spins me so his body is blocking my father's view of us. "For one, your gonna quit that damn job. Two, I'm gonna split your ass in half when I fuck you. Third, I'm gonna shut that smart mouth of yours with my fist."

Reaching into his pocket, he pulls out what looks like an old washer used to keep bolts from slipping.

"Here, your daddy was complaining I ain't give you a ring yet."

Holding the washer between my thumb and index finger. "It's a washer."

"It's your ring now, ain't it?" A humorless laugh leaves his lips, "Best be grateful I didn't go with my brother, Joe's idea."

Joe was Wesley's younger, and severely twisted younger brother. He lived deep in the woods behind the rest of the family.

Something sinister lurked in Wesley's eyes as he leans forward, the grease from the chicken still smeared on his chin. "He said you needed a training collar, maybe I'll get you one of those instead."

MONDAY MORNING, I climb the steps to Tripp Brothers Plastics with dread in my belly. Wesley would return today, his shift at the tire plant beginning in a few hours. Yesterday, I'd been able to stay home from church as I started my period. My parents have some odd belief a menstruating woman should refrain from entering the doors of a holy place, the blood leaving my body some form of evil in their eyes.

I used the time alone to sift through my meager belongings and separate what I would need and what I would leave behind. Working in an office, I assume I'll need the dresses hanging in my closet, but as I took them out, I couldn't help but think of how, just as moving away from here and starting new, I needed to leave them behind. Choosing the handful of dark skirts and blouses, I hung the rest back up, but not before carefully removing the map from the wall.

Walking into the office, I find Norma Jean and Dixie gossiping in the corner. Their chatter stops the second we lock eyes and I know it's about me. Taking my place behind my desk, I stash my purse in the large drawer at my left before turning on my computer to begin work.

With coffee cup in hand, Norma Jean crosses the room, her straight-as-a-board blonde hair courtesy of her sister's beauty shop down the road. She was born with the same red hair I have, but after a trip to the beach one year for Spring Break, she came back and dyed it blonde.

"You know, Elli. Just because you and Wesley are getting married, doesn't mean he will stop coming by and paying me a visit."

Waiting for my email to load, I shift my eyes from the anti-quated computer screen to her attitude-filled face, "I take it they threw a party this weekend."

The Owens brothers have one claim to fame around here, the massive parties they host on their property. Wesley's oldest brother, Moses, is the law in these parts. And with him standing in the door of their barn selling red solo cups at five dollars each, there were never noise complaints lodged.

"Of course they did," she counters, a smear of her red lipstick on her teeth. "But that ain't what I'm talkin' 'bout."

Leaning back in my chair, I cock an eyebrow as I wait for her to continue. Maybe my father is right about the evil present in a woman when she bleeds, as all I can think about is clawing that smug look off her face.

"Wesley is a fine, hard-working man with many talents." Norma Jean draws the hard-working part out as if it's something special to her.

"Wesley Owens, about yay tall?" I say incredulously, my hand-held above my head to emphasize his height. "Is hard working?"

Using the handle of the spoon sticking out of her cup, her eyes shift to her fingers as she stirs the liquid inside. "See, I told Lottie you didn't deserve him. You can't appreciate how good you have it."

Lottie is Norma Jean's sister who works at the shop down the road, recently divorced from her fifth husband, she moved her and her four children back in with the sister's grandmother.

With a witty retort dangling on my lips, the chime of a new email gives Norma Jean's ears a stay of execution. It's from Olivia, sent to me at four this morning, the subject line reading urgent.

Elli,
On behalf of Congressman Howard and myself, welcome aboard. Our understanding is your start date is scheduled for fourteen days from last Friday. With recent events, which I am not at liberty to share with you in this email, we are hoping you are able to push your move to DC to this Wednesday. The Congressman understands this may present a hardship financially, and therefore has authorized this office to reserve a room at a local hotel within walking distance to the Capitol Building at his expense. Please contact me on my direct line as soon as you receive this email with your decision.
Sincerely,
Olivia Wesson

Jumping to my feet, the overwhelming feeling of urgency fuels my movements. Digging my purse out of the drawer, I log out of my email and delete the program from the hard drive. Removing the photo of my mother and myself from my desk, I shove it into the confines of my purse.

"You know what, Norma Jean? You can have hard working Wesley with his burping and farting, and inability to scratch his own ass. You can spend the rest of your life chasing after him, picking up dirty dishes and holey socks, listening to him complain how hungry he is twenty minutes after you clean the kitchen. You can spend hours crocheting a blanket with the pile of lent from between his toes and inside his belly button." Throwing my purse over my shoulder, "And while I have no doubt you will love every second of it. I wish you luck in keeping him home at night, but then again, it sounds as if you already know he hasn't seen his dick without a mirror in a long time."

Cliff Tripp stands in the threshold between the offices, his eyes wide and mouth agape at my outburst. "Mr. Tripp, I know I said two weeks, but I quit today." Fishing the keys to the office from my pocket, I cross the room and place them in his hand. "Good luck to you, Mr. Tripp and remember what I said about scaling back."

TOSSING the last few items I need into a bag, my mother stands at the door to my bedroom, a dishtowel wadded in her hands. "Don't you care what people will say?"

Zipping the bag closed, "Momma, I love you, but I have to get out of this place before it suffocates me."

"But Wesley will be crushed."

Setting the strap on my shoulder, I take a final look around at the room I've lived in my entire life. "Wesley will be just fine; Norma Jean will make sure of it."

Hooking her hands on her hips, the beginnings of tears well up in her eyes. "And what about your daddy? What will he say when he comes home and you're not here?"

Wrapping my mother in my arms, "Unfortunately, Daddy will have mean things to say. Instead of feeling proud of what I've accomplished, he will resent me for going against him." Pulling back, "Momma, I can't tie myself to a man like Wesley. I can't spend one more day wondering what life is like on the other side of this mountain."

"Elli," my mother pleads. "It's rocks and trees, just like here. The sun still rises in the morning and sets of an evening. There's nothing special out there."

Maybe she's right, but I can't quiet the voice in my head which tells me there's a life out there for me, one I need to start living today.

"Then let me figure that out on my own."

I CATCH the last train out of Norfolk, my mother volunteering to drive me to the station and then hide my car until she could sell it. I told her to keep the money, save something for herself on the chance she ever wants to come to visit me.

Once the train pulls away from the station, I call Olivia letting her know I'm on my way. She gives me the information about the hotel where I'll be staying, Congressman's generosity extending until I can find a suitable apartment.

As the sun sets on my first night in Washington DC, the darkening blue sky gives way to the pinks and gold of the fading sun, I stand in the window of my hotel room, the Washington Monument standing proud, bathed in light from base up. Tomorrow will be the first day of the rest of my life, and I can't wait to see what fate had in store for me.

CHAPTER FIVE

RYAN

W atching the city come to life from the window of my condo as my feet pound against the belt of my treadmill, sweat pours down my face and clears my head. I'd managed to sleep ten consecutive hours last night, a personal record as I haven't closed both eyes in years. Perhaps it's my subconscious accepting Lindsey is really gone, and the war against the Konar family is over. I'll take it, whatever the reason, as I haven't felt this good in forever.

Judson Cane, my former boss, sits in my chair with his feet propped on my desk, a cup of overpriced coffee from a local shop in his hand.

"Well, well, well. What did you do, Ryan, save Congressman Howard's dog from choking?"

Ignoring his prodding, I set the empty box on my desk and begin packing my things.

"Because we both know, you don't have what it takes to get an appointment as a personal guard. Not to worry, Buddy Boy, a staff member is a fine bullet point to put on your resumé."

"Says the man who has been rejected thirteen times."

Just because I was chained to a desk, doesn't mean I sit and do nothing all day. Passwords around this place are a joke, half the guys in here call them out as they went to take a piss, Judson included. I've seen the folder he keeps of the rejection letters, along with the denied access to personnel records, including mine. He wants to move to the next building as badly as he wants his next sip of coffee.

Pulling his feet from my desk, "How the fuck do you know that?"

Opening the locked draw beside his left leg, "I'd tell you, but you don't have a high enough security clearance."

Judson stands from the chair, bending over to poke me in the middle of my left arm. "Mark my words, Biggs, when the shit hits the fan and you can't keep up, don't think for a second you can come back here."

Standing to my full height, towering over the pissed-off man I have zero respect for. "You listen to me, you little shit. Even if they took this job away today, I still wouldn't come back and work for an idiot like you. Keep on walking around here like you're some-thing special, maybe you'll be able to convince yourself it's true."

CONGRESSMAN HOWARD'S office is buzzing with activity as I walk through the door. A middle-aged woman with dark hair and tailored clothing stands behind a desk answering phones, while two suited men stand off to the side, cell phones to ears and White House Staff printed on the badge hanging from their necks.

"Can I help you, young man?"

With the phone trapped between her shoulder and ear, the woman looks directly at me as she speaks.

"Morning, ma'am. I have an appointment with the Congressman this morning." Stepping forward, balancing the box full of my possessions under my arm and the leather bag across my chest.

Glancing down to a cell phone in her hand, "You must be Mr. Biggs, one of our new staff members." Holding her finger up for me to wait, she finishes her conversation and places the phone back in its cradle.

"You will have to get used to this organized chaos, Mr. Biggs, never a dull moment around here."

Extending my hand out to her, "It's Ryan, Mr. Biggs is my father and while he's a great man, he carries the mister part better than me."

Her smile is genuine as she shakes my hand in earnest. "Pleasure to meet you, Ryan. I'm Olivia Wesson, Congressman Howard's personal assistant, please feel free to call me Olivia. You can come to me for anything you need. There are two more new staff members starting today, my assistants, but they are currently down with security getting their badges." Looking to her watch, "I'm giving them thirty more minutes and then I'm going down there myself to see what the holdup is."

Something tells me Olivia is not someone to upset. She reminds me of my mom, commanding but kind, and I would rather take on the Taliban with a broken arm and blindfolded than mess with her.

The phone begins to ring again, "Excuse me." She apologizes, as she reaches for the phone. A smile splits her face in half as she nods her head, "Yes, sir. I'll send him right in."

Placing the phone back in its cradle, she steps around the desk, her arm raised in the direction of the door at the end of the hall. "The Congressman is ready for you."

Following her down the short hall, I go to step around the two men with thumbs going wild on their cell phones. The frame of the door isn't wide enough for me to pass with them standing there, "Excuse me, gentleman."

The guy on the left, his badge reading Richard, looks up from his phone, craning his neck back as I'm considerably taller than him. "Hey, I know you, we belong to the same gym."

The minute I decided to become a SEAL, I drove to nearest the gym and called it my second home. Once upon a time, I was tall and skinny, but after joining that gym and earning the title of Gym Rat, I bulked up to the size I am today. This guy, Richard, may have a gym membership and spent a minute or two walking on a treadmill as he scopes out the girls who are looking for guys like me. Judging by the looks of his arms, the only weight he's dealt with is the time he spent leaning against the wall while they make that cup of coffee in his hand.

"Nah, man. I don't go to public gyms."

Richard scowls as he moves to the side. In a dick-move I don't regret, I bump his shoulder with mine, giving him the inspiration to drop the phone and use that membership for real.

Congressman Howard stands from behind his desk as Olivia closes the door behind me. Extending his hand, "Good to see you this morning, Ryan."

"Pleasure, Sir." Returning the handshake.

"Please, have a seat, we have a lot to cover before I take you to your new office."

Setting my box and leather briefcase in the chair beside me, I take the offered seat as he returns to his.

"First, let me say, everyone, including your former supervisor, Mr. Cane, thinks you're here as a congressional staffer and not as a member of my personal detail. I need you to blend in, not giving anyone who may be watching any reason to suspect anything."

"Understood."

"Here in a few minutes, I'll take you around, introduce you to people, and take a meeting with a colleague of mine, Congressman Hoyt. I need you to get a read on him, tell me what that gut of yours tells you."

"And what does your gut say, sir?"

Leaning back in his chair, "My gut said to hire you."

It's close to eight in the evening before I finally leave the Capitol Building. The meeting with Congressman Hoyt had been...interesting. He and Richard hit it off like two fraternity brothers, comparing the local clubs in town and sharing photos of girls they recently met.

My gut told me he would sell his own mother for the right price, spill closely-guarded secrets for a blow job and reach around. I wouldn't trust the motherfucker to walk my damn dog.

Walking in my building, Barton, the night concierge is waiting with a handled bag, the logo of a local restaurant on the side.

"Mr. Biggs, this was delivered about fifteen minutes ago with strict instructions to give it to you personally."

Taking the bag from him, I wait until I'm in my condo before exploring the contents. A card rests atop a foil takeout container, my name scrolled across the front.

Ryan,

I wish I could have been there to celebrate with you.
Congratulations on your promotion.
Love,
Eleni

Pasta has never tasted so good, and as I sit alone at my bar, I've never felt so loved. My team had no idea how lucky they were to have such women in their lives. The feeling carries me through as I watch the nightly news, spotlighting the girl who thought she broke me. Lindsey was undeniably beautiful, even a blind man could see it. She was convinced a pretty face was all she needed, her history proving her theory right. A large part of me can't wait for the day her looks fail her, providing her with the harsh truth of the world around her. Another part wishes her happiness, despite the shitty hand she dealt me.

The shrill of my phone pulls me from a dead sleep, the clock on my bedside table reads just after three am. Disoriented, I grumble my displeasure into the receiver.

"What?"

"It's time, Ghost."

CHAPTER SIX

ELLI

"*D*id *you see the hot new guy?*"
     I tried not to eavesdrop, focusing instead on the mandatory training Olivia instructed me to do. My co-worker, Ann Marie, and her friend from across the hall are taking their lunch together at Ann Marie's desk. She'd complained of her stomach hurting earlier, so Ms. Wesson told her to try and eat something.

"The one with the serious body, and eyes so blue they have to be contacts?"

Discreetly placing my fingers to my ears, I'm trying desperately to pass the test on human trafficking and proper use of a government credit card.

"So worth the risk of unemployment to climb that tree."

Ms. Wesson returns just as I finish, having excused herself when hit with a sneezing fit. So far this morning I've been fingerprinted, had my photo taken a dozen times, issued a cell phone and given my own desk, with a list of responsibilities. The one thing I had not been given, was the opportunity to see the new guy everyone spoke of. Apparently, he transferred from another department, senior staff with a much higher clearance than anyone else in this office. I'd been away from my desk when he came in, not that it mattered much as I wasn't here to fawn over some muscled-up man with blue eyes.

Besides, Ms. Wesson made the office rules quite clear, keep my phone on me at all times, never comment on anything the press says, and anything said in the office, stays in the office.

Walking back to my hotel, I stop at a corner store, selecting a few non-perishables and a for rent guide. While the hotel is nice, it isn't mine and I won't take advantage of my boss's generosity. I'll head out this weekend, find a place close enough to work, yet far enough not to break the bank.

Crawling between the sheets, I use the browser on the phone to read over some of the protocols for the office, next thing I know, the phone is ringing in my ear, jarring me from a sound sleep.

"Hello?"

"*Elli, it's Olivia.*" Sitting up, I wiped my eyes as she began to sneeze.

"God bless you."

"*Thank you, listen,*" her voice sounds scratchy as if she's smoked for a hundred years. "*I need you to get dressed, pack an overnight bag and get to Andrews Air Force base within the hour.*"

"Okay?" Glancing around the room at the open manuals and highlighters strewn about.

"*I'm sending a car, make sure you have your identification. I was scheduled to go, but I have the flu and can't risk giving it to the Congressman and Ann Marie is waiting to be taken into surgery for an appendectomy.*"

Recalling my training from earlier, "What about expenses, I don't have a travel card?"

"Don't worry, Congressman Howard will take care of every-thing. If you happen to spend money, get a receipt and we will fix it later."

According to Google Maps, the drive from my hotel to Andrew's should have taken thirty-two minutes. I use the time to familiarize myself with the protocol for attending events. Getting past the gates at Andrews took longer than I expected, some of my credentials were still in review, but one call to Olivia and they let us through.

In a rush to report to the Congressman, afraid my delay would cause him issues, I race up the steps, my bag dangling behind me, not stopping until the Congressman comes into view. Righting the bag on my shoulder, I take a deep breath, tugging my skirt down and making sure my hair is in place. With borrowed courage, I approach the white-haired gentleman I'd been introduced to yesterday.

"My apologies, Mr. Congressman, I got here as soon as I could."

Sparkling blue eyes glance up at me from his cell phone. "Ms. York," setting his phone to the side, raising from his seat. "Thank you for joining me. Sorry for pulling you from your bed, especially since this is technically still your first day."

"No problem at all, although," holding up my phone." I do feel ill-prepared as there were no scheduled events on your calendar."

Motioning for me to follow him, "You're correct. This wasn't scheduled, but I assure you, this will be a quick flight to New York, dinner on me and back in time for you to enjoy your first weekend in DC."

I follow the Congressman down a narrow aisle, my eyes searching the interior, the reality of where I am finally kicking in.

"Feel free to sit wherever you want. As soon as the rest of my staff and the crew arrives, we will leave for New York."

Selecting the first row of seats I come to, I lay my bag in the seat beside me. "Thank you, sir. If you need something, please don't hesitate to ask."

I wait until after the Congressman leaves before I let out the breath I've been holding. Never in my wildest dreams could I have imagined myself sitting on one of the most recognizable planes in the world.

Leaning back into the leather seat, I allow myself to surrender to the moment. I've worked hard to get here, defied the odds against me in finishing school and finding this job. I allow my inner self to throw a middle finger or two at the image of Wesley and his chicken grease covered chin.

"Wait until I show those bitches I'm on Air Force One."

My body flinches, and my image of Wesley crying like a baby disappears from my mind like the fog when the sun rises, at the sound of his voice. Waiting until the last possible second before opening my eyes in hopes he disappears like Wesley.

"The President isn't on board, so it's just an ordinary 747 headed for New York." The words are out of my mouth before I can think.

My eyes pop open to find the owner of the voice, Douglas Hayes, one of the Fact Checkers who works in the office standing with his phone raised above his head in the standard selfie pose, the presidential seal on the wall behind him.

"Yes, it is," lowering the phone and tapping on the wall. "See, President of the United States." Enunciating each word as if speaking to a child. His friend, Richard, I think his name is, nods his head like one of those dogs Mr. Tripp has glued to the dashboard of his truck. Something about the cockiness in their presen-

39

tation has me seeing red. I may not be the smartest girl on the planet, but from where I stand this is information the pair of them should have.

"Air Force One is given to any aircraft the President uses in flight. It doesn't matter if it's this 747 or a crop duster, once the President is on board, it takes on the name."

Doug looks to a now laughing Richard and then back to me. His eyes drop to my name badge; the curve of a smile creases his face.

"She's right," a deep voice sounds to my right, startling me and pulling the smile off Doug's face. Sitting not three feet from me is the most gorgeous man I've ever seen. Hauntingly familiar eyes, blue like the ocean I've only seen in photographs, hair cut short on the sides, with the top sticking up in a fashion which completely works for him. Broad shoulders and, from what I can tell from this angle, a trim waist. Despite his tailored jacket, it's evident he spends quite a bit of time in the gym. Try as I might, I can't place where I've seen him before.

"Elliott? Not a typical chick name."

Doug's dig pulls my attention back, tossing gasoline onto the flame his condescending attitude created earlier.

"My father wanted all boys, made it to number nine before his luck ran out and my mother had a girl. He'd already had the name chosen, so Elliott went on my birth certificate." And because I'd had years of men telling me what to do and making decisions for me, I let the snide remark dancing on my tongue free. "Besides, I wasn't aware Doug was short for Douche bag."

Laughter fell from Richard as the gorgeous guy to my right stands and removes his jacket, the smell of his cologne hits me, stirring something primal deep inside. Doug, not influenced by the muscles testing the limits on the man's pressed shirt, smacks his friend in the chest, resulting in Richard doubling over in laughter.

"Listen, Elliott. Take it from me, no dude likes a smart girl."

Muscle Guy glowers hard at Doug, his jaw clenching as he stares down at him. "Speak for yourself, Douche Bag."

CHAPTER SEVEN

RYAN

"All right, Gentleman, the pilot, and crew have arrived, so take your seats and we can be on our way." Congressman Howard pushes past the two idiots blocking the aisle, taking his seat behind me, squeezing my shoulder as he lowers himself into the soft leather.

He'd briefed me on what was in store for today, a quick flight to New York, then an appointment with the Deputy Director of the FBI as soon as we land. Since a full-crew is required for the 747 to fly for a scheduled maintenance check, Howard made a last-minute schedule for the aircraft, using the ruse of saving taxpayer dollars to camouflage the trip.

I assumed I was the first to arrive, outside of the Congressman, until my eyes landed on the woman sitting with her ankles crossed in the front row. Historically I've been team blonde, however as I take in her red hair pulled back in a severe bun at the nape of her neck, I know my future is colored in crimson.

My dick jumps to attention when she opens her mouth,

schooling the pompous ass in shit he should already know. My eyes drift to the center of her chest where her name badge hangs, my fantasy getting lost between the mounds of perfectly round and, thank-fuck, natural breasts.

As Thing One and Thing Two take their seats, I lean over the aisle, extending my hand in greeting. "Ryan Biggs, a pleasure to meet you."

Her blue eyes flashed from my outstretched hand to my face, a hint of a smile breaking out as she mimics my position. "Elliott York, but please, call me Elli."

"Elli." Trying it out on my tongue, "Cool name, although I think you totally rock Elliott."

A laugh bubbles out of her chest and I notice for the first time the splattering of freckles along her nose. I've always been a sucker for freckles, tiny kisses from the sun gods my mother called them, I call them sexy as fuck, especially on Elliott.

"Thank you. Although it has created a bit of a mess for me, especially when I enrolled in college."

"I can imagine," adjusting in my seat. "I heard you say you had eight older brothers, that must have been amazing growing up?"

Dipping her focus to her lap, running her fingers down the fabric of her skirt, "Amazing isn't the word I would use."

"Super protective, were they?"

The plane shakes as we taxi down the runway, causing Elli to grip the armrest of her seat, my question forgotten.

"Not a fan of flying?"

"Don't know," she swallows, her knuckles white from gripping the leather seat. "Never flown before."

My body acts of its own accord, releasing my seatbelt and jumping across the aisle to the seat beside her. Taking her hand in mine, I pull her close, kissing the top of her head as the aircraft rises higher and higher.

"Whenever I'm nervous, I close my eyes and think about my favorite place on Earth. It's a stretch of land owned by one of my best friends, in South Carolina. Have you ever been there?"

Elli shook her head, but I could feel her body marginally relax.

"It's beautiful, with the tall pine trees and lush vegetation, with hills and valleys and some of the nicest people you've ever met. There's a pond on his land, right behind his house, where no matter what time day or night, the catfish break the surface just to see what's going on."

Pulling to the side, her hand doesn't let go of mine as she looks up at me, "Sounds like a place near where my parents live. At night, the crickets and frogs sing you to sleep, while the hoot owls keep watch."

The shaking of the plane levels out as we reach cruising altitude. Elli looks down to our intertwined hands and attempts to pull away, placing distance between us. "You must apologize to your wife or girlfriend for me. I didn't mean to grab you like that."

Pulling her hand between both of mine, "Don't have either one. What about you, is there some lucky guy waiting at home for you?"

Her gaze stays locked on our fingers, "Didn't have time for boys growing up, between going to school and work, then coming home and helping on the farm." A visible shiver rocks her body, "Not that any of them could hold my attention."

I'm about to ask her if she will join me for dinner in New York when movement at the front of the plane catches my attention. Two men, maintenance crew by the looks of their uniforms and came on board with the pilot, are now standing, pulling bags out of one of the compartments overhead. Bags I know for certain they didn't bring with them.

Both have dark hair which curls around the edge of their ball caps. The one closest to me is taller than the other, with a clean, thin line of hair boarding the edge of his chin. He's heavier than his partner, by at least thirty pounds. But it's their shoes that has the hair on the back of my neck standing straight. Dress shoes, where boots or athletic wear should be, designer labels, the same brand which fills half of my closet in the condo.

Slipping from my seat, "Stay here, Elli." I use the ruse of grabbing my jacket to gain a better look at what they're doing, the smaller of the two looks in my direction, but continues to search for something inside the bag. Glancing behind me, I see the Congressman on his phone and as I look back to the two men, I find the larger one bounding down the aisle, a gun raised and pointed at me. His face is clear now, but unfamiliar, with dark eyes and a scar that runs from the bottom of his left ear to the corner of his mouth. A mirror image to the one Matt has.

"Put the jacket down, Pretty Boy."

Elli gasps beside me, and it's everything I have not to reach for her, taking the fear I can feel flowing off her away. But I keep the son-of-a-bitch in my sights, watching as he continues to come at me, his partner not far behind.

"I said," tipping his hand to the side, the gun dipping forward slightly. "To put the fucking jacket down."

"Please, Biggs, do as he says." Howard pleads from behind me, but it's the tiny whimper to my left which has me holding firm and standing to my full height. I can see her in my peripheral vision, bottom lip trapped between her teeth, knuckles white again from holding on to the leather of her chair, blue eyes locked on the end of the gun.

Raising my arm, I stare down the barrel of my gun, the man's forehead in my sights. "Do yourself a favor, motherfucker. Put the gun down before it's too late."

A sinister smile grows slowly on his face, white teeth revealed as he lowers his gun and for the briefest of moments I think I've won. But just as fast as he lowered it, he pulls it back up, fires a single shot and my world goes black.

CHAPTER EIGHT

ELLI

As if in slow motion, Ryan drops like a dead weight, his gun clattering to the floor beside him. Doug stands with a triumphant smile behind him, laughing as if he'd won some championship fight.

Springing from my chair, I ignore the two men wielding guns around and shouting orders in a language I don't understand. Kneeling beside Ryan, I check for a pulse, relieved when I feel his strong heartbeat.

The strangled sound of my name falling from the Congressman's lips pulls me from the muscled neck of the man who's been so kind to me. Standing, I look to the second row of seats to find my boss slouched in his seat, a dark circle forming in the middle of his thigh.

"Sir, you've been shot." His face contorts in pain, as blood drips down the chair and onto the floor. Looking around, I frantically try and recall the first aid article I read on the train ride here. I need to stop the bleeding, but with no idea, if there are medical supplies on board, I search the surrounding area desperately looking for something, until it hits me.

Stepping over Ryan, I grab my purse, searching inside for the single sanitary pad I keep for emergencies. Ripping open the plastic covering and tossing the trash to the floor, I open my overnight bag, removing a new pair of nylons.

Turning to go back to the Congressman, my path is blocked by the man holding the gun as he stands over Ryan while the other guy removes a shiny watch from his arm and the shoes from his feet, binding his hands together.

Doug stands to the side, cursing under his breath demanding to know why the fuck the internet isn't working, while Richard looks to be in shock, his mouth gaping and eyes locked on the gun in the man's hand.

With Ryan still unconscious, the men pull him to the side, propping him up against the seat as I slide past them. Reaching down, "Sorry, sir." I apologize as I use the hole left behind by the bullet to rip his pant leg open. He hisses at the intrusion, but slumps back in the chair, allowing me to press the cotton part of the pad against his thigh. "This is going to hurt, but we have to keep pressure on the wound."

Ripping the package of nylons with my teeth, my crimson covered fingers fumble as I unwind the pantyhose from the cardboard insert.

"Be calm and do as they say, Ms. York." Congressman Howard rasps, his eyes shut tight from the pain as I wrap the hose around his thigh, securing the pad to his leg. I'm not sure how well this will work considering the amount of blood seeping past.

A moan from behind me snaps my attention to a slowly waking Ryan. His eyes, like the Congressman's, are clamped tight. Dropping to my knees, I cup my hands against his jaw, running my thumbs along the apple of his cheeks. I can't explain the pull I have to him, maybe I'm under the same spell he has on the rest of my co-workers, but I never heard them mention his willingness to go out of his way to help them.

"Hey," his deep voice rumbles. The sexiness of it, despite our current predicament, stirs something in my core. Blue eyes, so deep and haunting, slowly open, the recognition of what's happened flashes in his eyes.

"Hey, how do you feel?" It's lame and I hate how stupid I sound, but it reflects my current concern. I know next to little about him, but desperately want that to change, to explore this new feeling, see if something wonderful could grow from it.

"How long was I out?"

"Ten minutes, give or take." I shrug, "Thankfully it was just a hit on the head for you. Congressman Howard was shot in the leg."

Ryan looks over my shoulder, "How bad?"

Following his gaze, "I'm no doctor, but it's bleeding pretty bad. I put a feminine pad and pantyhose over it."

"Good thinking." Motioning to the door at the back of the room, "If it gets worse, there are supplies through that door."

Turning around, I find the door he's talking about and wonder how Ryan knows so much about this plane. The information I have is limited, most of the details classified, including the layout and equipment on board.

"So much for my plans of asking you to dinner tonight," he jokes, looking down at this torn shirt and bound hands. "Which one of these fuckers hit me?"

Tipping my head to the right, "Douche bag Doug." Flashing my eyes to the two men with guns, a cellphone in the hand of the smaller one. "But those men took your watch and shoes."

Ryan cranes his head to see the pair, holding his focus on them for several minutes before turning back to face me. "I need you to do me a favor."

"Okay." I agree without hesitation.

"There is a necklace around my neck, inside my shirt. I need you to put your thumb over the face of the icon and hold it for a few seconds. Then, so no one can see, take it off and put it on."

"Why?"

"Please, Elli. I swear to tell you everything, just do it."

Nodding, I reach under his tie to unhook the first button, the blood on my hands now dry.

"Undo my tie so they think that's what you're doing."

"Good idea."

Pulling his tie free, I locate the silver chain around his neck, the icon of Saint Christopher in the center. I mash my thumb to the center, counting to ten silently in my head before unclamping the chain and removing it from his neck, my fingers brushing the warm skin of his muscled chest. Ryan watches my movements, his gaze intense and I wonder what he's thinking. Returning to my seat on the floor, I mash my thumb again before clasping the chain around my neck and tucking it inside my blouse.

Ryan sends me a wink as I sit up straight, the two men with guns none the wiser.

"Hey, dumb-ass Doug." His accurate description makes me smile, but quickly fades as the look in his blue orbs darkens to a level of anger that has me recoiling.

Doug leans over the back of the seat, his phone still in hand as he looks from the Congressman to Ryan.

"Mind telling me what the fuck made you sucker punch me from behind?"

Doug drops his phone, eyes shifting to the two men who are now shouting in a language I don't understand.

"Because you were trying to be a hero and get us all killed." He whispers, his eyes darting between Ryan and the two men. "Now we just have to wait for a mayday signal to go out and a gazillion fighter jets will bring us down."

"Look out the window, Einstein. How many fucking jets do you see? This plane isn't carrying the President; it's going for maintenance. Any signal they get will fall on deaf ears as a mechanical issue."

Doug's face falls as his body slumps in the chair, the color fading from his face as the gravity of this situation registers in his thick head.

"Our only hope is Ted Durant when we fail to land in New York." The Congressman adds, beads of sweat collecting on his forehead.

"Deputy Director of the FBI?" For the second time, today, words leave my lips before my body can stop them. Mr. Durant was once the Sheriff two counties over from the one I grew up in. Folks around town spoke of his departure to the Feds for weeks when I was a little girl. I tried, with great difficulty, to connect why the FBI would be involved if the Congressman missed a meeting, only to come up more confused than when I started.

"Not since a member of your staff canceled the meeting." Jolted, my attention drawn to the cellphone in Gun Guy's hand, a look of victory covering his face as he twisted the phone from side to side.

"And now, our friend Ghost is going to disable the transmitter system, so no one can track our progress." His foot connects with Ryan's thigh," Aren't you, Ghost?"

"Ghost?"

Gun Guy looks down at me, tips his head to the side, and then tosses it back in laughter. "You haven't told your feisty girlfriend who you are?" Lowering himself down to my level, dread fills my belly as he wraps an arm around Ryan's neck, placing a sloppy kiss to his face.

"Allow me to do the introductions. Mr. Pretty Boy here enlisted in the Air Force where he raced up the ranks with his ability to pick up the skills they taught him, crossing over from airplane mechanic to pilot in a matter of years. Then, out of the blue, he chucks it all, leaving the Air Force and joining the Navy to become a SEAL."

Unable to believe what Gun Guy is saying, my eyes shifting to Ryan who by the intensity of his clench jaw is about to kill someone. My grasp of what the SEAL's do is limited, but enough to know this man in front of me is a trained killing machine, able to get in and out of situations most other men fail.

Gun Guy lifts Ryan's wrist, "I took your handy little watch after seeing first hand all the clever little things it can do."

Tipping his head behind him, "And since we know how much you love tracking devices, your friends will be looking for your shoes at the bottom of the ocean."

My throat feels thick at the thought; this is how I will die. How ironic; my first flight, first opportunity to see another part of the country, only to die in a fiery ball at the bottom of an ocean I've never seen.

"Now, be a good sport, and do your magic on that transmitter."

"And if I refuse?"

Gun Guy's movements are so fast; I don't even register anything until I feel the metal of the gun against my temple.

"I'll blow your little girlfriend's brains out."

I can hear my heart beating in my head, feel the tears prick at the back of my eyes, see the absence of fear in Ryan's eyes.

"Go ahead."

CHAPTER NINE

RYAN

R elief washes over me as I watch Elli place her thumb over the sensor. The second the system doesn't recognize her thumbprint; it will send an alert to every program we have. Cell phones and computers will go crazy, sending my team information about whom the print belongs to. All of this is in theory of course, as I've never tested the system like I have the others.

Elli doesn't blink an eye as those two words leave my lips. Mr. Dead Man, the name I've given him, as the first chance I get, I'm ending him, pulls my gun away from her temple, pointing it to the ceiling and attempts to fire off a round.

When it fails to fire, "Another clever tool." Dead Man rejoices, examining my gun in his hand. "But something tells me she's still important to you."

Standing, Dead Man reaches down, yanking Elli by the bun at the back of her neck, pulling her to stand beside him. Her red hair falls from its elastic confines, landing in waves of beautiful red curls across her shoulder and covering her breast. "How about instead of shooting her, me and my friend fuck her while you watch?"

Clearing my throat, doing everything in my power not to launch myself at this motherfucker. "What is your name?"

Pushing Elli into the chair closest him, her hair bounces and covers her face. "Josef."

"Well, Josef, if you ever touch her again, I will cut your fucking fingers off and hold you down while she feeds them to you."

"You can try, Ghost. But where we're going, I'm the least of your worries. Now, do as I said, disconnect the transmitter."

Leaning my head back against the wall, "Not until you untie me so I can have a look at the Congressman."

"You're not in charge here, Ghost. I say when that bastard gets attention, not you." He roars.

"And you don't know how to disconnect the fucking thing. So, who's in charge again?"

"Open your mouth again, Ghost, and the girl will get my dick shoved so far up her ass, she will gag on the tip."

"I'd be careful, she's the baby of eight boys, chances are she could kick your ass and not break a nail. Now untie me and let me have a look at the Congressman. Then, and only then, will I disconnect the fucking transmitter."

Josef looks to the second man, conversing with him in Persian. They keep their sentences short and danced around any information as I'm fairly certain they know I understand every word. Glancing at Elli, I catch her eye and mouthed, 'Are you okay?' She nods once, her eyes shifting to the two men not ten feet from her and then back to me. I need to reassure her, let her know nothing bad is going to happen to her as long as I am breathing.

Josef finishes his conversation, the two agreeing the transmitter has to be taken out before we reach New York. With the clock ticking, and us traveling at five hundred miles an hour, we should reach New York in a matter of minutes.

Josef says nothing as he clips the zip ties from my hands and ankles. The second I'm free, I jump to my socked feet, grabbing Elli as I race down the aisle toward the closed door where the medical supplies are located.

Once through the door, I spin on my heels, pulling Elli into my arms. "Baby, tell me you're okay?"

We cling to each other; the smell of her perfume invades my nose and bleeds through my pores to become a part of me.

"I'm okay, but you scared me with the gun thing."

"I know," pulling her back, I look deep in her blue eyes. "Please, trust me when I say, nothing and no one will ever hurt you while I'm around."

"I trust you," she swears as she dives back into my chest, pressing her nose into the crevice where my neck and shoulder meets. "What is this transmitter Josef wants you to disconnect?"

"It's a signal the plane sends out, letting other aircraft and Air Traffic Control know where we are."

"Oh."

The heaviness of what it means to disconnect the device isn't lost on her. Once I sever the wires that connect it, we'll be one huge target for some unsuspecting airplane. This is foreign territory for me, this instant attraction and need to be close to another human. After less than an hour with Elli, the pain and humiliation left over from Lindsey has begun to fade.

"Come on, I need to have a look at the Congressman."

Opening the cabinet, I hand packages of gauze, quick-clot, and several Ace bandages to Elli. She never falters, a determined look on her face as she tucks each item I handed her in the crook of her arm

Pulling her back through the door, I drop to my knees beside the Congressman, his skin is pale and covered in sweat. "How do you feel, Sir?"

"Like I've been shot." He rasps, the beginnings of a chuckle coming through before he grimaces in pain.

"I know how you feel." I'd been shot twice, once in the shoulder and once in the arm, neither was enough to brag about, even though they hurt like hell. "Ms. York did good in wrapping this, but you're still bleeding. I can cauterize the area with this."

Ripping open the package of quick-clot, sprinkling the power over the open wound, Howard cries out and grips the seat as the chemical goes to work.

"Times up, Ghost. Disconnect the transmitter." Josef demands from behind me. Standing to my full height, sending a wink in Elli's direction, her warm eyes reflect back at me as she offers the Congressman a sip of water.

Spinning on my heels, I tower over Josef by nearly six inches, the cocky grin on his face makes me want to knock his teeth out. "It's Biggs, you haven't earned the right to call me Ghost."

As if I've said the most amusing thing in the world to him, he tosses his head back in laughter. With my gun shoved in the waist-band of his pants, he motions for me to walk in front of him, past the second man, and toward the cockpit.

Josef reaches around, sliding a key into the lock, twisting it until the door pops open, revealing a third man sitting at the controls, a notebook rests on his lap as he labels the instruments in front of him. A headset is still connected to the uninformed pilot slumped in the corner, a trail of dried blood down his neck, pooling on the collar of his shirt. There's no need to check for a heartbeat, as an exit wound resides where his right eye used to.

"Friend of yours, Ghost?" Josef laughs, pushing back the dead pilot's head with his foot, a new trail of blood leaves his nose. I won't dignify this piece of shit with a response, give him any fuel to add to the chaotic fire brewing in his head. Instead, I take a look around the cockpit, it's been a while since I stood inside one this size, my trips of late have been in the back of a helo and cargo planes.

A walk down memory lane of the last time I worked on one of these will have to wait until I have Elli safely back home.

My eyes land on a piece of masking tape secured along the edge of the instrument panel. The numbers, while written in Persian, are most definitely the coordinates of our final destination. Locating the panel housing the transmitter, I attempt to pull the cover away, but considering the intended cargo, the door is secured with at least a dozen bolts.

"I need tools to open this," I call over my shoulder, assuming there's no way they will hand me something I can use as a potential weapon. Josef motions to the guy sitting in the Captain's chair, who gives a look but hands over a screwdriver.

Shrugging, I wrap my hand around the grip and get to work on the bolts, it takes less time than I bargained for, as half the bolts are loose as hell and barely hanging on. Once inside, I lay the screwdriver by my foot, hoping the fascination of watching me take this thing apart will amuse the pair enough they forget about it.

The transmitter is right where it's supposed to be, the green light on the left flashing, letting me know it's working. Tugging the box out of its space, I turn it over, the disconnected wire staring me right in the face.

A battle rages inside me. It's one thing to pull the plug and allow these bastards the opportunity to die a fiery death, it's another to place Elli in harm's way, especially when I can do something about it.

Using the point of the screwdriver, I break open the box, removing the wire that sends power to the green light. Using the wire that feeds the recorder, I stick it in the secondary feed, the one I pray my team is listening to.

Returning to my seat, I pull Elli close, kissing the side of her head as I whisper in her ear, "I know where we're going."

CHAPTER TEN

ELLI

I lose track of time as I watch the sun skirt across the sky and then begin dipping toward the horizon. Ryan and I take turns checking on Congressman Howard, his leg has stopped bleeding, but Ryan worried about infection setting in. We exchange small talk, including how the men holding us captive spoke Persian, one of several languages Ryan is fluent in.

When the noise of the engines changes and the rays of the sun shift from the right side of the plane to the left, Ryan jumps to his feet. "Come on, Elli. Get to the back of the plane and strap yourself in, no window seats."

Following his instructions, I head down the aisle as he picks up the Congressman, tossing him over his shoulder, stopping long enough to point in my direction as he passes Doug and Richard. Neither move, only glancing over the top of their seats as I cinch the seatbelt around me.

Ryan is convinced the pilot is as green as shamrock when it comes to landing this plane. I don't ask how he knows or how the pilot managed to get us into the air. I trust him, the first man besides my father I felt I could put any faith in.

With the Congressman buckled in, Ryan leaps over the row of seats in front of me as the plane tipped so severely to the left oxygen masks drop from the ceiling and the exit signs begin to flash.

"Ryan," I scream as the motion sends him flying into the aisle. The plane starts to shake, shifting this time to the right, the sound of breaking glass and cries for help can be heard over the roar of the engine. Dangling oxygen masks sway with the rocking of the plane, another shake, and tip to the left, a wall of doors opens, their contents falling like an avalanche covering the seats we occupied not two minutes ago.

Another series of shakes, followed by a feeling of weightlessness, the motion strains my body against the straps of my seatbelt. More glass breaking and another dip, then a shudder, leaving me nauseous and terrified.

"It's okay, Ms. York." The Congressman shouts, "Just turbulence." While I appreciate his lie, it does little to ease the terror lodged in my throat. Gripping the edges of Ryan's pendant through my blouse, I begin reciting the Lord's prayer inside my head.

As the plane shifts again, a body bounces in the seat beside me. "He's right, Elli. Nothing to worry about, just pockets of air." Ryan's smiling face appears, a cut above his left eye dotted with blood. "But just in case I'm wrong," His right-hand reaches up, cupping the back of my neck and pulling me close until his lips cover mine. Shocked by his sudden moves, my lips open in a gasp. Ryan takes advantage and slips his tongue past my teeth, caressing his tongue against mine, twirling, sucking, and exploring every inch of my mouth. Hands hold me impossibly close as he dominates me. Never in my life have I experienced a kiss like this, unaware so much passion and raw need could exist.

But the events around us refuse to be ignored, as the plane takes another dive, the momentum separates us. "Arms around those knees, Elli."

Nodding, I lower my upper body to my lap, surrounding my thighs in a tight hug. Turning my head, I lock eyes with Ryan, finding all the confidence and assurance I will ever need in those orbs. Reaching out, he intertwines our fingers behind my legs, our gaze never breaking as a storm of debris rages overhead.

The plane shakes, and glass continues to break, while more shouts of not wanting to die ring around us. Ryan's hand never leaves mine, his eyes remain locked with mine, even through the sound of metal moaning from the strain of it all, he never looks away.

My ears pop, and nausea grows worse, the wind blowing dirt below my feet, in my hair and landing on Ryan's white shirt. The plane dips once more before bouncing twice with such force I see my hair lift in the air and hover, only to slap down on my cheek as gravity kicks in.

As the last bounce hits hard, something shifts, and it feels as if we're spinning. Ryan grips my fingers tight mouthing something I can't make out, his eyes dancing with mischief as the plane rights itself, shoving hard forward, sending my head into the seat in front of me.

The overwhelming smell of kerosene burns my nostrils, so I pull my body up to search for the source. Wind whips, sending waves of sand against my ankles, the tiny prickles scrape my skin and force me to pull them up.

Dirt and sand fill the cabin like a giant cloud over the prairie, invading my lungs and making me cough. Squinting my eyes, I look over the top of the seat in front of me, where once sat a monitor against polished teak wood, now is miles of endless desert. The middle of the plane is detached and turned upside down, the nose buried somewhere in the desert floor. Immense heat surrounds me, the sun blindingly bright despite its position at the edge of the horizon.

Ryan jumps from his seat, checking on the Congressman who sputters his answer of being fine. My eyes land on Doug, or rather what is left of him, as his body lays motionless under the wreckage of the plane, eyes wide open and arms above his head, the cell phone he treasured so much still clamped in his hand.

Off in the distance, I see two black objects I assume are cars by the way they move over the desert.

"Elli, you okay?" Ryan palms my face, his fingers rough from the sand, his white shirt torn in the front, his muscular chest on display. "Elli?" He calls once again, but my mouth won't work, won't form the words to answer his question. "Elliott, answer me, goddamn it."

Coughing, "I-I'm okay."

Reaching down, he unbuckles my seat belt and pulls my freed body to his, wrapping me in his sand covered arms. "We need to get out of here, it's not safe." The moaning sound of metal behind us confirms what he says and has me out of my seat.

Ryan heads toward the edge of the severed plane and jumps to the sand below, dancing on the heated sand until he leaps into the other half of the plane. I watch in fascination as he searches for something, pulling up wreckage until he finds what he's looking for.

Off in the distance, the cars are still approaching, they're close enough now I can tell they are jeeps, old army ones with big guns mounted on the hoods.

Movement to my right catches my attention, it's Richard, his jacket torn and body covered in sand. His eyes land on Doug and rushes to his side, dropping to his knees and staring at his dead friend. Ryan jumps from the wreckage, a pair of shoes on his feet. I doubt they are his, but I know why he took them.

Our crash landing wouldn't have gone unnoticed; the approaching jeeps are likely pirates looking for items of value or the reason we never made it to New York. Either way, I'm the only female and the little training I did yesterday spelled out exactly what is most likely to happen to me.

Richard notices Ryan standing beside him, more specifically the shoes on his feet.

"Take those off," he demands, jumping to his feet and charging Ryan. "You stole them, give them back to him."

Richard tries to shove Ryan, but it's like a small child trying to push a piece of furniture out of the way. Ryan stands his ground, allowing the grief-stricken man to pound on his chest, tears and screams precede Richard falling to his knees, his cries reveal the amount of pain flowing through his body.

As the jeeps move closer, Josef and the other man step from the wreckage, their uniforms exchanged for clothing I've only seen on the news and in pictures, long dress-like shirt over linen pants.

Josef jumps from the edge of the wreckage, steps over Doug's body and waves the Jeeps over. The second man follows, but his attention lingers on the body, staring at poor Doug with such intensity.

Ryan rejoins me, wrapping his arm tightly around me and kissing me softly as the sound of the engines grows closer. "I don't want you to be afraid, I'll kill any motherfucker who tries to touch you."

While his promise is heartfelt, I won't hold him to it, as there is one of him and at least five men approaching. When the first jeep stops beside Josef, I make a promise to myself; if today is my last on earth, I will make it count and die with dignity, not playing into some sick bastard's hand by begging him to spare me. Rising to my tiptoes, I place one final kiss to his lips and share the best smile I can conjure up, letting him know I believe him.

Outside the plane, Josef greets a tall man dressed in similar clothing, motioning over his shoulder in my direction. The tall man jumps from the Jeep; several others surround him as he walks with ease through the shifting sand.

"Salaam-Alaikum," the man says to Ryan, his right hand over his heart as he moves to stand before him, extending his left hand to Ryan as if asking to shake.

"Peace?" Ryan shakes his head, ignoring the outstretched hand. "You don't even know the meaning of the word, Aazar."

"How nice to see you again, Ghost. How long has it been, a year…two?"

I'm shocked by his near-perfect English and disturbed by the coldness Ryan shows him. What horrible things has this man done to earn such disdain from Ryan?

"Not nearly enough. Now, why the fuck am I here?" Ryan crosses his arms over his chest, his stance, like a Viking, taking on a storm. The action is both intimidating and erotic, stirring up needs I have no business entertaining.

"In due time, my friend, in due time." Aazar looks over his shoulder, says something in what I suspect is Persian. Josef and the second man jump into action, scurrying across the sand to stand beside him.

Aazar points to the Congressman, whose eyes are closed and, I suspect, has finally passed out from the pain and blood loss. He spouts off more words I don't understand before pulling out a gun and shooting the pair between the eyes.

Ryan shakes his head, dipping the top half of his body as he peruses the floor under his pilfered shoes. Leaning over toward me, "Apparently, they weren't authorized to shoot anyone."

Aazar pockets the gun, turning back to Ryan, his eyes bright as they land on me.

"My apologies, beautiful lady, I've failed to welcome you. My name is Aazar and we've been expecting you. Well, not a lady such as yourself, but I do hope you find the accommodations to your liking."

My father used to say dressing a snake up in the finest clothes didn't take away the venom in his bite. Something told me this Aazar was the first of many snakes I would encounter today.

"Come, the sun wants to set and the desert is no place for a man at night." Aazar snaps his fingers and several men from the jeep jump down, coming to pick up the Congressman from his chair and carry him back to one of the vehicles.

Richard stares wide-eyed as the men passed, his fear evident in the pleas which leave his lips, promises of secrets which he will exchange for his freedom. Aazar steps from the wreckage, pausing as he stands before Richard, extending a hand to help him to his feet, motioning to one of the men to help him.

"They're going to kill him, aren't they?" I whisper to Ryan.

"Yes, Elli. He'll be lucky to make it to where we're headed."

Ryan helps me into the jeep, settling in the seat beside me. Looking over the wreckage, the plane is broken into three parts. The nose is completely gone, lost to the layers of sand, the pilot no doubt buried with it. The wing on the left is partially covered in sand, only the shell remaining. The right is bent in half, the tip pointing to the sky above. If what I've read in books to be true, by the time the sun rises tomorrow, the sand will have shifted, taking the plane with it.

Aazar shouts a command, waving his hand high in the air, and the jeep lunges into drive, a caravan quickly forming as we travel away from the setting sun. Shifting my focus to the mountains in the distance, I see something shimmer at the bottom of one of the ridges. Brushing it off, I lean into Ryan, savoring the closeness of a man I wish I could explore more.

Drawing closer to the foot of the mountain, the light of the day nearly gone, the jeep in the middle, the one carrying Aazar and Richard takes a sharp right and disappears from my vision. Burying my face in Ryan's chest, keeping myself from watching what I'm sure is the end of Richard. Ryan pulls me tight, placing a kiss to my head. I can feel his heartbeat, the warmth of his skin as he traces his fingers up and down my arm. This is what I want to remember, being close to someone, not out of an arrangement made over coffee and my mother's apple pie, but out of the need to be close and wanting to be there.

The sun is nearly gone as we enter a gate, shouts in Persian ring out as the caravan passes through the structure. Men with rifles gripped in their hands stare down at us from the top of a massive wall. Inside is like a small village, children and dogs run around as women, covered from head to toe, stand lurking from the corners, their eyes following as we round a bubbling fountain in the center.

When the jeep stops, more shouts come as a pair of headlights dance in the entrance behind us. Aazar stands in the center of the approaching jeep, a gun raised high in the air as the people around us cheer. My eyes search frantically for Richard, but as all the men step from the car, he is nowhere to be seen.

"Welcome, welcome," Aazar announces as he walks with

purpose toward our jeep. Several men have the Congressman lifted and lying on a makeshift stretcher, carrying him into a stone building, several women rushing in behind them.

Ryan lifts his knees, balancing his foot on the edge of the door as he peruses the surrounding structures. The night is upon us and several security lights come to life as Aazar moves to stand on my side of the jeep, his hand held out for me.

"We have hot food and a shower if you like."

Something tells me any bites of food would be my last and the shower would be held with a captive audience. I won't clean up for anyone so they can rob me of the one gift I saved for my wedding night.

Ryan stands, offers his hand and helps me from the jeep. "She stays with me, Aazar. Any of your men get any ideas, I'll kill them with my bare hands. Feel me?"

Aazar bows, extending his arm in the direction of the tallest building in the compound. Its gold-domed top has to be the reflection I saw in the desert. Large windows, filled with stained glass surround the area below the dome. Arched entrances run the length of what I assume is a balcony, where more armed men stand sentry under the windows.

"It all looks so new," I whisper aloud as we follow several gun welding men past the fountain and up the sandstone steps of the large building.

"That's because it is." Ryan's head shifts from side to side, his eyes never staying in one place for more than a split-second.

Inside, the temperature changes from the humidity plagued air to a much more comfortable level, almost as if stepping into air conditioning. The interior resembles a palace with its shiny floors and gold accents about. The glass windows above look like paintings, illuminated from the security lights outside.

"This way, I'll show you to your room." Ryan's hands never leave me as we follow Aazar down a long hall, around several corners and two sets of stairs. A lone guard stands outside a pair of double doors, with ornate carvings telling a story of what looks like a battle.

The room is massive, the windows covered by a screen, with hundreds of diamond shapes cut from a single sheet of wood painted black and filtering out most of the light. A single bed, the comforter matching the colorful artwork on the walls, rich gold tones with red and an indigo blue tossed in the mix.

The door slams hard, causing me to gasp, as Ryan pulls me close.

"You know, it's okay to cry if you want to."

Stepping away, "Crying won't change anything or bring an end to the regret I feel for not doing all the things I've dreamt of doing."

Clearing the distance I placed between us, "Like what?" His eyes flick between mine, a genuine curiosity for what I have to say.

"I have a map on my wall, or I did until I moved to DC, a pin in every city I want to visit. My first flight ends in a crash and I have no earthly idea where I am."

Ryan reaches up, running his rough hand along my cheek, his eyes full of the same regret I feel.

"Is what they said about you being a SEAL true?"

Licking his lips, "Yes."

"And you know who that guy is and why we're here?"

Nodding, "I know who he is, but not what he wants or why we're here."

Just as I'm about to ask him where exactly we are, chanting echoes from what sounds like a speaker outside the window.

"What the…?"

"It's the Maghreb, the evening prayer."

Flashing my eyes to his, "Prayers?"

"Yes, you'll hear them five times a day. There will be one more at bedtime."

Crossing the room, I look through one of the diamonds to see the yard is empty, even the men on top of the fence are nowhere to be seen. The jeeps we arrived in are gone, the fountain bubbling away in the center. With a deep breath, I consider everything that's happened, all the things I've yet to experience. Turning from the window, my mind focuses on the one regret I have the ability to change. Standing before Ryan, my hands rest on the warm skin of his chest.

"There is something I never got around to doing, something I was saving for a later time."

Cupping my hand around his neck, I pull until our lips touch, dragging my left hand down his chiseled chest to the belt securing his pants, pushing my fingers past the material of his waistband to the softness of his skin beneath.

"Elli," Ryan breaks the kiss, his eyes bore into mine. "Are you sure?"

Kissing him once more, "If we survive this, I want to have at least one happy memory. I don't want them to take what is mine to freely give."

CHAPTER ELEVEN

RYAN

B lue eyes plead with me, shattering any reservations I have and fueling the desire I've possessed since the moment I first saw her. I've no idea how much time we have, or if Aazar will keep his men at bay or feed the hunger I saw in each of their eyes. The man is a loose cannon, one who has betrayed more than one leader he'd sworn his loyalty to.

"You deserve so much better than this. I swear, when we get out of this, I will take you to any city on that map of yours and love you until the bad memories of this day are gone."

Not waiting for an argument, I pick her up, cover her lips with mine and cross the room, placing her on the edge of the bed. I've never been with a virgin, but I know this will cause her pain, and it's my job to make sure she is as ready as possible.

Slipping my tongue passed her perfect lips, I reach over and begin removing her blouse. She follows suit, removing the remnants of the shirt I pulled from the dry cleaning bag this morning. I wouldn't think of the day I bought it, pulled from one store after the other, taking instructions from a woman who means nothing to me now.

My fingertips brush the skin on her chest, the chain of my pendant brings a smile to my face and a twitch from my dick. Rounding her back, I find the clasp of her bra and something silky covering it. Bewildered, I pull back to see Elli has a full slip on, something I assumed went out with pantyhose. As she pulls her skirt off, I notice she has a pair of those pulled up to her waist as well.

"Let me." Stopping her fingers from lifting off the slip, I drop to my knees raising the silky material, revealing untouched skin, her essence calling me. Reaching down, I slip off the tattered dress shoes, taking her foot in hand and relishing the soft feel of her silk covered toes. I've been with women who've paraded around in skimpy lingerie, something I toss to the floor without a second thought, but this was different. Elli wore this every day, taking an added step to make herself feel secure.

Setting her foot on my thigh, I run my nose up the inside of her leg as I reach up and pull the pantyhose down, trailing open mouth kisses down her leg until I reach the arch of her foot, where I use the flat part of my tongue to pull a moan from her chest. Repeating the other side, I sit her on the bed, legs apart, feet resting on my shoulders, her panties damp from the lubrication I'm creating. Reaching up, I push the cotton material aside, feasting on the sight of her virgin pussy.

Although groomed, she's not bare like so many I've been with before. The sprinkling of hair is thicker at the top and sparse on her lips, but the smell of her and the knowledge I'm the first man to see this sight has my dick begging to get inside.

With the tip of my tongue, I touch the bottom of her lips,

tracing the soft skin up and past her opening, circling the puckered clit at the top.

"Ryan," she moans my name aloud. The breathy way it fills my ears has my tongue sinking deep in her opening, as I shake my head back and forth and my nose brushes her clit. Her fingers find the hair at the top of my head, pulling me closer as my tongue fucks her tiny pussy. In and out, sucking her clit before repeating the cycle over and over. Her legs shake and she tries to lift herself off the bed, but I shift my body, replacing my tongue with a finger, my thumb to her clit.

Capturing her mouth with mine, tracing my tongue with hers giving her a sample of the incredible taste that is her. She moans into my mouth, her hips thrusting as I brush the rough surface deep inside her. With my free hand, I take her left nipple, kneading her firm mound in my hand rejoining at the feel of real flesh. Her hips start to jerk and I know she's close, breaking away from the kiss I latch onto the nipple in my fingertips, adding a second finger as I suck the nipple into my mouth, nipping with my teeth as she cries out my name.

"That's one, baby," I tell her with a smile, slowly removing my fingers from her pussy only to shove them in my mouth and moan around them.

Standing, I remove my pants and shoes, gaining a huge ego boost as she watches with a heated look in her eye as my cock slams against my stomach. Her pussy glistens with the juices of her orgasm, but I know how well-endowed I am, earning complaints from even the most seasoned of lovers.

"Elli, it will be easier for your first time if you control things by being on top."

Her eyes shift from my hard cock pointed at her, teeth holding her bottom lip hostage as nods her head and climbs to her knees.

Thankfully the bed has a decent sized headboard, something she can use to steady herself as she rides me. Moving to the head of the bed, I adjust the pillows behind me as I lean into the firmness of the headboard.

"Come here, baby." Stroking my cock as she crawls over, straddling my legs, her attention focused on my hand as it travels up and down my hard shaft. "You can touch it if you want."

Startled, her blue eyes flash to mine, a hint of pink reddens her cheeks. "Uh uh, baby, no embarrassment here, just two people falling slowly in love."

Reaching over, she touches the tip with her index finger, swirling the pre-come around the head and crown.

"Here, let me show you." Replacing my hand with hers, I cover her fingers with mine, showing her exactly how I like to be touched. In a bold move, she leans over, running her tongue along the slit of my cock, my thumb coming in contact with the edge.

"Fuck," tipping my head back, the innocence of her makes this so much better than any other time before her.

Tentatively, she wraps her lips around my head, kissing the flesh there before raising back up to look me in the eye.

"I want to do this, touch you, I mean. But I'm afraid I'll suck at this."

Cupping the back of her neck with my free hand, "That's the mechanics of it, you suck. Trust me, there is no way in the world you're gonna be bad at it."

With the same determination I've seen from her all day, she lowers herself once more, taking the head and about half of the shaft inside her pretty mouth. Being surrounded by her is too much, and I allow my head to flop back on the pillow behind me. This girl, who knows nothing of giving a fucking blow job, is rocking my fucking world.

She feels so good, it's everything I have not to grip her hair and fuck her mouth. Instead, I grab the metal of the headboard, letting her take as much of me as she wants. My balls ache for release, and just when I don't think I can hold off another second, she pulls away. Reaching out for the headboard behind me, a pink nipple suddenly in my face as she reaches down and lines herself up with my cock.

Gripping her hips, "You go as slow as you want, stop if you change your mind and don't worry about anything other than you and me." I whisper against her lips, her hair falling in sweet tendrils around us.

Her skin is slick as she allows me just past her lips, breathing heavily against my shoulder as she slowly continues. Reaching down, I run my thumb through the moisture left over from her fantastic blow job, pressing against her clit as she takes me further.

"Tell me what you want, sweetheart, and I'll give it to you. Kiss you, suck you, whatever you need to make this better."

Nodding her head, gasping on a sharp intake of breath as I slip further inside. "I like your thumb, keep doing that."

Running my free hand up and down the naked skin of her back I rub her clit back and forth, adding pressure randomly.

"Oh," she cries stopping her decent on my cock and I can tell I'm right at her hymen. Wrapping her arms around my neck, her eyes locked with mine, she licks her lips before dropping her weight and connecting her pelvis with mine, effectively taking me all the way inside of her.

"That wasn't so bad," she admits, a peal of slight laughter in her voice. Slowly she begins moving her hips back and forth as if she'd been doing this her entire life. "I expected to be ripped in half with the way my mother described it."

"I'd say your daddy was doing it wrong, but you do have eight brothers."

Taking me in deeply, rubbing her clit against the muscles of my pelvis, "Can we please not talk about my brothers right now?"

Smiling, I'm about to agree when she arches up, placing her luscious tits in my face. Connecting a hand to the back of my head, she rubs her nipple along the bottom edge of my lips. "Time for you to suck," she giggles, continuing to ride my cock in slow and even strokes.

"Yes, ma'am"

Taking her left nipple in my mouth, I knead the right, paying special attention to alternating the pressure on her nipples, as her thrusts increase. Keeping her left tit in my mouth, I reach down and grip her hips with my hands, holding her down as I thrust into her. She arches again, pulling her nipple out of my mouth, her tiny hands hold the underside of the opposite one, teasing my lips until I reach out with my teeth and nip at the tender flesh.

"That's it." She pants, increasing her thrusting as I suck hard on the nipple she offered, her free hand drops between us and I nearly come when I feel her fingers brush against the skin of my cock as she pulls at her clit.

"So close," she chants, and it's everything I have not to flip her over and finish her. However, her movements grow sloppy and by how fast she is rubbing her clit, I know she's almost there. The tell-tale signs of her walls quivering is all I need to let my orgasm free and as my cock swells inside of her, she pounds harder, calling my name and then slumping to my chest.

The chants of Isha sound from outside, surprising me at how quickly the time is gone.

"Time for bed, right?" She mumbles into my chest, a smile covering my face as my dick grows harder.

"Not for you, beautiful girl. Hard parts over, now let me show you how I feel about you."

* * *

ELLI SQUEALS as I pick her up from the bed, with her legs wrapped around me, I walk toward the bathroom I noticed when we came in earlier. There is fresh fruit on the table, but you couldn't pay me to eat it.

Stepping into the bathroom. Elli's lips attach to the skin at my neck and ear, making my dick harder as it slaps her ass with each step I take. There is a large grate in the corner of the room, a single handle sticking out of the stone of the wall.

"This might be cold, babe, but don't drink it."

Turning the handle, I find the water is lukewarm, instead of freezing. I want to wash the dirt and sand off us before I lay her on those sheets and love her until the sun comes up. Elli drops her legs, stepping under the spay, tipping her head back as the water rinses the desert down the drain. There is blood on my cock and her thighs, but I refuse to draw her attention to it, choosing instead to rinse it off, letting it join the sand wherever the pipes lead it.

"I'm sorry, but there's no soap or…" I begin, as I dip under the spray beside her. Her eyes spring open a split-second before she launches herself at me, commandeering my mouth with hers.

"Less talk," she pants. "More showing me how you feel."

Without hesitation, I press her to the stone wall, line myself up to her entrance and bury my dick deep inside of her. My left hand holds her ass cheek, my long fingers touching where my cock slides in and out of her. Between her cries of more and the way our bodies feel coming together beneath my fingertips, it isn't long before I spill into her again, my dick begging for more, spinning her around and taking her from behind.

I could watch my cock disappear into her all day, but as the ache in my balls stirs again, I reach around giving her clit attention with my right hand, while the left finds its home on her tit. She lifts her ass at just the right angle, bracing her hands against the stone as the water hits her in the middle of her back. It's too much, yet not enough as I come hard once again, this time, pulling her over the edge with me.

CHAPTER TWELVE

ELLI

"Tell me why you left the Air Force and became a SEAL."
Sleep was the furthest thing from my mind as I lay beside Ryan, our chests facing his semi-hard dick still inside me. He's shown me several times, and in a multitude of positions, how he cares for me. Now with the stillness of the night, I want to know as much about him as I can.

"Well," running his fingers along my shoulder, eliciting a delicious shiver from me. "Like you, I grew up in a huge family, each trying to outdo the other. One day I woke up, took a hard look around and decided living on a ranch in the middle of Montana wasn't for me. I kicked around several careers, but in the end, the love of an old HAM radio my grandfather gave me sent me to the Air Force recruiter."

Sliding out of me, he shifts us so he is on his back with me tucked under his arm, my head lying on his chest.

"I went to work every day, lived through several moves across the country, but still wasn't happy with the way my life was headed. One rainy afternoon, I was curled up in my room watching some stupid movie when a preview for another movie came on. I watched as a man, with his face painted in green and black, rose out of the water, his eyes full of determination and confidence. I shot up off the bed, wanting to earn everything I could about the SEAL's. The biggest was I would have to leave the Air Force and join the Navy."

Tracing the tattoos on his right arm, gliding my fingertips along the petals of the rose drawn there.

"I put the thought to the back of my mind, as the next day my boss walked in and told me he was putting me in for this achievement. I felt guilty for thinking about leaving when the guy is doing something nice for me. Less than a year later, there was an attack on a Navy boat as it sat docked in a harbor. SEAL's were sent in and, in less than a day, captured the men responsible, bringing them back to the states. The next day, I called a friend of the family and asked him what I should do. He told me to think hard, which I did. I left the Air Force a few months later and enlisted in the Navy."

Lifting my head, looking at his face, "Are you happy now?"

Reaching up, he cups my chin with his hand, gently touching his lips to mine. "As a SEAL, yes. Here with you, absolutely."

Kissing him back, I lay my head back down, relishing in the beat of his heart,

"SEAL training was one of the hardest things I've ever done, I nearly rang the bell half a dozen times. I got lucky, and they put me with a group of guys who became more than just my team, they became my family."

"Can you tell me about this mission, the one you're on?"

Clearing his throat, I brace myself for him to say it's classified.

"I left the military over a year ago. My teammates and I formed

79

a corporation, you might call it. Taking on jobs other men can't or refuse to do. At first, I was there to offer a little help as I had accepted a position as a Secret Service agent, but even that got screwed up. A few days ago, I was called away from a friend's wedding to escort your boss to New York."

Reaching under my chin, he pulls my face to his, laying a toe-curling kiss to my lips. "Now, beautiful Elli, tell me everything about you."

Raising myself up on my elbow, my fingers keep tracing the ink on his arm. "You already know I have too many brothers," I tease. Ryan takes my hand from his arm, placing several kisses before nipping at my knuckle.

"My parents are extremely religious, so much so, my mother has never worked a day in her life, or owns a pair of pants. She does everything my father asks, including washing him and cutting up his food. My brothers, whose names all start with E, live in trailers lined up along the drive to my parents' house. Each has a wife just as subservient as my mother. Last year, my father decided it was time for me to get married, so he came to an agreement with the son friend of his, Wesley, to marry me."

Ryan drops my fingers, "So you're engaged?"

"Oh god no," I add, laying my hand on his cheek in an effort to calm the anger I feel rolling off him. "Wesley is a horrible man. He tossed one of the washers you add to make a bolt stronger at me and said it was my engagement ring. He never asked, and I would never have agreed. I left town the next day and here I am, with you."

Ryan looks deep into my eyes, "Swear to me you're not engaged to or with him."

"I swear it." My eyes flash back and forth between his, "I would never do that to you."

Ryan doesn't say a word as he flips us over, spreading my legs and entering me fast and furious. Leaning back, he holds himself up with one arm as he tosses my leg over his shoulder with the other. His face is feral as he pounds into me, chanting, "Mine," over and over. Roaring my name, he comes hard, dropping the weight of his body on me.

When the chants for morning prayers begin, Ryan is wrapped around me, placing gentle kisses to my neck and shoulder. "I'm sorry for earlier, taking you hard like that."

Looking over my shoulder, "You have nothing to be sorry about, you were gentle the other dozen times you entered me."

Pulling me closer, he buries his face in my hair, his hand kneading my breast, his hard cock sliding between my thighs. Reaching down, I guide him inside me, needing to feel him one last time before the torture our captors have planned for me.

"Elli," He whispers as he sets his rhythm, a perfect blend of pain with pleasure." Once this is over…"

Turning over my shoulder, I stop his words, capturing his mouth with mine. I don't want to think about when this is over, what evils await on the other side of that door. I know he is keeping things from me, how he knows Aazar, where we are, and why the plane was hijacked. But it doesn't matter, none of it matters as if this is my last morning on earth, I have no more regrets.

Removing him from inside me, I flip over, straddling his hips as I lower myself onto him one last time. Leaning my hands back on his thighs, I allow him to see what he does to me, the pleasure of being with him.

Opening my eyes, I watch him watching me, the way his eyes linger on my breasts as they bounce with my movements, my fingers as they coach the incredible tingling sensation out of my clit. I can feel his cock grow harder, the look in his eye of his approaching orgasm. We've been this way countless times since the door closed hours ago, but as I feel his hands grip my hips, his mouth as it suctions my nipple, and my clit as he pushes my hand away, replacing it with his own, we find the end of the cliff together, crying out each other's names.

CHAPTER THIRTEEN

RYAN

I felt horrible for keeping Lindsey from her, especially after I'd fucked the name of her so-called fiancée out of my mind. The thought of anyone touching Elli besides myself, had me seeing red. I've never been this possessive over another woman, never really cared if another man looked at a girl I was with. Envy has become expected when dating someone as high-profile as a news anchor.

Elli stirred something within me, a level of emotion I've never experienced. And now, like the damn drugs I've fought hard to take off the streets, I'm addicted to her.

My dick has never been this ready, not even when I was nineteen and constantly horny, but I can't get enough. Even though her breathing tells me she's asleep, I crave her, taking her breast into my hands, rubbing my ever-hard cock against her ass.

Nipping at the delicate skin of her shoulder, palming the natural tit I want to put in my pocket and keep with me, she beings to stir and my cock twitches, begging to be sheathed into her warmth. Elli arches her back, sending that tight ass of hers exactly where I want it, but as I reach down to check to see if she's ready for me, the sound of rapid gunshots fire off in the distance, followed by the rumble of an explosion hitting the side of the building. Jumping from the bed, I pull on my discarded dress pants from last night, sand and dirt tumbling to the floor as I raise the zipper.

When the second explosion rumbles, Elli shoots straight up in the bed, the sheet we slipped between covering those glorious tits.

"What's going on, Ryan?"

Tossing her blouse to her, "Get dressed, baby."

Sliding my feet into my shoes, I spin around as the door to the room bursts open. Aazar and several of his men stand, guns in hand, the welcome from last night forgotten.

Elli fumbles with her shoes as she comes to stand beside me, I take a step forward effectively shielding her body from those bastards.

"Long time no see, Ghost." A hauntingly familiar voice calls from behind the line of men. "You and I never had to the chance to play, such a pity."

Vivian, a nurse we escorted across the Korengal Valley, steps around the men, her body squeezed into a tight-fitting dress, her black hair slicked back into a tight ponytail, a line of rhinestones along the part at the top of her head. She walks toward me, like a lioness stalking her prey, stopping just short of my position, running her nails up and down my exposed chest.

"Perhaps he'll let me keep you." She purrs, drifting her fingers lower to my crotch.

Remembering how much trouble she gave Viper when she and her friends nearly got us killed the last time I saw her. "I'd rather have my dick cut off and forced to eat the motherfucker before I'd let you touch it."

Vivian tips her head back in laughter, "Careful, Ghost. I have the power to make that happen."

A third explosion rocks the building, the smell of sulfur hitting my nose.

"Come, gentleman, our guests have arrived." Vivian turns on her heels swaying her hips as she exits the door. Aazar commands his men in Persian, to grab me, leaving Elli for him. I use the same language as I warn him if he touches her, gun or no gun I will kill him.

Aazar turns to Elli, "Come, beautiful lady, I have someone who would like to meet you."

Extending my hand back to her, I'm met with blue eyes full of fear with a determined face denying it. "Come on, baby. Everything will be fine."

Walking back through the same hall, the gun-wielding men lead us back to the first floor where we entered last night. The sun has begun to rise, but not enough to shut off the security lights. Elli's hand trembles in mine as we make our way to an interior room, a study by the looks of it, but the ceiling is composed of the stained-glass windows from under the dome.

Standing with his back to me is a man with a phone raised to his ear. The light in the room makes it hard to tell who he is, but as he turns in my direction, anger like I've never known, floods my body.

"How the fuck are you still alive?"

A laugh I haven't had the displeasure of hearing in over a year echoes in the room, bouncing off the glass windows and clouding my better judgment with anger.

"Don't you know, Ghost, you can't kill the devil?"

Aarash Konar stands not fifteen feet away, his dark eyes full of more evil if that is even possible. Motioning to the guards, they pull my hands behind my back, slamming me down into a chair. More gunshots ring out behind me, and I turn to tell Elli to get down, but I'm too late, Aazar has her, pulling her to the front of the room beside Aarash.

"Well look at what we have here?"

Glancing over my shoulder, I watch as two men drag a still unconscious Congressman into the room, placing his body on a long table at the front. Aarash leans over the man, mutters something under his breath and turns back to Aazar.

The hair at the back of my neck prickles as an eerie quiet fills the space. I try to send Elli an assuring look, but she isn't stupid and knows this a bad situation.

A loud bang rings out, causing Elli to scream, and Aarash's smile to elongate. His gaze follows something behind me and I can hear the soles of shoes hitting the floor.

"Have I missed anything?"

Confused, I watch as the suit-clad man with a sling over his left shoulder walks to stand beside a now waking Congressman. I glance quickly at Elli, whose face has as much confusion on it as mine.

"Hello, old man. Didn't think you'd see me, did you?"

Another explosion sounds outside, closer this time as I can see the smoke roll in through the open windows.

"Ah," Aarash exclaims, far too chipper than he should be, considering. "Finally, our guests have arrived."

I hear it before a single word is spoken, the static of an earpiece going out of range. My pulse increases as I ready my body, as if on cue the members of my team stand at the corners of the room, dressed in full fatigues with guns at the ready.

Aarash pulls Elli to him, his gun pointed at her temple. "Careful, gentleman. Wouldn't want to spill the blood of an innocent."

"Ryan." Elli cries, her bottom lip trembling and the brave face she's had from the beginning lost to the terror she feels.

For the first time ever, I lose my edge, pushing the men holding me down away, raising my hands in the air, begging my team leader to break our number one rule.

"Stand down."

Staring Viper in the eyes, his face covered in sand and sweat, gun pointed at Aarash and sadly, Elli.

"Please, Viper. Tell them to put their guns down." My voice shakes, emotion wrapped around each syllable.

Viper nods once, giving the signal, and I feel defeat creeping in as Aarash orders his men to take their guns.

A slow clap sounds from behind, "Very good, gentleman." A second females voice fills the room, one I wondered if I'd ever hear again. Rachel Cutter enters the room, her extensions back in her hair and the designer purse dangling from her arm. Her high heels click against the tile as she makes her way past Chief and Havoc to stand beside the man in the suit. "We've been waiting for you."

"We?" Chief shouts off to my left, "Who the mother fuck is we, you sadistic bitch?"

Rachel cocks her hip to the side, "Ah, having issues moving on, Aiden?"

"If you mean fucking something that wasn't made in a factory, as moving on, then yes. I'm having a real hard time keeping my fucking hands off her."

Rolling her eyes, Rachel moves to stand by Aarash, licking the shell of his ear. "You always were so vanilla." Sliding her hand under his shirt, "Never letting me have it the way I wanted."

Moving from Aarash, she eyes Elli up and down, "And this is the new Lindsey?" Shaking her head as she lifts a strand of red hair from her shoulder, "Tsk, tsk. What is it about the lot of you down-grading?" Hooking her hands on her slender hips, "Ghost, you have the perfect girlfriend, with a body for sin and will to let you fuck anyone you want. And you chose this?"

Before I can blast her ass on her choice of fucking Aarash, a voice echoes in the room, one that has all of us turning in his direction.

"Gentleman, I'm sorry for being late, but your entrance last night caused quite a traffic jam."

Senator Green walks from the back of the room, a cane in his left hand assisting him with a limp in his leg. Moving to sit on the edge of the table Congressman Howard is lying on, Senator Green lays his cane on the wood, a triumphant smile on his face.

"I suppose you're wondering what we're all doing here?" Turning to his left, he motions for Rachel to come to him. A coy smile covers her lips as she walks with that same sway in his direction. "Hello, darling." He greets her, pulling her to him, mouth open and tongue extended. She returns the kiss with eagerness, lowering her hand to his crotch much as she did for Aarash.

"Gentleman, I'd like you to meet my husband, Senator Green." She says with pride, her eyes never leaving his, as her bottom lip becomes a prisoner to her teeth. "However, I do believe you already know, Logan, don't you, babe?"

Green slaps her on the ass, sending her back to Aarash who shamelessly fondles her fake tits as she kisses Aazar. Vivian stands beside the trio, apparently waiting her turn.

Green directs his attention to Doc, "I've kept track of you for a while, Logan. Waiting for the right time to take my revenge."

"Revenge?"

"Did you really believe I moved you to the front of the line, ahead of more qualified men, in order for you to become a doctor?

Speed you through the process of BUDS training, and then allow you to leave your contract early, all from the kindness of my heart?"

Doc cleared his throat, confusion written all over his face. "I assumed you were a friend, one my father said I could trust."

Standing from the table, "I hate your fucking father, he stole something from me."

"Stole something? He gave you several more years with your wife, you wouldn't have had otherwise."

"I hated her." He shouted. "Cursed the day I had to marry the frigid cunt."

"So why didn't you divorce her? Marry the bitch over in the corner?"

Green tosses his head back in laughter, "And give up all the money? My dreams of having it all? No thank you. I wanted what your father had, not what he wanted to give me."

"Which was?"

Green shakes his head, resuming his seat against the table. "Let me tell you a story, Logan, one I'm certain you've never heard. Years ago, I fought my way into one of the country's best colleges for political science. In my younger days, I was quite the looker, able to sweet talk my way into my fair share of more mature, and bored, housewives' beds."

His claim wasn't hard to believe, even as a mature man, his dark hair with only a touch of gray by his ears gave him an edge. His blue eye stood out, and it's clear by the small number of wrinkles around his mouth and eyes, he takes care of himself. Take thirty years off him, and I would have considered his competition.

"They wanted a young dick and I wanted tuition, so we came to an agreement. One of those wives, Jillian Stratton, introduced me to a lovely woman by the name of Meredith Reese, you know her as Mommy."

Doc's jaw clenches as Green continues, the look of hate building in his eyes. Jillian Stratton lived in the same building in New York as his parents, she married well and outlived her last three husbands. She tried for years to get Doc to fall for one of her daughters, he never did, but she never stopped trying.

"From the moment I laid eyes on your mother, I wanted her. However, she was too busy floating from charity to charity, funding one cause after another, never giving me more than a hello. I watched her, thought of her when I fucked other women, pretended to be her friend, all while waiting for her to fall for me."

Doc shifts his stance, "But since my mother has taste, she chose my father over you."

Narrowing his eyes at Doc, "I sat in the church as she married him, watched as she brought your screaming ass home from the hospital. When she learned she couldn't have any more children, I knew Weston would pack up and leave."

This time it's Doc who tosses his head back and laughs, "Leave her? My father doesn't leave my mother's side for anything. Those two are so in love, I'm not sure even death will have an effect on that love. So, if you're still waiting around for him to grow tired of her," Doc shakes his head, adjusting his stance. "You might want to find a new hobby, cause it's not going to happen."

Green shifts his attention from Doc, dipping his head as he looks toward Aarash. "I think our guests will be more comfortable in a chair for the remainder of this conversation."

Aarash commands his guards to put the six of us in chairs, binding our hands behind our backs. Green watches with rapt attention, his fingers drumming on the table as two guards cinch a rope around Doc's wrists.

"As I was saying, when she learned there would be no more children, I waited for Weston to leave, but the devoted bastard stayed. So my plan had to change, if he wouldn't leave her, maybe I could take him out of the equation. When my wife became sick, I called my dear friend, begging him to save my wife. I'd planned her death down the day, fed her a carcinogenic, exposed her to elements which should have grown twelve tumors instead of one, the one your father took away."

Reaching my fingers into the belt of my pants, I pull out the razor hidden inside. Out of the corner of my eye, I see Reaper doing the same, the muscles in his arms flexing, using the blade from his watch the guards failed to remove.

"I did my research, found your uncle who was wallowing in debt, but too full of pride to do what most businessmen do and take it. I befriended him, got in his head and made him realize the money his in-laws were giving away was his, to begin with. In the nick of time, he finally came around, giving me the perfect opportunity to initiate my plan. You needed tuition and I had a solution."

Rachel moves to stand beside Vivian, a knowing look on their faces as if hearing the story unfolding in the room. Aazar places himself between the pair, an arm around each girl's neck, while Elli slips back against the far wall, making me feel slightly better.

"I make a call, scratch a few backs and, like magic, you're off to med school. Then, September eleventh happens, and as I watch the towers fall, I contact another friend, one who makes sure you're on a plane to Afghanistan, and almost certain death."

Doc's brow furrows, "Certain death? I was at a field hospital, not on the fucking front lines."

Green places his hands on the table, supporting his weight as he leans over in Doc's direction. His jacket falls open, revealing a nine-millimeter in a shoulder holster. "Come on, Logan, you were born with a silver spoon in your mouth. You paid people to do the shit work you didn't want to do."

"Doesn't make me a fucking pussy." Doc roars, his Park Avenue childhood a sensitive subject for him. Each of us has suffered a split lip or black eye when we've breached his request to leave that subject alone.

"No, but your need to solve the world's problems became your downfall and one of my greatest assets." Raising his upper body, Green crosses his arms over his chest, stretching the leg with the limp.

"You wanted to join the SEALs and, even though you didn't meet all the requirements, I paid the psychiatrist to change his recommendations, and stream-lined you in. Once you graduated, I made sure your first mission was the most difficult."

"But we fucked up your plans when we succeeded."

"Yes, which made me reevaluate and think hard as to what makes a man do stupid things. All I had to do is look in the mirror to gain my answer. I did some research, found a company on the brink of bankruptcy, put my personal attorney on it and within a week had a medical staffing company. Which is where I met my beautiful wife Rachel. She wanted to keep her job and showed me for several days how far she was willing to go, inviting a friend of hers, Vivian, to join us. As you can imagine, I fell for the pair the instant I watched them enjoy each other, but it was Vivian who first introduced me, in a way, to Aarash when I found her shooting up heroin in my bathroom. Being in the position I am, never one to involve middlemen, I traced the heroine back to the source and my good friend—"

"Aarash," A collective chorus rings out, stealing the thunder from Green.

"Very good, gentlemen," Green mocks, the disdain evident in

his voice. "Aarash was understandably hesitant at first. Having a member of the Senate contact you out of the blue doesn't an illegal deal make. However, when an associate of mine, Kumarin, vouched for me, we struck a deal."

Aarash didn't appear to be listening, too busy with Vivian against the wall, his dick pounding into her from behind while Rachel was on her knees with Aazar.

"So, you used your wife and her friend as a distraction. When she didn't end up with Doc, she fucked around with Chief."

Green nods his head, catching a glimpse of his wife sucking another man's dick. "You're correct, Ghost." He sighs, shifting his gaze to the floor underneath him. "I didn't account for Aarash and Vivian having a connection. Her job was to turn Logan's head, distracting him long enough for Aarash to kill him. Instead, she created a toxic environment, one, as you know, ended with all you of flying out of there alive."

Looking to Chief, I see the relief on his face from dodging a huge bullet with that hot mess. He had a good woman now; one he knew would never betray him as Rachel had.

"Then the investigation with Virginia Greyson and her ties to Kumarin made it to my ears. I called Aarash, who had the perfect plan for getting rid of Kumarin, any thoughts of him testifying about what he knew and making all of you think you'd won and killed Aarash and put an end to his smuggling of heroin. And it seemed to work as the group dismantled, you came to me and wanted out, Aarash offered to have his brother, Ecnal who was in the states, kill you. But when that failed, I knew I had to take drastic measures to end this. So, I devised a plan to bring you all back here, to see your faces as you took your last breath, watch as the life leaves your disbelieving eyes."

I've cut through enough of the rope keeping my hands behind

my back to break away easily. Keeping the blade between my fingers, Viper lets us know he is free too.

"So, hold up," Havoc interjects, his cockiness returning, something I'd assumed would end with his marriage. "What exactly is your end game? I mean, I've had some pussy in my life, damn good shit I wanted to fucking dive back into, but never have I wanted to go to war over a piece I ain't sampled. No offense to your mother, Doc."

"None taken, Havoc."

Doc and Havoc are both free as well, which leaves Reaper and Chief.

"Oh really, Havoc? You chased Eleni, killing Aaron because of her."

"Hold on, motherfucker. We didn't kill Aaron for Eleni." Reaper pipes up, tipping his head in Havoc's direction. Which leaves Chief left to free himself.

"No, that fucking pussy took himself out. Filled his veins with the last of the shit he bought off you, Aarash."

And there we were, all of us free and ready to fight to stay alive.

"My brother was a fool," Aarash shouted, pushing Rachel to the side, his face bent with anger, taking several steps toward us. "Allowing the pretty face and open legs of a common whore to compromise our plans. His job was to kill you, Havoc, not fall in love." Aarash steps back, registering what he's just admitted, having knowledge of what Aaron was doing all along.

"He's right, Aarash, and I agree Aaron was a weak man, you did us a favor by driving him to the edge and eliminating himself. But to answer your question, Havoc, my end game is more than getting revenge." Slapping the chest of the Congressman, "Which is why this bastard is here too."

Green stands from the table, grimacing in pain from his leg. "I have plans to run for President, naming my friend and colleague, Mr. Vale here," motioning to the suited man who'd remained silent standing to the side since he walked in. "As my Vice President. I've agreed, based on the help he has provided, once your wives come out of hiding, he may revisit Kennedy and rekindle an old flame. Kennedy Forrester will make an excellent Second Lady."

"Vale? Where have I heard that name from?" Viper questions, his brow furrowed and mouth tight as if he leading the man on a path he knows the ending to.

The man in the suit steps forward, "Pleasure to officially meet you, Mr. Forbes. Kennedy and I were to be married, or at least I was led to believe she would consider me. Unfortunately, you came in the picture. I worked for her father until Senator Green offered me the position of his personal attorney and the chance to take a role I've always wanted as Vice President and ultimately Kennedy's husband."

Doc stared at the leg, nodding his head slowly as his chin lifted in ponder. "I have to hand it to you, Green, this was an amazing plan. Even with all the pitfalls, you managed to do what few others have, pulling the wool over our eyes." Tipping the front legs of his chair back, rocking several times before letting them fall to the floor as he continues. "You get revenge on a girl who turned you down over thirty years ago. This dude," tipping his head in Aarash's direction. "Gets to keep selling his shit."

Doc turns his head to the left, "Do you want to tell him where things went wrong, Viper?"

Shaking his head, Viper tips his chair back and holds it. "Nah, he was talking shit about your mother, you go ahead."

"Yeah, but he has you buried and your wife running the damn White House."

"It's fine, Doc, Kennedy is too smart for him. Besides, Mrs. Michaels prefers her man to spend more time in the gym, than behind a desk."

A smile tickles my lips, for as prim and proper as Kennedy is, she does appreciate Zach's physique.

"Your first mistake was Vivian over there. I don't claim to know everything about women, but I do know if you shoot at one, they ain't gonna wanna cuddle in your bed. Trust me, Vivian was practically straddling your boy Aarash here when we transported them to camp. Second, every time I came to you for help, magic happened, it was as if a Leprechaun lived inside your ass. Shit was handed down from your office that shouldn't have been. And let's face it, Green, my family is fucking loaded, I could have bought out my contact anytime I wanted. Something else you didn't know when you handed me the transfer to Virginia, Ghost had been hearing chatter for weeks. We knew Ecnal was there, just not where he was hidden. Aaron and his twisted mind smoked him out for us."

Doc shifts his attention to Aarash, "Another thing Green didn't know, is how you grew tired of him fumbling with all these ideas of his, each one costing you more time and money. Which is when you decided to bring on the company in America you own, Medinet. When Jeb swore an alliance to you, he told you about his brother, Jackson, who was this brilliant chemist. You paid him a lot of money to step out of the lab and into the role of Sheriff to watch over the bullshit Green's guys were slinging. But Green didn't trust Wolfe, and for good reason, as he was playing both sides. Green called in a favor from Angel who spoke with Wolfe, making him think he was working for him and had Carlos killed as an example of what could happen to Wolfe if he wasn't careful. Now, Angel may have no boundaries, but word is, he had someone on the

96

inside tell him to back off. Which is why he met with Aaron and severed ties. Green knew the Romanian's were stealing from Stavros, so he added that in as a distraction. Too bad the smoke screen cleared and showed Stavros who else was stealing from him. Seems your planning has started a mafia war."

Green's face grows red as he listens and looks at the emotion-less face of Aarash. Double-crossing a man can sure stun you silent.

"What you didn't count on, Aarash was Rayne stumbling upon those guns, or Jordan interrupting Rachel's last attempt at redemp-tion. When your girl realized she'd fucked up again, she wanted protection, something Aaron's puppet, Cory, offered. She knew you would toss her out once you learned she suffered from Ovarian Failure, all the shots and pills in the world weren't going to give you a baby to brag about since she was born without any eggs."

Reaper tips his chin in Rachel's direction, "But it was your gift to her that tipped us off as to your involvement. Harper has a keen eye for discerning the difference between a fake and a real designer handbag, one Rachel refused to surrender to a TSA inspector when she boarded a plane for Afghanistan."

Silence fills the room as Green shoots Rachel a hard look, his eyes boring into hers as she rubs Aazar's chest.

"You know, Senator Green, for the longest time I couldn't figure out why you contacted us and had us put a tail on Congressman Howard. So, one day as I was out on a run, I came across him and flat out asked him if there was bad blood between the two of you. He took me out to the cabin where he showed me a report Special Agent Steele had given him, detailing your involve-ment in the OPM scam and the deal you made with Kumarin. First of all, you both should know, Kumarin agreed to the deal with you because he was dying of cancer. No one, including his son Drew, knew this. He was looking for fast money, as he knew the men in his inner circle would never follow his son, and he was right. You provided him with money and, I would imagine, a painless death. You got the added benefit of making everyone believe you were dead, including Aaron. However, when it came to Steele, as you are both aware, he couldn't be bought. So, you had him killed in front of his house and kidnapped his daughter, who worked in the office as her father's assistant and knew everything about the case. You decided you wanted to kill her yourself, but knew there was a chance we would be listening, which I was."

Keeping my eyes locked on the Senator, I show him a fake smile and bat my lashes. The action causes the Congressman to laugh, which leads to a coughing fit.

"I get a call from the Congressman, we jump on a plane and find the girl in less than ten seconds. You showed up with Mr. Vale here, Havoc shot you in the leg when you took off on the snowmobile. You can't go to a hospital, cause they'll ask questions. Even the mob doc in Detroit, who studied in Guatemala, wouldn't take out the bullet for fear of killing you, leaving you with a limp and unable to fuck Rachel, if I'm guessing right based on her fucking these two for the past hour."

Doc sets his chair down hard, "I'll take it out, Green. I don't give a shit if you live or die." Laughter rings out, but Doc's stare is ice cold, leaving no room to question the seriousness of his statement.

"But that didn't explain why you had us sitting in the middle of the woods in the pouring rain." I continue. "It wasn't until we discovered Aaron listening in on our conversations at Doc's wedding that we did a sweep of all of our homes and businesses, finding the little listening devices your idiots tried to hide. Just like Aaron, the two of you have been hearing what we've wanted you to for a while. Which is how you knew we would be aboard the 747 headed to New York."

Green looks to Vale who shrugs his shoulders, and then back to the Congressman who has begun to cough again.

"Jesus Christ, Green, at least let Doc take a look at him," I shout, my fingers ready to snap the rope.

"Why?" He shouts back, jumping to his feet and nearly stumbling. "He's going to die just like the rest of you anyway."

Looking him cold in the eye, "No he's not."

"Oh really? He's bleeding all over the table, and the six of you are ten seconds away from having a bullet in the back of your head." Green seeths, his face turning purple with the force he's using to get his point across.

"Because you both forgot one tiny detail."

CHAPTER FOURTEEN

ELLI

"What would that be?" Senator Green fires back at Ryan. His harsh tone makes me take another step back, something I've been slowly doing since Aazar let go of me so he could have sex with the two girls who joined them.

"Tombstone, Diesel and Black Widow."

Not a second passes before Ryan and the other men spring to their feet, the ropes the men used to tie them tossed to the side as a series of popping noises sound from above. Red smoke fills the room as the windows above are smashed, the glass falling to the floor as three men rappel from black ropes.

Aarash reaches out, pulling me to him. I fight with everything I have, clawing at his face and kicking as hard as I can. The sound of gunfire is all around me, men shout and more smoke fills the air. Fear fuels my movements, and when Aarash tries to pick me up from behind, I open my mouth wide, sinking my teeth into the flesh of his arm, causing him to stumble back, hitting his head on one of the gold accessories. The momentum sends me to the ground, kicking my feet to back away from him, my hand lands in something wet and sticky, but I don't dare stop to see what it is until I'm far from Aarash's reach.

"Hold your fire." I hear one of the men shout, a second before something large crashes into me, rolling me along the floor and coming to rest against the wall.

"Elli," Ryan's face appears above me, his desperate eyes searching mine. "Are you okay?"

Am I? I'm not sure, but as I look to my left, I see the aftermath of what just happened. It's Aarash's body lying in a pool of blood that has me pushing Ryan off me.

"Oh my god, is he dead? I didn't mean to kill him, Ryan, I just wanted to get away."

Ryan pulls me from the floor as the one he called Doc bends over Aarash and feels for a pulse. Looking over his shoulder, "Darlin', you ain't killed him. Just knocked some manners into him, that's all."

Ryan shoves my face in his chest, kissing the top of my head as the sound of two shots ring out, followed by the ping of shell casings hitting the floor

"Now he's dead."

Ryan pulls me back, his eyes roaming over me as I try to look for myself at the dead body of Aarash.

"Baby, you're bleeding." Looking at my hand in Ryan's, the source of the wet and sticky substance covers my left hand.

"Calm down, Romeo, it ain't hers."

The man Ryan called Reaper kneels over the body of one of the two women, the one Green said was his wife. Her eyes are open, but there is a deep gash across her throat, the lower half of her body naked and exposed.

"I'd wash that hand in bleach if I were you," Reaper adds,

standing to his full height, kicking a knife from the hand of Aazar, who lay motionless, a bullet hole in the center of his head. The second woman, the one whom Aarash kept against the wall, lay two feet from the first, an identical gash to her throat.

The one they called Viper has the attorney on the ground, his foot in the middle of his back, while the one they call Chief has Senator Green bent over the table, his hands tied behind his back.

"Elliott York," the handsome one they called Havoc approaches, a welcoming smile on his face, his glove-covered hand extended in my direction. "Alex Nakos, a pleasure to meet you."

Glancing from his hand to his face. "How did you know my name?"

Raising his hands as if in surrender, "My apologies, I assumed Ghost told you about us."

"Hell no, he was too busy shagging her, you can smell the sex rolling off him." One of the men who broke through the ceiling teases, sending a wink in my direction.

"Fuck off, Diesel, you're making her nervous." Ryan pushes me behind him, his long arms keeping me close to his back. Looking past him, I'm transfixed as Doc goes to work on the Congressman's leg. Giving him something I assume is pain medicine to swallow. He works quickly, dressing the wound and placing him on a stretcher I have no idea how it got here.

"Ignore him, Elliott," Havoc returns. "It's the pendant you have around your neck. When you pressed it, you triggered several things. One, a tracking system and the second a fingerprint recognition program. When your prints weren't a match for Ghost's, the system went to work to find out who you were."

Reaching down, "I forgot about this." Lifting the chain to remove it, "It sounds important, I should give it back."

Ryan halts my progression, his fingers wrapping around mine as he lowers the chain back to my neck. "Keep it."

"Oh really?" Havoc murmurs in shock.

"Yes, really. Her name is Elli and she's important."

* * *

THE WALK out of the compound was much different from the one in. For starters, the place was deserted, not even the dogs who played with the children were around. Second, the jeeps were replaced by Humvees, military grade and air-conditioned on the inside. Reaper drives the one Ryan and I climb into, the Congressman with Doc and Chief following behind us.

The sun is high in the sky and I'm grateful to be in the protection of the truck, the harmful rays of the sun unable to touch me. After a while in the truck, where Ryan and I held each other and slept, we arrive at what looks like an abandoned military base.

"What's this place?" I yawn as I look at the weathered structure beside me. A gate has been pulled wide open, several tumbleweeds roll across the yard littered with various sized tents the wind had torn to shreds.

"The last place we were together as a team."

Ryan opens the door for me, the sun bright, forcing me to squint my eyes as the other truck pulls alongside. Doc jumps from the truck, Chief moving around to pull the Congressman out of the back.

"Come on, Elli, this way." Ryan guides me, around the back of the Humvee to where a jet sits waiting. Apprehension fills my belly as we approach a man in a uniform standing with a stack of what looks like rolled up towels on a silver tray.

"Gonna need more than that, Bernard," Doc instructs the man

as he and Chief carry the stretcher up the steps and into the belly of the plane.

The man took one look at me and my blood covered hand, turning abruptly and racing up the steps. Ryan guided me by the hand up the steps into a room straight out of a magazine.

Doc stood in the center of the aisle, a black bag in his hand, tossing it to Ryan as we continue down the aisle. I am at a loss for what to do, activity flutters around me as men climb aboard, Green and Vale with hands bound and strips of tape over their mouths.

"Here," Ryan stands in front of me, a clean black shirt and pants that matched everyone else's. His borrowed shoes replace by black boots which gave him an edge. Handing me a stack of clothes. "There's a bathroom in the back. Bernard says ladies first, so please don't use all of the hot water."

"But..." shaking my head, handing the clothes back to him.

"Elliott, if you don't go change, Bernard will never let us leave the ground, and my wife is expecting a call from me, which I can't make until we're in the air." Doc huffs as he takes a seat near a window.

"It's Elli, only my preacher calls me Elliott." I return, taking the clothing and heading toward the back of the plane. I have so many questions, but as I close the door, everything except the grandeur of the room fades away.

The room is huge, almost the size of my bedroom back in Virginia, with a glass-doored shower and two sinks with carved mirrors above. Setting the clothes on the counter, I turned on the water, letting it run over my hands, taking the blood with it.

Remembering Ryan's warning, I fill the sink with hot water, strip off my clothes and use a washcloth to wipe myself down. I hissed at the soreness at the apex of my thighs, a smile lighting up my face as I recall the reason. The water in the sink turned to a dark brown by the time I was finished, I found an extra trash bag in the container, placing my dirty clothing inside.

The clothes Ryan handed me are miles too big, but as I place them to my nose, I close my eyes relishing in the smell of him. Slipping on the shirt, the hem hits me at mid-thigh, the pants so big I have to roll them several times, but they're clean and I feel a little more human.

Opening the door, I find the guys all sitting around, the television screen on the wall playing some movie I've never seen. Ryan stood from his seat, extending his hand for me to take, "Feel better?"

Nodding, I slipped past him, "Yes, thank you." Taking my seat, I secure my belt and look around.

Eight sets of eyes reflect back at me, the movie muted and forgotten. I could feel the plane as it started to move, although different than the 747.

The way they all looked at me made me question if I'd accidentally flashed them "Did I do something wrong?"

Ryan grabs my hand, "No Elli, you're perfect. They just can't believe you're with me."

My heart speeds up, I know we discussed if he was married or had a girlfriend. I knew first hand he wasn't gay.

"Jesus, Ghost, now you're making her nervous." Diesel stood from the chair, tossing the remote in his hand to the table beside him.

"Elli, please forgive me for being rude earlier. My name is Chase Morgan, but these guys call me Diesel. This guy here," placing his arm on the guy shoulder beside him, "Is Aiden, but we call him Chief. You already know Ghost beside you, although, we are all aware you call him Ryan."

Several of the guys snicker, as Ryan mumbles something under his breath. "This is why I never bring a girl around you guys."

Doc moves down the aisle, "It's your own fault, Ryan. You had to know this would happen when you moved on."

Turning away from the conversation, thinking back to the woman who picked up a piece of my hair. "Ghost you have the perfect girlfriend, with a body for sin and will let you fuck anyone you want. And you chose this?"

"Hey, hey," Ryan captures my face, pulling me away from the memory. "These guys are assholes. Okay, I had an on and off girl-friend, Lindsey. These guys hated her. She and I broke up, you and I are together."

Ryan unbuckles his belt, stands in the aisle, one hand hooked on his hip while the other raises as if to make a point. "Yes, fuck-ers, you heard that right. Lindsey is history and Elli is my girlfriend."

Several things happen all at once, the guys break out in cheers, a few saying "It's about fucking time." My favorite is Reaper, who introduced himself as Matt, when he crosses the aisle, pushes Ryan out of the way and hugs me.

After introductions were made, and Christian names confirmed, I learned Tombstone wasn't really part of the team anymore but owed them for rescuing his children from a terrible situation. Chase, along with his two brothers, ran the bounty hunting part of the team. They lived in Charleston, South Carolina, however, Chase has been an honorary member of the SEAL team until he left the military. Black Widow, or Bradshaw, was a state trooper also from South Carolina. He'd helped them with a recent situation and offered his services if they needed him.

"So, Elli, you're one of now. After everything you've seen, you must have some questions."

Once we're at cruising altitude, Logan opens the bar and galley, serving everything from a bag of chips to my personal favorite, a toasted bagel. My mother doesn't go to the grocery store for food, she goes for staples she can' make herself, salt, pepper, and detergent.

"Well," swallowing my current bite, and setting the rest on the paper plate. "You said something about how Aarash got the benefit of pretending to be dead, even to his brother?"

Zach shoves his last bite of sandwich into his mouth, crumpling up the napkin before tossing it on his empty plate. "Over a year ago, Matt, Aiden, your boy Ryan and I received intelligence about where Aarash was held up. Long story short, we found it, filled it full of explosives and blew it sky-high. We saturated the Dark Web with Aarash's death and sat back and watched. Matt and I had a bet Aarash would stay hidden until after we neutralized his brother, Aaron, but he couldn't do it. Last summer when Logan and Harper got married, we found a drone hovering in a field across the road. Initially, it contained one IP source, but the longer Aaron spoke, Aiden was able to spot a piggyback, although the source was encrypted. A few weeks ago, Ryan was able to hack into Aaron's computer, where he found the same encrypted address. This time he was able to break it, which led us back to Aarash. This guy," pointing to Alex. "Decided to get married and instead of running off to Vegas for a bachelor party, the six of us flew here, hiked the mountains and located where Aarash had been hiding for the last year. Plus, we found the new compound he'd built from the heroin money he was no longer splitting with Aaron."

Ryan picks up my hand, "I'm sorry you had to get in the middle of this, but I'm not sorry I met you." He kisses my knuckles, his blue eyes full of truth and, dare I say the L word.

"It was my first day. My boss called me at three in the morning, she had the flu and my coworker was going into surgery, so I had to go." I shrug, a feeling of utter joy falling over me.

"Well," Ryan starts, his eyes remaining on me as he spoke to the room. "When your boss contacted me to help him take down Senator Green, I was supposed to escort him to New York where he could meet the Deputy Director of the FBI. They wanted to show Green's involvement with Kumarin and Aarash, forcing him to pull away from the presidential race, allowing the Feds to prosecute him for Steele's death and Virginia Greyson, the woman who ran the OPM scam from her home. Someone and I have a suspicion of who tipped Green off to the plan, which is why it was such a cluster-fuck hijacking."

Sleep found most of us during the long flight back to the States. Ryan curled up with his head on my lap, arms wrapped around my middle. My eyes pop open the second the sound of the landing gear engaged, fear from the last time this happened filling my chest.

"It's okay, Elli," Logan assures, his hands busy securing Congressman Howard to the stretcher for landing. "This will be the total opposite of the last time you landed."

"You sure about that?" My voice deep from sleep, the aches in my pelvis from yesterday intensify as I shift under Ryan. I can't wait to get back to my hotel and soak in a hot bath for hours.

"Positive, only a lunatic lands a 747 in the middle of the desert. Those wheels didn't stand a chance."

Logan was right. Forty minutes later I barely felt anything as the plane touched the tarmac, which woke the rest of the team, including Ryan.

"Hey, beautiful." Leaning over, he places a kiss to my lips and raises his arms high above his head in a stretch. His black t-shirt rode up, exposing the muscles on the lower part of his stomach, revealing the veins which rest under the skin and above the muscle. Reaching out, I trace the one closest to his bellybutton, gaining a moan which has me pulling back.

"Later," he teases, with a wink and second kiss.

"All right, listen up." Aiden stands from his chair, his cellphone in hand. "The news has gotten out about the attempt on Congressman Howard's life. The FBI and Capitol Police are waiting, as are a shit-ton of reporters. Doc, Ghost, and Elli are the only ones who will exit the plane with the Congressman, Vale, and Green. The rest of us will remain on the plane until Green and Vale are taken into custody and the Congressman is on his way to the hospital."

Whispering into Ryan's ear, "Why aren't the rest of them coming?"

"Doc owns the plane. You and I technically work for the Congressman, everyone else has to keep their faces out of the media."

Leaning back in my seat, looking out the window I see Aiden is correct. Just beyond the fence stands a sea of reporters, news vans and several cars with red lights flashing on top.

Two men wheeling a stretcher approach the plane as soon as the engine is turned off. Ryan and Logan meet them at the door, sliding the Congressman into their hands. Ryan turns, pulling Vale from his seat, handing him off to Logan, and then does the same with Green.

My hands shake as I take the first step off the plane, the sounds of cameras flashing and people calling my name makes my anxiety worse. Ms. Wesson's warning of not speaking to anyone suddenly flooded my mind, as I follow the man in a Capitol Police uniform in the direction of a waiting ambulance.

I ignored the questions being tossed at me, internally rolling my eyes when one guy asked if I was scared.

I was nearly to the ambulance when a microphone was shoved in my face, the shock of it pulls my head up and leaves my mouth open.

"Elliott York, have you spoken to your fiancée, Wesley? Does he know you're safe?"

"Uh..." My brain is a clouded mess, lack of sleep combined with what I'd just experienced leaves me unable to respond.

"Will you push up the wedding now that you've been rescued?"

"I-I..."

The blonde pulls the microphone from my face, spinning on her heels as she spoke into a camera.

"Lindsey Jennings coming to you live with an exclusive interview with a member of Congressman Howard's staff who just exited the plane returning from Afghanistan after being rescued by our very own SEAL with Honor."

The second I hear her name; images fill my memory. Rachel, back in Afghanistan, called her Ryan's girlfriend. An article years ago I read of an American SEAL and this woman, and how they fell in love.

"You're engaged?" Ryan's angry voice breaks through the photo of the couple I recall, taken at an awards banquet in her honor. Now, as the two stand beside one another, I remember where I know him from, those blue eyes which had made an impression on me back then, haunt me now.

"No, I told you about him."

Lindsey steps between us, "Will you be at the wedding now, after rescuing her?"

Ryan hooks his hands on his hips, clearing his throat. "I wish Ms. York luck in her nuptials, but I was only doing my job."

The ice in his words wraps around my heart, shocking me stupid. I know the tears will come, as well as the pain, I just pray to whoever is listening, it waits until I'm far away from here.

"And you, Elliott. Do you have anything to say to your rescuer?"

There are so many things I want to say to him, demand to know if what we shared was part of his job or something to pass the time?

"Thank you, Mr. Biggs. I do hope you receive a medal for what you've done." My voice cracks at the end, but I swallow hard, forcing the hurt down. Approaching the back of the ambulance, I can't help but look over my shoulder, Lindsey stands triumphant, handing her microphone to the cameraman as she smiles in my direction. Ryan lives up to his call sign, disappearing into thin air.

CHAPTER FIFTEEN

RYAN

Water cascades down my body, the sting from the intense spray keeping the memory of Elli's devastated face in my mind. Logan caught the conversation between Elli and myself, having seen Lindsey approach a second too late for him to stop her.

My neck still hurts from the slam into the side of the news van he'd given me, as he demanded to know what my goddamn problem was. It was a valid question, one I couldn't answer, not until I got a few of my own.

Stepping from the shower, my phone vibrates on the bed as I slip past it and turn on the television. I know it's Lindsey. All these months of wanting her to call, now I wish she'd leave me alone. The news has been nonstop coverage of what happened or at least a watered-down version. Green's face is plastered on every channel, his Senate seat suspended until further notice.

This morning, an anonymous file was sent to the FBI, detailing Green's involvement with the murder of Selena Ramirez, the stripper from Tampa who'd been beaten to death. His DNA was found on her body, an imprint of his college ring identified on her shattered jaw. Green is looking at a long stay in prison, and my role in all of it is complete.

Congressman Howard phoned not long after he came out of surgery, he will need months of physical therapy, but the surgeon agrees with Doc, Elli's quick thinking saved his life. He asked me to stay and work for him, turn the promotion we created as a ruse to a permanent one. I'd asked for some time to think about it, which he granted, neither of us mentioning Elli.

Slipping into a pair of jeans, my phone vibrates again. I've half a mind to ignore it, but as I glance at the screen, I see my mother's smiling face.

"Hey, Momma."

"*You are alive.*" She teases into the phone; her laughter brings back the smile I'd lost yesterday.

"Barely."

"*Uh, oh. What happened?*"

Dropping my body to the bed, head in my free hand, I tell her as much as I can about what happened. It felt oddly good to have someone listen, instead of demand through clenched teeth for me too, 'figure my shit out.'

"*Ryan Oliver. I've never known you to have a mean bone in your body, but your father and I saw the article and read about what happened. Coming from a woman's perspective, that girl had some powerful hurt in her eyes. I'd hate to think one of my sons was responsible for putting it there.*"

My mom has a gentleness about her making it much worse when you do something to disappoint her. She feels everyone deserves an opportunity to show who they really are before passing judgment on them. She never spoke an ill word about Lindsey, but she wasn't exactly warm to her either.

"You know there are three sides to every story, and you've heard one. Maybe it's time you listen to another."

Shooting off the bed, I throw open my closet and begin packing. "Mom, do you have any idea how smart you are?"

Laughing, the tinkling sound a welcome addition to the conversation. *"I've had years of practice."*

Tossing my bag in the passenger seat and sliding my body behind the wheel, I reach over, shifting my phone to hands-free mode as it rings in my ear.

"What's up, dickhead?"

Turning left out of my garage, I spot the Capitol building in the distance. I doubt she's at work, but it doesn't help I'm not sure where she is.

"Am I welcome at your house?"

"Son, I'm the last one to hold a grudge against you for hurting a girl. Now Rayne, well, that's a different story."

I expected nothing less when it came to her. Matt worked hard to earn her trust after telling her he didn't love her. But as similar as our situations are, they are just as different.

"I need to spend some time sitting beside your pond, see if I can figure this shit out."

"You flying or driving?"

"Driving, I have another stop before I reach your place."

"All right, but don't say I didn't warn ya."

It wasn't hard to locate where Elli's family lived. The news made her into a heroine, Lindsey's competitors did at least. Congressman Howard made a statement from his bed on how she was to be commended for the immense bravery she showed, how the town of Jupiter, Virginia should be proud of their hometown girl.

Four hours later, I pull off the highway and onto a two-lane road. There is a truck parked off to the side in a gravel area, a spray-painted sign propped against the side of the cab, reads of boiled peanuts and fresh tomatoes. I nearly stop as I recall the first time I tried them; Rayne made a pot and I'd turned up my nose, which caused her to shove a bowl full into my hands. One hesitant bite turned into a second helping, the flavor something I instantly loved. Maybe once I'm done here, I can sweet talk her into making a batch.

"Your destination is on your right in five hundred feet."

According to Google maps, Elli's address didn't exist. However, she did mention her family was a bit primitive, perhaps keeping their identity away from the prying eyes of the government. With a quick look in her personnel file, I locate the address of the last place she worked, a plastics factory on the verge of bankruptcy.

Turning off the main road, my small car bounds over the potholes as the wooden building comes into view.

The white sign over the door has seen better days. Tripp Brothers Plastics Plant, the faded letters providing a true telling of how the company is about to fade away. Pulling my car along the side of the building, I turn off the engine as I take a look around. Just as Elli described, it's a lot like Matt's property with its tall pine trees and lush vegetation.

Rounding the corner, I climb the three steps, the now hiring sign catches my attention as I reach for the handle.

The wooden door creaks in protest, the ancient hinges announcing my presence to the room. Inside, the office is bare-boned, with two desks that have seen better days and a computer monitor on each that was mostly left over from the ninety's.

"Can we help you, Darlin?"

A blonde woman who reminded me of Lindsey, stands from her seat behind one of the desks, her blonde hair in a mess of curls around her head, the ends frizzy as if she accidentally touched electricity.

"Afternoon, I'm looking for the York place."

"Oh my god, you're him. You the hot guy who saved that government guy."

Rounding her desk as if it were on fire, the blonde separates the distance, calling for her friend over her shoulder. "Dixie get out here, you ain't gonna believe who's here."

A second woman rounds the corner, a cup held firmly in her hand. Blonde hair, just as over processed as her friends, pulled to one side, the dark roots of her natural hair showing. "What in the world are you shouting about, Norma Jean?" The second girl stops short as she sees me, her eyes growing wide as she takes me in.

"Well, hello." She purrs, setting the cup on the edge of an empty desk, swaying her hips as she approaches.

"It's that guy from the tv, the one who works with Elliott."

Dixie adjusts her tits, appearing to not give a shit who sees her. "I can see that, what can we do for you, handsome?"

Clearing my throat, I raise my hand to scratch the back of my neck. "I'm looking for the York place. I know Elli used to work here and was hoping to get directions."

Norma Jean shares a look with Dixie, the flirtiness gone from her face, a more possessive one replacing it.

"If you're here for the wedding, it's too late." Raising her left hand, showing off the silver ring on her finger. "Wesley changed his mind and chose me." Wigging her fingers, as if this is the biggest news since Neil Armstrong walked on the moon.

Leaning forward, I squint my eyes as I take a closer look at the ring, "I'm sorry, but is that a washer?"

Norma Jean drops her hand to her side, "It's just until he can save up. We had to find a new trailer and everything after Elliott runned off."

Hiding a laugh behind my hand, I fake a cough when it begins to slip out. "I understand." And I did, I understood why a girl like Elli would want to run as far as possible from these people. Separate herself from a man who thought it was okay to slide a piece galvanized metal on a girl's finger and call it a marriage. Mostly, I understood once again I'd allowed Lindsey's bullshit to sully the feelings I have for the incredible girl whom I chased away and had no idea how to get back.

"Wes is up at the York place if you're wanting to talk to him."

"Yes, ma'am. If you'd give me directions, I'll be on my way."

Norma Jean drew a map for me on a paper towel, using a hot pink pen. She gave step by step details, including if I pass the big oak tree I'd gone too far and to watch out for York's dogs as they've been known to bite. "Next time you see Elli, you tell her not to come looking for Wesley. That man is finally happy."

The property was just as Elli described, a washed-out road with a large double wide plus a deck and garage to the left. Eight smaller trailers are parked at an angle on either side of the drive, their exteriors free of clutter, except for the one end which was still up on cinderblocks.

Just as Norma Jean warned, four dogs came barking from the woods surrounding the property, teeth bared and hackles raised. Spending most of my life around animals, I knew to be cautious, but show no fear. Rolling down my window, I spoke softly to the quartet, when one of them began to wag his tail I continued until all four were standing on hind legs against the side of my car, enjoying having their ears scratched.

A tall man, approached the front of my car, wiping his hands with a red cloth. He couldn't be more than thirty, with the same blue eyes as Elli.

"You lost, Mister?"

Opening my door, the dogs take off, back into the woods. "No, sir. I'm here to speak with Mr. York."

Adjusting the cap on his head, "Which one?"

Embarrassment heats my face as I close my door. "I'm sorry, my name is—"

"I know who you are, just not why you're here?" He interrupts, shoving the rag in his back pocket before crossing his arms over his chest.

"I need to speak with Wesley Owens, I was told he was working with Mr. York."

Rocking back on the heels of his mud-covered boots, "Working ain't the word I'd use when it comes to Wes." Holding out his hand for me to shake, "I'm Elijah, Elli's oldest brother. Come on, my wife just made some jalapeño jelly and where there's food, Wesley ain't far. That a Porsche?"

"No, it's a Jaguar, a gift to myself when I let the military." I'd spent the majority of my adult life driving trucks. When I purchased the condo, I needed something small to fit in my parking space.

Wiping the mud caked on my boots as I climb the four steps to the tiny deck, the smell of sugar and spices fills the air as I clear the top step. Elijah held the door open as the sound of running water greets me.

Inside the furnishings were old and terribly outdated, but it was immaculate, not a trace of the mud which seems to cover every-thing outside.

"Nancy, we got company," Elijah announces, his voice a little sharp for my taste. A tiny woman, her hair pulled tight at the base of her neck in the same fashion as when I'd first laid eyes on Elli, came around the half wall in the center of the room. An apron is tied over her ironed dress, a pair of flats covering her pantyhosed feet. She stands not five feet from him with her head bowed as if waiting for permission to speak.

"Wesley here yet?"

With her eyes fixed on the laminate floor, she runs her hand down her apron, as if there are a million wrinkles. "Yes, Sir."

Elijah drops his body onto the recliner in the corner, Nancy rushes over and drops to her knees, removing his muddy boots and replacing them with slippers. She wraps the boots in the body of her apron, scurrying to the back of the trailer.

A loud belch to my left shatters the disbelief in what I've witnessed, the level of servitude I've not seen in years, and defi-nitely not in the US. A man, as round as he is tall, waddles across the room, his ball cap on backward, a plate stacked high with corn-bread, several crumbles dusting the hair of his beard.

"Wes, this fella is here to see you."

"I'm busy," he mumbles around a large bite of cornbread, drop-ping onto the cushions of the couch, the unmistakable sound of a wet fart makes me cringe. "Come back t'maro."

"Hoss, by the looks of you, I don't think you'll make it till tomorrow."

Wesley stops his chewing, pounds his fist into the center of his chest until a second belch leaves his gut. "Whatcha want city boy?"

Squaring my shoulders and crossing my arms over my chest, I

make sure he gets an eyeful of every muscle I have. Before I can tell him why I'm here, the front door opens behind me, the man who walks through is no doubt Elli's father. Nancy rushes in, a new apron around her waist, Elijah's boots, clean as the day they were purchased in her hands.

"Bettie said somebody was looking for me."

Mr. York is an older version of Elijah. White hair peeking out from a straw hat, a sharpened carpenters pencil in one of the pockets on the front of his bib overalls. A red bandana tied around his neck, contrasting the black-rimmed glasses on his face.

"Afternoon, sir. My name is Ryan Biggs, and I'd appreciate two minutes of your time."

Holding my hand out to Mr. York, he gazes at my fingers for a minute, then offers his own. "Ervin York, but I suspect you know that. Come on, Bettie has lunch waiting."

The sound of wood cracking precedes several grunts. Glancing over my shoulder I watch in amusement as Wesley struggles to get up while balancing the plate of cornbread in his hand.

"Not you, Wesley. That motor ain't gonna put itself in." Ervin calls back, his face remaining forward as he descends the steps and heads for the double wide at the end of the drive.

Following behind, I notice a truck parked in front of the garage, its hood has been removed and a cherry picker straddles the front, an engine dangling from several chains above it.

"That a seventy-six Ford?"

"It will be if Wesley can ever fix the engine."

Walking in step with Ervin, "We had a couple of those on our ranch growing up. My brothers and I rebuilt a few engines, it's not too hard."

Opening the door of the double-wide, "It is when you have to eat every three minutes."

Inside is much the same as Elijah's trailer, with exception of the massive table in the middle of the room, and the rest of Elli's brothers seated around it.

"Boy's this here's, Ryan Biggs," Ervin announces, handing his straw hat to a woman I assume is Bettie, Elli's mother.

"Starting on the left," Ervin points, "Is Eric, Emmitt, Ethan, Ezekiel, Everett, Eugene, and Earl."

Each man nods as Ervin ticks them off with his finger, Elijah takes his place beside Earl. "And you already know Elijah."

"Pleasure," tipping my head as I waited for Ervin to take a seat. Scanning the room, I notice an old radio in the corner, a doily laid over the top, with a blooming plant in the center. My passion for vintage radios overshadows my reason for being here.

"Is that an original Zenith?"

"It is," Ervin takes his place at the table, as Wesley comes through the door, the plate from earlier empty, but still in his hand. "Ain't worked in ten years. Can't find nobody who works on 'em anymore."

Crossing the room, an idea fresh in my head. "Tell you what, Mr. York, how about you talk to me about Elli for as long as it takes me to fix this."

Ervin looks at me, his hands tented as if ready to pray. "Suit yourself, but if Wesley's eating there won't be a stitch of food left when you're done."

The beauty of the vintage radio calls to me, my mother having one exactly like it in our living room back in Montana. These things were built to last and usually needed a good cleaning to get them running again.

"That's all right, sir, I have my whole life to eat, but the questions I have won't wait."

Carefully removing the plant and doily, I pull my multi-tool from my pocket. Unscrewing the back, I wait as Ervin says grace, his head bowed and eyes closed. Wesley is practically foaming at the mouth, licking his lips as he stares at the bowl piled high with mashed potatoes.

"Amen." Rings around the table, not a second too soon as Wesley grabs the bowl, dumping half on his plate.

Pulling off the back, I immediately see the reason it hasn't worked. Lifting the tube, I blow the dust out of the way and clean the prongs. Carefully placing it back, I wipe my hands down my jeans.

"You said you had questions."

"Yes," leaning my back against the paneled wall. "I'm assuming you've seen your daughter on the news as of late."

Ervin continues to chew but doesn't move to acknowledge.

"A comment was made about her engagement to a young man. Wesley as a matter of fact."

Wesley is like a pig in a trough, not even the mention of his name can pull him away from his plate.

"If you mean what that woman and the man she brung with her was asking, then it ain't me you need to talk to."

Pushing off the wall and carefully stepping around the radio, a deep suspicion on my tongue. "What woman?"

Wesley mumbles something, but his mouth is overflowing. Reaching into my pocket, I pull out my phone, turning the photo I have of her as my screen saver in Ervin's direction. With a glass of what I suspect is tea raised to his mouth, Ervin studies the photo and nods his head.

"Spent the better part of an hour with Wesley. The man with her stayed in the car."

Pocketing my phone, there's no doubt in my mind who the man was. I walk around the radio, reattaching the back and plugging it in. The smell, like the first time a furnace is turned on in the fall, fills the room as the sweet sound of a country song floats through the speakers. Bettie stands in the door, her hands covering her mouth as a gasp escapes. Her eyes are filled with unshed tears as she sets a plate of pork chops in the center of the table. Wesley is the first to reach his fork over, but Ervin slaps it away with a fly swatter.

"Boy, Norma Jean ain't my daughter. You best take yourself outside and talk to this man, and then get that truck of yours off my property."

Wesley's fork clatters to his empty plate as he searches the faces at the table. Using the end of the tablecloth, he wipes his chin before pushing himself away from the table and waddling toward the door.

"I appreciate your time, Mr. York," I say, holding my hand out for him to shake.

"You never did ask me a question, so how much do I owe you for fixing Bettie's radio?"

With a smile, "How about I ask my question after I speak with Wesley, then call it even?"

"I'd hurry if I were you," tipping his head in Wesley's direction. "He's been known to eat food that's fallen under his truck seat."

Jogging out of the double-wide, I take the steps two at a time, breaking out into a run as I round the house. Wesley is propped against the side of the truck, staring down in the space where the engine is supposed to go.

Coming to stand beside him, I stare at the engine as it dangles above the empty space. A laugh fills my chest as I consider whether or not I want to burst his bubble on why the engine isn't going to fit.

"You do realize that engine isn't going to fit your truck, right?"

Sending a glare in my direction, he tips his head to the side. "And pray-tell why not?"

Pointing at the mount, "This is a Chevy engine, and Ford and Chevy aren't friends."

Wesley takes a harder look at where I'm pointing, dipping his head as he kicks the tire. While I've never been in his shoes, I have broken the same sort of news to other men. It's been my experience to let a man have a minute in his grief.

"Whatcha wanna know, City Boy?"

"First off, I grew up on a ranch, I live in the city now because of my job. I can still run any piece of farm equipment you put me in."

I won't tell Wesley how much I hate bailing hay in the summer, the long hours spent in the field getting dirty and sunburnt.

"Guy on the television said you was in the military." It wasn't a question, so I remain silent as I study the engine, allowing plenty of time for him to gather his thoughts.

"I could've joined the service if I wanted to." Wesley turns his head in my direction. "But I don't care for no man telling me what to do or when to get up."

Ignoring his ignorance, as everyone has someone who tells them what to do, I lean on the edge of the truck. "Ervin mentioned the reporter from Washington, DC paid you a visit recently. Mind telling me what she wanted?"

A smile cracks his face in half before the earth-shattering sound of a belch fills the air. I have to take a step back as the overpowering smell of corn and gravy floats under my nose. "Dude, your breath is toxic." Waving my hand over my face as Wesley lets another fart rip.

"Hey, that Lindsey woman didn't mind."

Taking two steps back before the smell of his colon meets my nose. "What do you mean?"

Lifting the ball cap off his head, he scratches his scalp before replacing the hat. "She came by, just like you, and wanted to know about Elli, 'cept she called her Elliott. So, I know'd she wasn't a friend like she claimed."

Wesley pauses as he reaches into his pants pocket, pulling out a half-eaten candy bar and shoving it into his mouth. "Wanted to know about where she grew up and stuff. Whether she had a boyfriend or husband."

Another belch leaves his mouth, thankfully he turns his head in the opposite direction as he sets it free.

"What did you tell her?"

With a fond look on his face, he turns to me, a smile not the product of gas lights up his face. "I told her it would cost her."

"So she paid you?"

Wagging his eyebrows, "Not with money, she didn't."

Astonished, "She let you fuck her?"

Wesley looks back at the trailer, searching I suppose for Ervin or Bettie, and then back to me.

"I told her how Elli didn't have the trailer cleaned for me like I told her to. How she went off and took every penny she made from old man Tripp, instead of buying plywood to cover up the hole in the floor. I spent every dime I have on this engine, and now I've got no money for anything until I get paid again. My momma already gots plans for my room, so I was counting on that trailer."

"So why didn't you take money from her, then?"

Wesley leans close, "Cause she offered something better than money."

I wasn't about to say it, not as I had the man standing in front of me, knowing how picky Lindsey is about everything.

"Which is?"

With the most prideful look I've ever seen on any man, his back straight and eyes full of honesty. "She sucked my pecker."

Letting out a huff. "No way, dude, not Lindsey Jennings." Shaking my head as I adjust my stance.

Slamming his hand on the truck. "Swear it on a stack of bibles. She took me all the way to my balls, I ain't never had a girl able to do that, not even Lottie, Norma Jean's sister, and she's gots four kids." Nodding his head once, as if it were gospel. "Even let me squeeze her boobies," the skin between his eyes puckers. "Although she did have something in them, felt like a balloon trapped inside."

Bile rises in my throat, I know exactly what he is describing. Lindsey spent a fortune on those 'balloons', giving her the ability to increase or decrease the size depending on if she was going to the club or gym. "Anything else you got? Lots of girls have things in their tits."

"Yeah, she had a pretty necklace, two C's but one of them was turned backward."

Reaching into his pocket, he pulls the platinum and diamond necklace out. "I must've got carried away with those boobies. After she left, I found this on the ground."

The Chanel necklace I got her for Christmas, rests among the chocolate smudges on his palm. She begged and begged for it, not blinking an eye at the five-figure price. It was the last gift I'd ever given her.

"Tell you what, Wesley. I'll give you what this engine cost you for that necklace."

Squinting his eyes at me. "You got five hundred dollars?"

Reaching into my pocket, "How about we make it an even thousand? You did say you needed money until payday." Counting out the bills, I chuckle a little as his eyes grow glassy, dollar signs dancing in his orbs.

Reaching out his hand for the money, "You got yourself a deal."

Pulling the stack of hundreds back. "Not so fast, Wesley, I've got one question I need answered before I hand over the cash."

Not bothering to look up, he waits like a dog getting a steak bone.

"Were you and Elli ever engaged?"

Walking back to my car, Lindsey's necklace shoved in my pocket, feeling a lot better than when I'd arrived. Ervin calls my name as he walks down the steps.

"I ain't forgot about what I owe ya."

Resting my foot on the edge of my open car door. "Mr. York, I've hurt your daughter in the worst way, believing a lie when I knew the person who said it possessed a forked tongue. If I ever make things right with her, can you forgive me?"

CHAPTER SIXTEEN

ELLI

M oving into your first apartment is a monumental event in
a young adult's life, especially when it comes furnished
and at a price well within your budget. Looking out my living
room window, I feel more like crawling into a ball and crying
instead of arranging the furniture to achieve perfect Feng Shui.
Holding the picture of me and my mother, the photo was taken the
night I graduated from high school, I trace her delicate features,
her pride-filled eyes reflecting back at me.

I'd sent an email to my old pastor back in Jupiter after I left the
hospital, asking him to please tell her I was safe and would send a
letter when I could.

Bettie York, like most of the women in my family before her,
can't read or write. I'd tried to teach her, but there's always work
to be done. Anything needing a signature or explanation she takes
to the pastor for help.

I was given a promotion for my heroics at work, moving up
from assistant to Fact Checker. Doug and Richard's funerals are

scheduled for tomorrow, even though neither of their bodies would ever be found. I briefly wonder if he'll be there but chastise myself for allowing my mind to think of him.

I'd gone back to my hotel from the hospital, shrugged out of his clothes and cried for what felt like forever under the spray of the shower. I gave myself one day, twenty-four solid hours, to get it out of my system before I refused to shed any more tears.

We'd had one crazy adventure together, survived a near-death experience and had, in my opinion, a night of incredible passion. All of this combined doesn't equate to exchanges of I love you's and wedding bells. I laundered his clothes, placed them in a box ready to return, but no matter how hard I try, I can't remove the necklace from around my neck. My mind has no trouble rationalizing it, it's my heart who refuses to get on board.

My new apartment isn't as close to the Capitol as the hotel was. Its location forces me to ride past the White House each day, wondering if he is guarding the President, or if the speculations are true of a reconciliation between America's Sweetheart and the SEAL with honor.

"Are you excited about next Friday?"

Jennifer, my new coworker, and apartment-finder, questions from over the top of my cubical. She's pretty, with a glowing personality, and always planning an event or attending one.

"Of course, it isn't every day you get to meet the President in person."

Truth is, I don't care about this medal they want to present me or the cash award that comes along with it. I want to go home, change into my pajamas, and get lost in a book about killer zombies. There's a strong possibility he'll be there, as he is the real hero in the equation. I'd been too nervous to ask, instead of using the time to shop for new clothes to replace the ones I'd left back home.

"Awesome, I'm so excited. Oh, before I forget, I'm having a little get together this weekend in the community room at the apartment. I've invited the guy in 3A to come."

Jennifer is obsessed with the guy who recently moved into our building. Granted, he is cute as hell, but the last thing on my mind is men.

"Put me down for a maybe, I might have to work."

It wasn't a complete lie, there's always an opportunity to work on the weekends, but it's generally only a few hours in the morning when the media shares what it invents overnight.

"Nice try, Elli. Either I see you at the party, or I bring the whole thing to your front door."

MUSIC THUMPS as I step off the elevator. Another one of the perks Jennifer boasted about is the community room on the first floor. It's free for residents to use and includes an entrance to the indoor pool.

Crossing the short hall, I use my swipe card to open the door. "Elli, you made it." Jennifer slurs, her arms wrapped around a guy I don't recognize. She tried to pull away, but the dark-haired man holds her close as he rubs up against her.

Sending her a wave, I spot a table pushed against the wall, an ice chest in the middle with stacks of red cups to the left. Reaching for a cup, I instinctively recoil when I come in contact with another hand.

"I'm so—"

"Forgive—"

Stepping back, I'm surprised to see the smiling face of the guy from 3A looking back at me. I can't help but notice he's much cuter up close, with dark hair and eyes.

"Please, you were first." Handing me the cup in his hand. "I'm Marc, by the way, just moved into the building. I'm in 3A." Tossing his thumb over his shoulder.

"Elli," purposely omitting my apartment number, another warning from Ms. Wesson. Taking the cup, I reach for the lid to the ice chest.

Reaching around me, he picks up a bottle of tequila from the table. "You here with anyone?"

Marc is cute, handsome by some standards, but everything about him is wrong. I shouldn't do this, shouldn't compare every man I meet to the one who is more than likely holed up in some luxurious apartment, having sex with his beautiful girlfriend. It isn't fair to Marc, or any guy I meet, to pay for a crime he didn't commit against me. While I know all this, I can't stop myself from doing it.

"I'm sorry, Marc," handing the red cup back to him. "I have to go."

* * *

It feels as if a thousand butterflies have been set free inside my stomach, each one trying desperately to escape as I'm escorted into the White House. I've barely slept over the past week, too concerned with how I'll react when I see him. Thankfully, I've been able to avoid seeing Lindsey's face on the news as she is a prime-time anchor. All that would change today, as it was announced she is one of the journalists invited to attend.

No matter how many times I remind myself to keep my eyes forward, the second they bring me in the room, my body betrays

131

me, searching the room for those blue eyes of his. It's both a blessing and curse when I come up empty, landing instead on the handsome face of Logan Forbes.

He's surrounded by a small group of people, a young beautiful brunette tucked under his arm. I assume she's his wife, the one he spoke of calling once the airplane got in the air. Based on his close ties to Ryan, she could be his great adventure.

"Are you doing okay?" Ms. Wesson, although no longer my superior, has remained my mentor. When the powers that be decided this award was to be presented, she was the first one to congratulate me.

"I'm fine," I lie, keeping my attention on the group as they, like me, wait for the President to arrive. "Just don't see the need for all of this when there is work to do."

Logan's eyes scan the room, stopping abruptly when they land on me. Kissing the forehead of the brunette, he heads in our direction.

"Everyone needs a hero, Elli, someone who does extraordinary things for the benefit of others. Today that someone is you. Take the award, pose for pictures, and hope some little girl out there is watching and waiting for the brand of hero you are."

Opening my arms wide, I hug Ms. Wesson. "Thank you." I offer into her ear, holding back the tears I've battled for weeks.

"Pardon the interruption," severing the hug as Logan's deep voice puts an end to the moment. "But could I possibly borrow Ms. York?"

Ms. Wesson kisses my cheek, then blends into the crowd of dark suits and camera flashes. Shifting my attention to a waiting Logan, the last thing I want is for the moment to be awkward.

"Congratulations, Dr. Forbes," It's lame, but the best thing I can offer.

Surrounding me in a hug, "Dr. Forbes is my father. Ryan's stupidity doesn't change the fact you are one of us. As a matter of fact, my mother insists you join us for dinner after this. Before you argue, I warn you she isn't one who takes no for an answer."

A temporary stay of execution comes with the announcement of the President's arrival. I'm pulled from the conversation to take my place next to the podium with the presidential seal on the front. The media takes their seats behind the chairs reserved for honored guests as the doors are opened wide for him to enter.

My heart falls a little when I fail to see him walk in the room. Everything I'd heard since the crash was of his selection for Presidential detail within the Secret Service.

For fifteen minutes, I get the pleasure of listening to the President tell the world the account of what happened, reliving the events of a day I will never be able to forget.

"It is with pride I inform you Agent Biggs is unable to accept his medal this afternoon, due to an assignment he bravely accepted."

I have no idea what the President said after that. I smiled when he shook my hand and placed the ribbon over my neck. Clapped when Congressman Howard struggled to stand and salute Logan. I stood where they told me, held the medal dangling from my neck as they showed me.

But when Lindsey Jennings approached me with a microphone, my mind pressed play on real time. In an instant, the room is too bright, the air muggy and thick, my need to escape clawing inside my chest.

My view of her is blocked by the solid mass of muscle belonging to Logan. "You've fucked enough things up, Lindsey." I hear him say as the brunette pulls me to the side and out an open door, down a hall and into a waiting SUV.

"I'm sorry about her," the brunette speaks as she fastens her seatbelt. "I can't wait for the day she gets everything she deserves."

Reaching for the door handle, "Um, who are you?"

Warm eyes, big as the state of Texas, blink back at me. "Oh, lord. I forget you haven't been introduced to the rest of the group, that usually precedes telling you about what they do." Extending her manicured hand, "My name is Harper, I'm Logan's wife. And may I say, you are so much better than Lindsey."

My rebuttal is forgotten as the door I have a hold of wrenches open and Logan's massive body appears, motioning for me to scoot over. He fluidly climbs inside, shutting the door tight, he places an arm behind me as another couple enters through the door to the seat in front of me.

"Oh, thank god, I thought we'd never get away from that horrid woman." Checking her reflection in her compact, her eyes land on me, applying her lipstick forgotten.

"Elliott York." A warmth I haven't felt in quite some time rushes over me as the woman I recognize from the media shares her smile with me. Extending her hand over the seat, "Meredith Forbes, a pleasure to meet you."

Her skin feels soft against mine, and the genuine smile on her face is contagious. For the first time in weeks, I feel remotely happy.

"I do hope you're not a vegetarian, Elliott. I promised Weston we would dine at a restaurant he's been wanting to try for ages."

"No, ma'am, I was raised on meat and potatoes." Releasing her hand, "And please, call me Elli."

Idol conversation springs up inside the car, thankfully none of it requires a response from me. Less than ten minutes later, the driver pulls under the awning of Davenport's, a well-known chop house in the district. The line to get in was wrapped around the front of the building, eager patrons perusing the menu in anticipation of gaining a seat. Logan helps me from the SUV before turning and pulling his wife into his arms, extending his elbow to me. It was no surprise when we bypassed the line, the maître d' opens the door and escorts us to a table in the back.

Weston helps me with my chair as one of the many waiters lay my napkin across my lap before filling a glass with water. "Order anything you like, it's on Weston." Meredith teases, leaning over and kissing her husband's cheek.

Logan has his phone in his hand, a mischievous smile on his, leaning over he shares what is on the screen with Harper.

The butterflies from earlier have been unable to find their way home, still plaguing me with unease. I keep my choice in food light, sticking with water as the rest of the table enjoys the rich foods.

As the dishes are cleared, Meredith spots someone she recognizes, excusing herself and Weston to go say hello. Logan takes the opportunity to lean across the table, his hands folded in front of him.

"Listen, Elli. I know things with you and Ryan don't look good right now, but you need to know his background before you write him off completely."

Reaching for my water glass, "He has a girlfriend. One who, according to a woman I've never met before, implied they have an arrangement."

Harper looks at me with sadness, "Please, Elli. Just listen."

Leaning back in my seat, nodding for him to continue.

"Ryan met Lindsey when she was a nameless reporter trying to climb her way out of the masses. Somehow, she landed an assignment to report on the treatment of refugees in a Syrian camp.

When shit got heated, she cashed in, twisting the truth to make it suit her. Ryan was this young, single guy riding the same wave of adventure the rest of us were, only she made him believe they were different. When the documentary was picked up by the network, America bought the bullshit she was selling. Sadly, so did Ryan."

Logan pauses long enough to take a sip of his drink, his eyes staring off behind me, over the rim of his glass.

"I wish I could count the number of times Ryan caught her in a lie. Not small shit like what time she got up, or what she had to eat, but big shit; like where she spent the night and in whose bed she woke up in. They'd break up and she'd come begging after him, always with an excuse and a camera in tow, their reunion making the rounds of the talk shows. Ryan's career as a SEAL made Lindsey the success she is, and anytime she feels threatened she pulls bullshit like she did at the airport. Now, I'm not saying Ryan isn't to blame, he has plenty of shit he needs to pay for. But this time, things are different. He made you one of us when he stood up and announced you were his girlfriend. And in this family, we take care of our own."

Taking the edge of my napkin between my fingers. "Those were just words, a feeling based on the heat of the moment. Besides, he hasn't contacted me or checked to see if I'm okay."

"Just because you don't see him, doesn't mean he isn't watching."

Lifting my eyes from my fingers, "What do you mean?"

"Ryan is getting his shit together with Matt's help. As I said, give him time before you write him off." Logan's eyes drift back to the place behind me, my curiosity peaks as I glance over my shoulder.

My breath catches in my throat. Not ten feet away, Lindsey sits at a booth with two men, one to her left and the second seated

136

across from her. Both men I recognize from the Capitol building. The man seated across from her has his body leaning to the side, her barefoot in his lap. The second, has his hand under the table and under her skirt, while her eyes are boring into the man across from her.

Disgusted, I turn back to the table, "That's..." A chill surrounds me as I search for the right word.

"Lindsey," Logan finishes. "A whore in every sense of the word. Ryan's been avoiding her calls, so she's been making the rounds."

"I was going to say horrible, but what you said works too." Pausing as I consider how to properly phrase my next question, "You said something earlier, about how he always takes her back. Who's to say he hasn't this time?"

Meredith and Weston return to the table, but Logan's focus remains on me. "As I said, this time is different, you're one of us."

After leaving the restaurant, the Forbes insisted on driving me home. A part of me wants to refuse in the attempt of keeping the location of where I live a secret, but Logan shot that down when he rattles off my address to the driver.

Kicking off my shoes as I enter my apartment, placing the box containing the medal on the shelf where I keep the photo of my mother, I'm suddenly overcome with a wave of dizziness and nausea. Rushing to the bathroom, I barely make it to the toilet before emptying the contents of my stomach into the porcelain bowl.

"Dang it," I swear, wiping my mouth with a cold rag. The flu has made its way around the Capitol building and until now I'd been able to avoid it. Changing into my pajamas, I crawl under the blankets and pray for sleep to take me.

CHAPTER SEVENTEEN

ELLI

R yan
Thwack

Raising the ax above my head, I swing down hard once again, splitting the cut log in half.

Thwack

I'd helped Matt clear a bunch of dead trees away from the house. With the weather getting colder, it's too risky to leave them so close in the event of an ice storm.

Thwack

It'd taken me longer than I thought to get here, having stopped several times to explore the area where Elli grew up, even buying peanuts off another vendor on my way out of town. I spent the first few days letting the road under me take me down the backroads of Virginia as I made my way south. I ate at roadside restaurants, watched a group of boys play baseball in a run-down field. I stopped at a festival, bought several of the wares the ladies sold, filling my truck with quilts and yard ornaments.

Lindsey continued to call, and I kept ignoring her until somewhere about day eight when she lost her mind and kept calling. I stopped for gas and blocked her number, only to have her use a different phone to call me. That's when enough was enough and I shut it down, tossing it into the truck with all those quilts.

That evening, I'd pulled into another town looking for a motel to rest for the night. I asked the clerk for the best place to eat and he directed me across the street to a dance hall. The last thing I'd wanted was to place myself in the middle of female attention, so I walked up to the bar and asked for my food to go. As I'd waited, I drank a cold beer, watching the people around me, keeping myself in the corner and away from any attention.

All my efforts were tossed to shit when I saw this asshole laying his hands on one of the waitresses. By the way she turned her head and recoiled from him, I had been able to tell she didn't appreciate his attention. After setting my beer on the bar, I crossed the wooden floor, placing my body between them. The guy tried to act big and bad, but I hadn't had a good bar fight in quite a while. When his two friends had stood up, I knew my dry spell was over.

Five punches later and the man was out cold, his buddies who'd insinuated they had his back, were gone before the second punch landed. The owner of the bar wanted to buy me another round, but I declined, took my food and returned to my room.

After scarfing down some of the best barbecue in my life, I'd fired up my laptop and checked my email for the first time in over a week. There was a number from Aiden which included attachments, I hadn't had to question what they contained. Clicking on the oldest, a photo of Elli and I asleep on the plane had filled the screen. My arms were wrapped around her middle, with those delicate fingers of hers buried in my hair. The next was of the look on her face as Lindsey prodded her about Wesley. My heart shattered in a thousand pieces at the devastation on her face. I'd sworn to protect her, but I never thought I'd be the one to hurt her so bad. The third was of Elli getting off a city bus, Namur dressed in a hoodie following behind her. Aiden included a bill for Namur's time, which I gladly paid. The final one was a copy of a lease for an apartment, Elli's name and address located at the top. A canceled check was also included, the amount totaling half the rent for the length of the lease. A note from Logan, reminded me we take care of our own.

That night, I slept until the manager pounded on the door, kicking me out as it was an hour past check out. I paid him for an extra day and crawled back under the sheets, sleeping well into the evening before climbing in my car and driving the rest of the way to Matt's house.

Memories of taking the same road with Eleni in the car came to life as I'd arrived in the wee hours of the morning. The porch light switched on as I parked my car in the drive. Climbing the steps, Rayne opened the door, a sour look on her face.

"I'm—"

Her hand connected with the side of my face, the sting nearly blinding me. She had shoved a pillow and blanket into my chest, shouting, *"Jack asses sleep in the barn."* Before slamming the door in my face.

It took her the better part of a week before she would look me in the eye, allowing me into the house to eat at the table with the two of them. The television was always on, turned to the national news, the story of the plane crash on repeat. A small penance I needed to pay I suppose.

I'd learned through sources of Elli's promotion, Congressman Howard sorry to see her go, but felt the position was well deserved. I wanted to send her flowers, but Rayne forbade it, claiming doing so would send a message I wasn't ready to. She hammered home how important it was for me to free myself of the chains Lindsey held me captive with before even thinking about winning Elli back. She helped me understand how wrong it was to jump from one relationship to another without knowing myself first.

Rayne was right, from the moment the words left her lips I knew it. And when the choice came between accepting an award from the President or helping Chase with a bounty jumper, I chose the jumper. While I wanted nothing more than to see her shine, I didn't want to ruin the moment for her. I saw firsthand the environment she grew up in, the lack of respect placed on the women who lived under the same roof. She deserved to have the most influential man in the world shine the spotlight on her.

For three days Matt, Chase and I trailed this guy through some of the most secluded parts of North and South Carolina. Finally locating him hidden in a cave at the base of a mountain. A brown bear did most of the work for us, as the guy picked the same place the bear chose as its spot to hibernate in until we passed.

Chase and I watched in awe, Matt approached that bear, spoke with him as if he was making a deal for moonshine, slipped past him and put the jumper in cuffs.

Thwack

When we returned, Rayne was standing in the gazebo Matt built her, face covered in tears. Her father, Sheriff Winters, had delivered the news the remains of her former boss were found in the wall of the basement in the house she inherited after ultrasound indicated the presence of something behind the brick. Rayne threw her arms around Matt's neck telling him she didn't want any more time to think, she was ready to marry him. When she turned to me, the sadness vanished and the anger from weeks prior returned. She made it plain as day, I was invited to their nuptials, but only if I brought Elli.

Thwack

Burying the tip of the ax into the stump, I wipe the sweat off my face as I stare out over the pond. How many nights have I sat out here, listening to the song of the bullfrogs and crickets, wishing like hell Elli were beside me? Its been a month today since I let her walk away, climb into the back of that ambulance and out of my life.

"Looks good, Ryan. I'm glad you stuck around to help out." Matt pulls me from my mental ramblings, their effect on me has changed of late. While I still wish they hadn't happened, I've moved from regret to grateful. I'm finally ready to move on.

"Me too, thanks for putting up with me. And letting Rayne smack me around."

Handing me a beer, "It's what she does best. Slap people with a dose of reality, make them take a look at themselves."

Kicking one of the logs I split, watching as it tumbles to join the rest. "I'm just glad she's on our team."

"You look better today," he adds, taking a seat on the stump with the ax buried in it.

"It's time I go home, Matt. Start working on getting Elli back."

CHAPTER EIGHTEEN

ELLI

M s. Wesson had been right, a week after the President handed me a shiny medal, an early winter storm created a massive pileup on an interstate, creating a new batch of ordinary heroes who risked their lives saving others. What I assumed to be the flu, turned out to be a twenty-four-hour bug, as I was fine by the following Monday.

"Hey, Elli?" Lifting my focus from my computer screen, I raise my eyes to Jennifer who's standing in the door to my cubical. "Look what just came for you."

Placing the large vase of white roses on my desk, she stands to the side, placing her hands behind her back. "Well, aren't you going to see who sent them?"

Lifting the card from the plastic stick, my name and work address splash across the front from a computer printout. Thinking of you is all the card says, no signature or any indication of who sent them.

"They're from Marc, aren't they? He asked about you last

night, so they have to be. You should totally go out with him, we could double you know."

I've run into Marc several times since Jennifer's party, mostly in the early mornings when I'm headed to work and by his rumpled appearance, he is just getting home. Jennifer never seems to shut up about the guy.

"No, they're from my father. My birthday is coming up; he sends me things when he remembers."

It was a lie all the way around. My father wouldn't know the first thing about sending flowers or have the means to do so. My birthday was in two days, not that I had any plans to celebrate it, at least not with Marc and Jennifer.

"Oh, well, I guess I'll see you in the meeting, then."

"Yeah, I'm headed there in a minute."

Shoving the card into the locked drawer of my desk, away from prying eyes. We'd recently gotten a new supervisor, who insisted on weekly meetings. Personally, I felt the time is wasted as once he gave out information which could be sent in an email, the rest of the time is spent spreading gossip about other departments.

Standing from my chair, a wave of dizziness forces me to sit back down and get my bearings. Once the dizziness passes, I slowly stand again, this time with no problem.

The conference room runs along the front of the building, with windows along the far wall. A long table takes up most of the room, high-back chairs surrounding. The meeting was well underway as I slip inside, taking an empty chair along the wall.

"So good of you to join us, Elliott." Mr. Cane stands with one arm crossed, the other holding a cup of coffee from a shop down the street. "Were you too busy accepting another award to show up on time?"

Mr. Cane had been none too happy when he was notified I was

to have time off to receive the award. I didn't understand the hostility he showed me as I'd never had any dealing with the man prior.

"Sorry, Sir. I had a small issue at my desk."

"I saw your issue, Elliott. Those flowers are distracting, take them home and tell your boyfriend not to send any more."

"I don't have a boyfriend," I mumble as bile rose in my throat.

Spinning on his heels, his overpriced coffee sloshes over the rim of his cup. "I don't give a shit if the goddamn Pope sent them. I don't want to see them in this office, are we clear?" He roars, his face red with anger.

Before I can mutter an answer, nausea, as I've never felt, hits me. Standing to my feet, I dash down the hall, bust through the ladies room door and vomit in the closest sink. Thankfully the room is empty and no one has to witness my repeated prayers to the porcelain god. Rinsing my mouth with water, I can still taste the bile on my tongue. Making my way back to my desk, I pull out my purse in search of the gum I bought last week at the grocery store. When my fingers don't immediately find it, I begin removing items from my purse and placing them on my desk. Glancing at the bottom, I see the pack of gum beside the sanitary napkin I placed there when Congressman Howard's wife gifted me the purse, as I lost mine in the plane crash.

Grabbing the pad with my fingers, I sit hard in my seat, calculating back to when I had my last period. It was two weeks before I moved here, fifteen days before my night with Ryan. Bolting from my chair, I barely make it to the bathroom before the dry heaves begin.

Not bothering to check out with Mr. Cane, I return to my desk long enough to grab my purse and head out the door. There's a pharmacy not far from my apartment. As I purchase a pregnancy test and a sports drink, the cashier sends me a sad smile. The directions recommend waiting until morning, but I ignore them and sit on the toilet, peeing on the tiny stick.

Fifteen minutes later, I stand shocked in front of my living room window, the positive test still between fingers as the phone rings in my ear.

"Good afternoon, Dr. Bakers office, this is Alicia. How may I direct your call?"

"Hello," my voice sounds odd even to my own ears. Clearing my throat before I continue, "I need to make an appointment, please. I think I may be pregnant."

MR. CANE WAS WAITING for me when I arrive the next morning his cup of coffee staining the pristine desk calendar I kept under my keyboard.

"I should write you up for leaving without telling me yesterday."

My nausea stuck with me for the rest of the night and continued into this morning. There is nothing left in my stomach, even the sports drink didn't survive long.

"Lucky for you, everyone heard you throwing up yesterday. I'm going to need a note from a doctor that states you're healthy enough to work here."

Mr. Cane chose the wrong day to be an asshole to me. Lifting his cup from my desk, "Policy stipulates I must be absent for three consecutive days before a physician's note is required." Forcing the cup into his hand, before motioning for him to get out of my chair. "Lucky for you, Mr. Cane, I have an appointment this morning and will be happy to provide you with a note upon my return."

Standing to his full height, his intention to intimidate me failing miserably. "I want a leave chit on my desk in five minutes."

Shoving my purse in my drawer, "The rules say an email is fine and has to be submitted within twenty-four hours of the absence."

Leaning over my desk, "You think you're so smart? Well, guess what, your little boyfriend who sent those flowers, does that for a lot of girls. You're nothing special, just something to pass the time."

Two hours later, I stand with a bag full of prenatal vitamin samples, an appoint for a month from today for my next visit and a black and white sonogram photo with a tiny circle where Dr. Baker said my baby is growing beautifully. As I walked out the door, Mr. Cane's harsh words come back to me. It's clear Ryan wants nothing to do with me, those flowers weren't from him and it'd been over a month since everything happened. I'm on my own, and too prideful to tuck my tail between my legs and crawl back to Virginia. Fishing my phone from my purse, I locate the number of the adoption agency I fact-checked a few weeks ago.

"Hello, I'd like to make an appointment to discuss giving up my baby for adoption."

CHAPTER NINETEEN

RYAN

"*Hello, you've reached the desk of Elliott York. I'm currently away from my desk, but if need immediate assistance, please contact Jennifer at 555-1234.*"

It feels like forever since I've heard her voice, even with the sullen tone to it, I can't erase the smile on my face. Ending the call, I punch in the numbers and hit send.

"*Good morning, this is Jennifer, how can I help you?*"

"Hello, Jennifer. I'm trying to get in touch with Elli, her message says she's away from her desk. Is she in today?"

"*I'm sorry, who am I speaking with?*"

"Special Agent Biggs, I work for Congressman Howard's office."

"*I'm sorry, Mr. Biggs, but Elli is at an appointment today, not sure if she is coming back, she wasn't feeling well yesterday.*"

Crossing the room to my computer, praying she still has the pendant I gave her on the plane. It's a long shot, one I wouldn't be surprised to find at the bottom of the Potomac.

"Thank you, Jennifer. I'll try her later."

Ending the call, I punch in my password and log into the program. A thousand scenarios flash through my head of what could be wrong, but as the map of DC comes to life and the red dot flashes inside a medical center not far from here, I slam my laptop shut and head out the door.

Parking my car, I grab my phone from the passenger seat, the red dot still blinking. Taking the steps two at a time, I throw open the door and follow the red dot down the hall. My heart begins to pound as I read the name on the door; Dr. Samuel Baker, Board Certified Ob/Gyn.

Reaching for the handle, I'm taken aback when it opens and there stands the most beautiful girl in the world, her phone to her ear, and a sonogram photo in her hand.

"Yes, thank you September ninth will be fine."

I'm ready to jump out of my skin as she ends her call, tossing her phone in the leather bag over her shoulder.

"Ryan?"

"You're pregnant?"

Our questions overlap, the door to the office opening again, as a woman advanced in her pregnancy tries to step out.

"I'm so sorry," Elli apologizes, as I instinctively reach for her arm, pulling her toward me and out of the way. Her face is pale, making those sexy freckles stand out. The pouty lips I adore now cracked and chapped, but not enough to make me not want to kiss her. The woman smiles and waits until the coast is clear, thanking Elli before making her way to the elevator.

Unable to release her, "You're pregnant?"

Nodding, she drops her eyes to the sonogram photo in her hands. "We didn't use protection...so..." She shrugs.

Remembering back to how incredible she felt around me,

always ready for me each time I took her. "You're right, we didn't." Taking a step closer to her.

Straightening her back, adjusting the strap on her shoulder. "I don't expect anything from you," shaking her head. "I have an appointment with an adoption agency in a few weeks."

Fear grips me, rendering the words I rehearsed on the drive from South Carolina useless. Spouting off the first thing that comes to mind, "I spoke with Wesley and your father."

Tipping her head to the side, her eyes half closed. "Why?"

Lowering my head, looking at her through my eyelashes. "Because I needed to hear it from him, see for myself the relationship was over. He's disgusting, by the way, the smells coming from him could kill a Troll."

Elli covers her mouth to hide a laugh, "Trust me, I'm all too familiar with his odors."

"I miss your laugh," I admit, wishing I could record the sound and listen to it constantly.

"Then why did you leave?"

"Because I had to find myself before I could really close the door on Lindsey." I want to confess it all, but I need to show her how good we can be. "Listen, I know you grew up in the south and there is a three-day weekend coming up for you. Please, come to South Carolina, Matt is getting married and I can't show up without you. Come give me the opportunity to prove to you who I am, without the guns and plane crashes."

Her eyes fall to the photo in her hand, "I don't know, Ryan. Things—"

"Please, Elli," I beg, willing to drop to my knees if it will help.

The war raging inside her head is written all over her face. I imagine she is trying hard to guard herself, and yet remain fair to the father of her child.

"Okay, I'll come with you."

It hasn't escaped my attention my pendant is still around her neck, not shoved into her purse, lost among old receipts and empty ball-point pens. The image of the silver chain creates a smile on my face I keep long after dropping her off at work.

Parking my car, I know something is up the minute I make eye contact with the gate guard, the heaviness as if he's just gone three rounds with a heavyweight champion while blindfolded. Exiting the elevator, I find Lindsey sitting outside my condo, talking loudly on her phone, her back on the floor, legs, and ass against the wall, the heel of her overpriced shoes making a dent in the drywall.

When she notices me, she ends the call, doing her best Sharon Stone impression as she lets her legs fall to the side, exposing her bare pussy. I've seen what's between her legs, hell, half the city has, so when my eyes remain on her face, she flips over onto her stomach.

"You changed the locks, why?"

Entering the code into the keypad, the locks click open and I see her in my peripheral vision climb to her feet. "Because I'm selling it."

"Why? It's a fabulous space."

Not bothering to invite her in, I walk through the space to my bedroom, grabbing the bag of clothes I sorted earlier. "Oh, today it's fabulous when a month ago it was last season." Stepping around her, I toss the dirty laundry into the machine and start it.

Lindsey leans against the doorframe to my laundry room, arms crossed, pushing her tits to her chin. "Are you going to apologize?"

"For what?"

"For ignoring me, not returning my calls," her arm outstretches, pointing to my front door. "Changing the locks."

Closing the lid of my washer, "How does it feel, Lindsey?"

Dropping her arms, "Fine, you made your point, now get naked, I'm horny."

"How does it feel, I said?" Knocking her hands away when she reaches for my shirt.

"I said you made your point, what else do you want?"

Crossing my arms over my chest, "How did you know about Wesley and Elliott's engagement?"

"Who?"

Pushing past her, I round the corner back into my living room. "Don't play with me, little girl. Now tell me how you knew?"

Plopping herself on my sofa, "Fine. When the word got out one of the President's planes had been hijacked and you were on board, I did some research of who else was involved."

Crossing her legs, she picks up one of the pillows beside her, tucking it to her chest.

"When I found there was a girl on board, and you were the only 'single' guy," she uses air quotes after the word single, rolling her eyes to drive her point home. "I speak from experience as to your need to protect. So, there was this strong chance you would develop feelings for her based on the situation. I mean if I thought I was going to die, I'd want to fuck the hell out of everyone." She laughs as if near-death is a fucking aphrodisiac.

Lying her open palm on her chest, "I spoke with my sources and found out her information. One call to her previous employer and they told me all about the two of them. I knew the second you stepped off the plane you were head over heels for the girl."

Uncrossing her legs, she reaches down and pulls the hem of her shirt over her head, those tits she loves so much on full display. Adjusting her skirt, she opens her legs wide as she begins to play with her nipples.

"Do you even know how to tell the truth?"

Her fingers pause, "I report the facts, with a little flare." She shimmies, her tits bouncing from side to side.

"You didn't call anyone, Lindsey. You drove down to Jupiter, pulled up to where her family lives and sucked the dick of the vile man who told you he was marrying another woman, and not Elliott."

"That's a lie, Ryan." Slapping her hands on the leather of the couch, a slip of hair falls across her eyes.

Reaching into my pants pocket, "You left this behind. Wesley wants a call when he can play with your boobies again." Slamming the necklace onto the glass tabletop, her mouth opens wide, hands reaching out to take the necklace as if she were Gollum.

"You begged for that goddamn necklace, got pissed at your producer when he forbade you from wearing it on air, claiming Chanel doesn't pay for commercial time during your segment. Since the moment you got the damn thing, you've had it close to you."

Clenching the necklace in her fist. "Okay, fine, I did go to Jupiter, but I love you and I couldn't stand the thought of you leaving me for someone younger." Tears form in the corners of her eyes, a slight tremor in the last few words.

"You left me a long time ago, or don't you remember?"

"We fight Ryan, but we always work it out. We're good together."

Shaking my head, "Not this time, Lindsey. Things are different."

"You love me, I love you, nothing has changed."

Unable to hold back, "Elliott's pregnant."

"So?" She huffs, condescension coating her tongue.

"It's mine."

"How do you know? Maybe Wesley was being forced to propose. Kinda per—"

Unable to stomach her slashing of Elli's character, I interrupt with the truth. "Because I took her virginity, that's how."

Pulling back her mouth gapes like a fish. "Wow, I didn't think those still existed," tipping her head to the side. "Although, she is rather…plain."

"Shut your fucking mouth, Lindsey. At least her sheets don't have frequent flyer miles on them." I seethe, regretting the night I allowed her to stay in my cot.

"So make her get an abortion. It's easy, I've done it at least a dozen times. Couple grand, half an hour, it's over." Reaching for her purse, "I have the name of a fabulous doctor, excellent technique with very little downtime."

Holding up my hand, "Wait, did you just say you've had a dozen abortions?"

Shrugging, "Give or take, yes."

Anger, shock, sorrow, all swirl together inside my veins. "How many were mine?"

If there is one thing in this world I have wanted to become more than being a SEAL, it's being a father.

Without an ounce of regret in her voice, "One or two, maybe more." She shrugs a satisfied smirk on her botoxed lips.

All this time, lies I believed just to keep what I assumed was the perfect relationship. A girl who understands my need to do my job, never complaining when I cancel plans last minute to disappear for weeks. I'd told Eleni I wanted Lindsey to listen to me, hear the love I had for her. Seeing her now, knowing the ultimate betrayal she's shown, it was I who hadn't been listening. But I am now, and I hear her loud and clear.

"Get out," I demand, walking with purpose to the door and throwing it open. "Get the fuck out of my life."

Lindsey rolls her eyes, allowing a humorless laugh to leave her lips as she grabs her belongings. "You know, Ryan, we both know when you've had time to think about this, you'll come crawling back to me like you always do. I'm not about to let your sense of decency ruin what I've worked for."

Stomping across the room, I grab the chain from her hand, snapping the pendant in half before throwing the two halves onto the floor of the hall. "There, go have your producer bend it back like he did when he fucked you over a table in New York."

Not bothering to cover her naked chest, Lindsey stomps down the hall, knocking over a table holding a single lamp.

"You're going to regret this, Biggs." She tosses over her shoulder as she bends to pick up the mangled necklace.

"I regret many things when it comes to you. Telling you goodbye won't be one of them."

CHAPTER TWENTY

ELLI

L istening as Mr. Cane drabbles on and on over limiting personal items on our desks, and prohibiting personal phone calls while on government time, makes me wish I'd taken the whole day off. I don't understand why he focuses so much energy on things which really don't matter.

"It's clear to me, my predecessor was quite lax in matters of requesting time off." Keeping my hands under the table, counting the minutes until it's time for me to go home.

"In the future, all leave will need to be approved thirty days in advance."

Several grumbles are heard about the room. Mr. Cane can try and create all the rules he wants to, but with a room full of Fact Checkers, he's going to lose badly. Besides, Cane is a position hopper, staying in one position long enough to go to the next. According to Jennifer, he's held six positions in the last three years, including this one.

A knock at the door sounds just as the clock on the wall ticks the end of my day. The cherry-stained wood opens to reveal Ryan, with a huge vase of flowers in his hand.

"Sorry to interrupt." Shifting the flowers to his hip, the action brings my attention from the cocky smile, complete with thumb swiping at the edge of his lip, to the sexy-as-hell way his jeans hang off those hips. "There was no one at the receptionist desk and I heard your voice from the elevator."

Mr. Cane tosses his notebook to the table, casting his attention to Ryan. "No problem, Biggs. What can I help you find?"

"Already found her," Ryan tips his head in my direction, the tenor of his voice creates a welcomed chill down my spine.

Jennifer leans over, her shoulder pressing into mine. "Tell me you've hit that?"

Refusing to give anything to add to the gossip pool, I stand from my seat, making my way around the table in his direction. "Hey," not wanting to assume anything when it comes to where Ryan and I stand. I've made it clear I don't expect anything from him, but his presence here does plant a seed.

Leaning over, he sets the flowers on the table, then pulls me in for a kiss. "You're done for the day, right?"

Before I can answer, Mr. Cane clears his throat. My hand's act of their own volition, folding themselves in front of me as if caught doing something I wasn't supposed to. Glancing to the side, I find Mr. Cane pointing to the enormous vase of flowers, "We have a strict policy against items like this in the office. Clearly, Elliott has forgotten to pass along the information to you since the last arrangement you sent."

Ryan's fingers dig into my hip, his sweet breath dancing across my face. "What arrangement?"

Mr. Cane tosses his glasses to join the notebook, "The white roses you sent yesterday."

Steadying myself against Ryan's arm, a wave of dizziness rushes over me. "Woah."

Ryan helps me into an empty chair, "What is it?"

Shutting my eyes tight, trying desperately not to throw up, "Just dizzy, is all. Happens a lot lately."

Lowering himself to his knees, his warm hand caressing my face. "When was the last time you ate?"

"Breakfast, nothing really stays down except crackers."

Ryan waits patiently as the dizziness subsides, running his fingertips gently up and down my arms. I recall with fondness the last time he did this, lying in bed beside him completely naked and perhaps following the moment we created this miracle inside me. I can hear my coworkers leave the room, pushing their chairs in while bidding me a good night.

"Better?" He questions as I open my eyes.

"Much," I agreed. Raising my head, the room still moving slightly but not as bad as a few moments ago.

"Good." Placing a kiss to my temple, he raises off the floor and takes my hands in his, steadying me as I stand. "Let's get you something to eat, I'll call Logan and see what we can do for this nausea."

"I have something," I blurt out, instantly regretting the admission.

"Good, when was the last time you took some?"

I haven't been this embarrassed since a science fair I participated in during sixth grade when I didn't have the money to purchase the boxed lunch everyone else did. I'd sat off to the side, eating my sandwich my mother wrapped in one of her kitchen towels.

"I haven't," I whisper, feeling the heat of my reddening cheeks forming.

"Then come on. Let's get your purse and get a dose in you before I take you to dinner."

When I didn't move as Ryan pulls me toward the door, my fingers begin to shake in his hand. His blue eyes search me, breaking me down until the embarrassment becomes too much, the tears building in the corners of my eyes.

"Talk to me, babe."

"After you dropped me off, the pharmacy called to say my prescription Dr. Baker phoned in was ready. After I gave the lady my insurance information, she apologized and said it was not a covered item."

"How much is it, Elli?"

"Fifteen hundred dollars."

He doesn't blink an eye at the figure, instead of tracing his thumb under my eyes to collect the tears. "Which pharmacy are we stopping at?"

"I—"

"Please," he interrupts, his whisper full of emotion. "You're growing my baby, taking care of you is my privilege and priority."

An hour later, I sit across from him sipping chicken broth, celebrating each drop as it fills my stomach and warms me through. He'd held my hand as we stood in line at the pharmacy, handing over his credit card as the cashier surveyed him, refusing to back out of the space until I placed the medication under my tongue.

"I can't thank you enough," I admit, leaning back in my chair as I swallowed the last of my broth. Ryan was elbow deep in the steak he ordered, devouring his salad in what seemed like two bites.

"No need to thank me, sweetheart. You're doing all the hard work, I'm just grateful I get to be a part of it."

His fork loaded with a slice of his steak hovers close at his mouth, his eyes trained on something behind me. Following his gaze, I find the source interrupting his meal, as two tables over Mr. Cane sits alone with his phone to his ear, a glass of red wine resting untouched in front of the empty seat across from him.

"Elli, was there a card with those roses delivered yesterday?"

Reaching for my purse, "Yes, although it doesn't say who sent them." Handing him the card.

Ryan flips the envelope over, then pulls out his phone, pressing the screen before holding it to his ear.

"Good evening, my wife received a delivery from your shop yesterday. The card wasn't signed, and we would like to thank whoever is responsible. If I give you her name, can you help me with that information?" My heart stops at the title he's given me, and while I know it's just to gain the information he wants, I can't help the thrill it gives me. "Great, her name is Elliott York, the arrangement was delivered to the Capitol Building."

Adjusting the silverware on the table, twisting the butter knife round and round. "Really, you're sure? No, there's no need to send a replacement, we just wanted to thank the proper person. I appreciate your help."

His joyous smile is contagious, but as he ends the call, the smile fades a half a second before a neatly manicured hand slaps on the table in front of him.

"You win, Ryan," Lindsey shouts, gaining the attention of the entire restaurant. "I'll let you knock me up, just don't choose her over me. Not after everything we've been through."

Ryan, who is unfazed by her outburst, cuts another bite from his steak. "Your theatrics are wasted on me. Go back to your producer, he will appreciate them."

"You're seriously doing this? Breaking up with me for someone you've known ten seconds?"

"Are you listening to yourself? This has nothing to do with Elli. This is the great Lindsey Jennings throwing a colossal-size tantrum because you're not getting what you want."

I cannot help but feel at least a little bad for her. I know what it's like to have a taste of Ryan, get him under your skin and then suddenly lose him.

"And you," Lindsey shifts her fury to me. "Do you seriously think he would be sitting here with you if he hadn't forgotten to wear a fucking condom?"

And just like that, my sympathy for her turns to empathy. The bold woman who fought her way to the top in a male-dominated world is no different from Norma Jean or her sister, Lottie, back home. Willing to claw each other's eyes out for the chance at a man.

"Hey." Ryan snaps at her. "You want to scream at me, go the fuck ahead, but don't even think about saying shit to her."

Lindsey stands silently, staring at Ryan's serious face. The battle lines which had been breached by her coming here, now reinforced.

"Pull this shit again, Lindsey and I promise you, hell will rain down on you."

Taking three steps away from the table, Lindsey raises her finger and points it at Ryan. "This isn't over, Biggs, not by a long shot."

Turning abruptly, she stomps her way out of the restaurant, unconcerned with the line waiting to be seated, plowing through them like a bowling ball taking down pins in an alley.

Ryan stands from his side of the booth, rounds the corner and slides into the seat beside me, pulling me tight against his hard body.

"I'm sorry about her, and what she said to you. It isn't true, I'd be here even if you weren't having my baby."

Soaking up the warmth he provides, "I know. Logan told me a little about her and the way she treated you. She showed up at the same restaurant..." I trail off, the memory of an evening at the restaurant comes to me and the identity of the man sitting across from her.

"What is it?"

"He was there."

"Who was where?"

Shifting in my seat to face him, "The night I had dinner with Logan, Lindsey was in a booth, she was with two men." Shaking my head in disbelief, "She had her foot in the crotch of the man across from her..." Shutting the image away of the other with his hands buried under her skirt. "It was Mr. Cane."

Ryan tosses a wad of money onto the table, holds out his hand for me, gently helping me from the booth, and then wraps a protective arm around me. He ushers me out of the restaurant and into his car. Reaching across the seat, he takes my hand in his. "I'd like you to come stay with me."

Purposely looking out the passenger's side window, "I don't think that's a good idea."

"Why?"

Turning to him, my head against the seat. "Because it will mean something to me you may not intend."

With his head forward, his left hand dangles off the steering wheel. "Such as my wanting to wake up with you or talk to the baby growing in your belly in the middle of the night. Bring you crackers when you wake up, hold your hair the next time you throw up, and one day, earn back the privilege to love you the way I did in Afghanistan."

Call it pregnancy hormones, clarity from proper caloric intake, or the honesty I know lives in his heart, but the happy tears fall and as he pulls into the parking lot of my apartment, I allow them to coat my answer as it falls from my lips. "Let me grab a few things for work."

I feel underdressed as I walk into Ryan's condo. Between the tight security and the high-end material they used in the construction, I refuse to touch anything out of fear of breaking it. Ryan comes in behind me, tossing my bag on the luxurious sofa as if it were nothing.

"Wow."

"Yea, I thought that too when I first saw it."

Glancing around, I take in the unobstructed view of Pennsylvania Avenue the wall of windows provides. The massive flat screen hangs over the fireplace, making me long for a cold night to burrow under a blanket while enjoying a movie.

"You can have your choice of bedrooms, I'm not partial to any of them. They're basically all the same."

Turning around to face him, "You don't sleep in the master?" Based on the length of the relationship he had with Lindsey, I assumed they shared the space.

"I can count on one hand the number of nights I've slept in a bed here." Picking up the remote, he points it at the television, "My work keeps me up to all hours."

Nodding, "I assumed you and Lindsey shared the master."

Ryan rounds on me, tossing the remote to the couch beside my bag before gripping my shoulders in his hands. "Lindsey spent less time in this condo than I did. Never, not once, did she ever spend the night."

Several hours later we curl up on the couch, the sleeping situation still up in the air. Ryan gave me control of the remote as long as he could hold me as we watch. I'm perusing the news channels, making mental notes of any information I'll need to check in the morning when I land on the station in direct competition of Lindsey's.

"Washington DC's very own SEAL of Honor has been at it again, dumping his long-time girlfriend, Lindsey Jennings for the newest damsel in distress, Capitol Hill Fact Checker, Elliott York. An anonymous video of the couple was sent to us a few hours ago, giving the patrons at Landmark Grill a dinner show they will not soon forget."

THE VIDEO IS of Lindsey pleading with Ryan not to leave her for me, the bouncy view is clearly from a cellphone captured by someone close to our table.

"Ms. Jennings nor CNN were available for comment. However, our sources confirm she was absent from the news desk this evening. We will continue to follow and bring you any new developments."

I WOKE up alone on the couch the next morning, under a soft blanket with a cup of herbal tea Ryan spent well over an hour researching, alongside a sleeve of crackers I mentioned, open on the glass tabletop.

"Good morning, beautiful."

Ryan's hair is still wet from a shower, the wonderful scent of his body soap fills the space around us, his deep voice wakes the most feminine parts of me. He looks rested and happy, bending over to place a kiss to my lips.

"Hey," my fingers find the spattering of hair at his chin, running along the dimple there. "Are you working today?"

Kissing my fingertips, "I have a project to finish this morning, then a little something I'm working on for this little miracle." His fingers drift to the skin at my stomach, circling my bellybutton before laying a tender kiss there.

"Okay, let me get dressed and out of your hair so you can get busy."

"I happen to like you in my hair...arms..." Wiggling his eyebrows, "Bed."

Forty minutes later, I push him away as I swipe my badge on the keypad. Watching over my shoulder as he climbs back in his car, promising me he will pick me up when I'm done.

Mr. Cane is standing outside my cubical as I walk in, his arms crossed, absent of his signature coffee cup, the video from last night plays on the monitors behind him.

"I tried to tell you." Sliding my purse into my drawer, his cocky attitude threatens to ruin the excellent mood Ryan placed me in this morning. "Biggs is a player, always has been. Give him a month and you will be in the same boat Linds is."

I wouldn't dignify him with a retort, remind him how "Linds" brought this on herself by allowing the relationship to die after repeatedly cheating on Ryan.

"By the way, you left those hideous flowers in the conference room last night. I won't tell you again to get rid of them."

Slamming my drawer hard, I push past him. "They're not hideous, you jealous shrew," I mutter under my breath, too low for him to hear me.

Standing inside the conference room, I stare at the bouquet, or what's left of it. The majority of the blooms have been ripped to shreds, scattered over the table and floor. Dropping to my knees, I painstakingly pick up each piece, tossing them into the trash, my anger building with each handful.

As I scoop the final bloom from the glossy table, the door to the conference room bursts open, an angry Lindsey standing in the threshold. Her normally perfect appearance is disheveled, face contorted in red-furry, hair a crazy mess.

"It should have been you that died instead of Doug," she seethes, clearing the distance between us, pulling her hand back and slapping me hard. My instincts kick in, and I twist my stomach away from her.

"I hate you." She shouts, shoving me in the center of my back, my arms reach out to block my fall. "You're fucking ugly." She shoves again, my hip slamming into the edge of the table. "I'm perfect for him and you're nothing." Grabbing my hair, pulling me down to the floor. "Nothing," she shouts again, kicking my bended knee. "Nothing." she roars, screaming at the top of her lungs. She picks up the vase from the table, slamming it down with such force it shatters, covering me in glass and water.

My heart is pounding, as I tuck myself into the fetal position, pain rips through my right arm as she kicks me one last time before disappearing down the hall, screaming for my boss. Fear paralyzed me, keeping me on the floor, silently praying she didn't hurt my baby. Footfalls sound toward me, my body flinching as Jennifer's face appears before mine.

"Oh my god, Elli." She reaches out for me, helping me to sit. "You're bleeding, love."

Following her gaze, I see the chunks of glass sticking out of my arm, rivers of crimson mixing with the droplets of water. My vision blurs as I begin to ask for help, "I need…" As Jennifer's face fades to black.

CHAPTER TWENTY-ONE

RYAN

"The offer is well above asking. There is, however, one condition."

Scrolling through the photos of the cabin I'm considering buying, pausing as I pictured Elli lying naked by a roaring fire as the snow falls outside, my pendant dangling between her breasts. Her belly swollen with our baby as I loved her in every way possible.

"Always is. What do they want?"

"They're refusing the furnishings."

Tipping my head back in laughter, knowing exactly how these folks feel. "Fine, I'll donate the furniture to one of those shelters, write it off my taxes." Not like I want any of this shit to follow me to Georgia if I'm able to convince Elli to move there with me.

"So you accept the offer, with the condition?"

The alert for an incoming call sounds in the background, pulling my phone away from my ear to check the screen, it's a number I don't recognize. Sending the call to voicemail, "Hell, yes, I accept the offer. I can be out of here by dinner."

"I'll let the sales office know of your decision."

"Thank you, sir." Ending the call, I reach for my cup of coffee, stretching my back as I swallow the last sip. This morning has been amazing, waking up with Elli snuggled against my chest, smelling the freshness of her perfume as I come back to the condo after dropping her at work. I'm gone for her, head-over-mother-fucking-heels in love with the girl. The tone for my video chat slaps me back from my Elli haze, Aiden's middle finger avatar fills my screen. Clicking accept, I wait while the call connects, Aiden's face appearing on the screen.

"What's up, fuck face?"

"Not as much as you, apparently. You big two-timer you."

"Fuck you, Aiden." I laugh, forcing him to crack a smile and join me.

"Jordan beat you to it this morning, but I'll pencil you in for later."

My phone vibrates on the desk, the same unknown number as before.

"Do you need to get that?"

Sending the call to voicemail, "Nah, they can talk to my secretary. What's new?" Tossing the phone back to my desk.

"Last night after watching you break poor Lindsey's heart, I got to wondering about something."

Leaning back in my chair, resting my boots on the edge of my desk, I lace my hands behind my head as I listen. "Glad to see I could inspire your brain cells to work again."

Aiden shoots me a look, flipping his ball cap backward, a sure sign this was about to get real.

"Why would Lindsey give a shit if you had moved on? It ain't like she hasn't been doing the same fucking thing for years?"

Sadness replaces the anger I'd experienced when I first heard of her deception. I'd put off talking to everyone about it in order to wrap my mind around everything. Clearly, my time is up and I need to let them in.

"I know exactly why she's pulling this shit. Before I say anything, let's get everyone else on, I only want to say this once."

Aiden snaps his head; the side of my screen lights up with the names of my team. One by one a new box pops on my screen.

"Morning, Hollywood." Havoc teases, his chest glistening with drops of water from what I assume was his shower.

Ignoring his banter, "As you all most likely saw last night, Lindsey and I are toast. Rayne was able to knock some sense into me, but it was a confrontation with Lindsey that hammered the final nail in her coffin."

Five sets of eyes reflect disbelief back to me. I can't fault them for it, as this isn't the first time I declared an end to the relationship. "When I came back to DC, I went looking for Elli. She wasn't at her office, so I took a chance and tracked her. Lucky for me, she was still wearing the pendant Eleni gave us."

I can't hold back the smile which split my face, the elation of news I want to shout from the rooftop too much to contain.

"I found her coming out of her doctor's office."

Even the vibration of my phone ringing can't spoil this, pressing ignore on my screen, "Elli is pregnant, with my baby."

Disbelief turns to elation, a choir of congratulations competing for my ears.

"You know, Ryan," Logan begins, his smile the biggest of them all. *"I've always believed one day you'd \ find rock bottom when it*

came to Lindsey. While I'm happy as shit for you and Elli, I'm a little concerned. I mean, you did turn your back on her once already."

I expect this from him. Logan is the most rational of us all, his ability to dissect a situation in a matter of milliseconds a positive for the success of more than a few missions.

"I know where you're going with this, Logan. Believe me, there is no going back to Lindsey, not after she admitted to having over a dozen abortions. More than a few of them mine."

We all knew the lines we could never cross with one another, for me it was fatherhood.

"She's agree—"

The vibration of my phone strikes a nerve. Whoever this bastard is, he's about to get a fucking ear full for interrupting me.

"What the fuck do you want?" I yell into the phone, Aiden laughs and shakes his head.

"Ryan, thank fuck." Namur pants into the phone. "Lindsey attacked Elli at the Capitol Building. She was bleeding really bad, so they took her by ambulance, but the building is on lockdown until they can find Lindsey."

I'm out of my chair and down the hall, not giving a shit about securing my computer or telling my team a fucking thing.

"I can't get out, and all cell service is interrupted while they search."

Taking the stairs, "Where are they taking her?"

"George Washington University."

Ending the call, I jump in my car. Weaving in and out of traffic, my heart hovers in my throat at the thought of losing her or the baby. Namur said she was bleeding, but from where and how bad?

Running through the doors of the emergency room, I search from side to side before spotting the information desk in the corner.

Slamming my hand on the counter, "My wife was brought here by ambulance, I need to see her."

The older lady sitting behind the desk peers at me over the top of her glasses, perusing me with her hazel eyes, the hint of an appreciative smile graces her lips.

"Your wife's name, sir?"

"Elliott York. She was brought here by ambulance from the Capitol Building."

Those hazel eyes flash back to me, the smile disappearing with what I assume is judgment fed to her by the media.

"Trauma three," pointing to a set of double doors. "Through those doors and to the left." Her eyes never leave mine as she purses her lips and pushes a button, releasing the doors to my right.

"Thank you," I call, slamming my shoulder into the door. Inside is organized chaos, doctors and nurse's running around a central desk, beds full of patients behind them.

Turning to my left, I'm nearly run down by a tiny nurse pushing an IV pole. "Excuse me," I toss at her, as I dive around her, spotting the large number three painted in blue against the yellow door.

Raising my hand to the door, I lean my head against the cold metal, saying a silent prayer I can handle whatever awaits me on the other side.

Elli sits in the middle of the bed, her red hair pulled to the side as a man in a lab coat shines a light in her eyes.

Carefully I approach, my eyes fall to the gauze wrapped around her right arm, large dots of crimson seeping through the mesh.

"Ryan," I hear Elli's emotion-filled voice call my name. My focus shifts to her tear stained face with three angry-red lines on her cheek. "How did you know I was here?"

"A friend of mine was in the building, he called me," I'll save the confession of having her followed since returning from Afghanistan for a later time. Unable to refrain from touching her, I place a kiss to the top of her head.

"Is she going to be okay?" Directing my question to the man with the lab coat, the name above his pocket reading Lee, MD. The man stands back, replacing his penlight into his pocket.

"And you are?"

"This is Ryan, my…" Elli's voice fades off, and damn Lindsey Jennings all to hell, it's clear she did more than just scratch the hell out of her face and cut her arm. She got in her head, spewed her favorite brand of venom, killing the seeds I planted yesterday of how much I care about her.

Standing to my full height, I extend my hand to Dr. Lee. "Ryan Biggs, boyfriend to this gorgeous lady and proud father to the little one she's carrying."

"Pleasure to meet you, Ryan, as I was telling Ms. York. There are several large pieces of glass embedded in her arm. It's hard to tell by looking if there will be any lasting damage after we remove them."

Adjusting my stance, tabling my anger for when I can do something with it, I reach down, taking her uninjured hand in mine, squeezing her fingers tight in assurance.

"I'd like to get an ultrasound. Even though Elli denies any vaginal bleeding, I'd still like to see for myself your baby is doing okay."

The prospect of seeing the baby for myself is huge and while I know it's too early to see anything, I don't want to miss a moment of my baby's life. Elli placed the one she'd got during her first doctors visit on her refrigerator. Hopefully soon, we can add it to the one I'd like to share with her in Georgia.

Dr. Lee leaves the room, promising a nurse will be in soon to set up the equipment to remove the glass from Elli's arm. As soon as the door closes behind him, I lean over the bed, taking her face in my hands, kissing her gently on her lips. Sitting on the edge of her bed, I place her hand in my lap. "I need you to tell me what happened."

Elli lies her head back, and I notice the tiny slivers of glass stuck in her hair. She looks over at her wrapped arm, her fingers caked with dried blood, telling me the detailed story of what happened in her office this morning.

My heart soars when she spoke of curling into a ball, preventing Lindsey from doing any harm to our baby as she kicked her.

Elli grew nervous as the nurse returns, unpacking several trays before Dr. Lee comes in behind a woman pushing what I suspect is the ultrasound machine. Dr. Lee slides on a pair of gloves before removing the gauze covering Elli's arm.

I've seen some shit in my day, come across burn victims, beheadings, and a few severe accidents. However, as I look at her arm, the jagged pieces of the vase I brought her yesterday sticking out of her skin, a new level of rage sparks to life inside my soul.

I hold Elli tight as Dr. Lee numbs the area, distracting her with stories of my team. "This reminds me of Aiden, and a fight he got into not long ago."

Her eyes lock tight with mine as Dr. Lee injects the medication into her flesh, grimacing, but she never says a word.

"The guy who challenged him, used broken glass, adhering it to a piece of tape and when he wasn't looking, punched him in the chest with it."

"Bitch move," Dr. Lee mumbles under his breath, his prover-bial slip of the tongue gaining a laugh from Elli.

"Exactly," I agree, pleased as fuck for the moment of reprieve his humor grants her from the discomfort.

"How is Aiden? And his…?"

"Jordan, his girlfriend. Aiden is doing well. I was on the phone with him when I received word of your accident."

"Oh, Ryan. You were working, it's important—"

Interrupting her rambling with a kiss, savoring the taste of her while keeping it rated G. "You, my love, are the most important thing in the world to me. My team knows this, especially Aiden." I assure her as the sound of a piece of glass collides with something metal.

A knock at the door forces my attention away from the tiny freckles across her dainty nose to the dark hair of the man looking around the edge of the door. His regret-filled eyes tell me not only am I not going to like what he has to say, but things are about to take a dramatic change.

"Marc, what are you doing here?" Elli's grip tightens, reflecting the unease in her voice, while pushing into me a little further.

Namur keeps his back to the door, his eyes dancing between the two of us and I know judgment day has finally arrived.

"Elli," I begin, gripping her hand tight between both of mine. "I know you recognize him as Marc from your building, but his real name is Namur Havid. He works for me and has been keeping an eye on you while I was away."

"I don't understand, why would I need to be watched?"

Bringing her hand to my lips, savoring the scent that is uniquely her placing a lingering kiss to her knuckles before returning my eyes to hers.

"You remember the conversation we had in Afghanistan, about what I do?"

"Yes," she nods, the confusion lingering for a brief moment before her mind connects the dots. "Oh," she swallows hard, dipping her head down.

"Hey," reaching out, I place a finger under her chin, pulling her face up. "I didn't lie when I said you're important to me."

Her watery smile nearly crushes me, the single tear escaping her lids has nothing to do with Dr. Lee and his needle, but everything to do with the bullshit I've put her through.

"Ryan," Namur calls from the door, his voice coated in apology. "I need to speak with you about Lindsey."

"What about Lindsey?" Anger punctuates each word Elli speaks through clenched teeth.

Namur glances to me, "I'll come—"

"No," Elli interrupts, pulling her hand from mine. "I won't be kept in the dark anymore. Tell me, did they find her?"

Namur takes a step in the room. "Yes, they found her, but she denies having anything to do with the attack. Your co-worker, Jennifer, didn't see anyone leave the room when she found you. Her producer is claiming she was with him all morning."

"So she gets away with this?" Elli's angry voice echoes off the wall, momentarily halting Dr. Lee's stitching of the gash on her arm.

"No, babe." Pulling her attention back to me, "I swear to you, she won't get away with this." I silently plead with my eyes for her to trust that I will tell her everything as soon as we're away from here.

Elli darts her eyes to Dr. Lee as he finishes the last few stitches. She reaches out, taking my hand in hers, squeezing in agreement. Shifting her focus to Namur, only to find the spot where he stood not a second ago is empty.

Dr. Lee stands from his tiny stool. "Good news is," tossing his gloves in the trash by the sink. "While the glass was embedded enough to require stitches, I'm confident there is no nerve damage."

"And the bad news?" Elli beats me to the question, her strength through all of this inspiring.

Dr. Lee approaches the bottom of her bed as he dries his hands with a paper towel. "The bad news is glass is clear, and I can't say for sure I've been able to remove all of it. Only time will tell if we need to go back in and search for more."

The nurse who assisted Dr. Lee has cleared the table away, replacing it with the ultrasound machine. Handing him a clean pair of gloves, Dr. Lee removes what looks like a dildo from the side of the machine, slipping a condom over the head like a pro.

"I'm assuming you've had one of these before since you mentioned Dr. Baker is your Ob."

"Yes," Elli agrees as the nurse helps her to scoot down in the bed.

"Good, you will find ours is a bit more high-tech than his." He smiles, an obvious story behind it.

He presses several buttons before lifting the sheet across Elli's legs, the probe disappearing between Elli's lifted knees.

"Pressure," Dr. Lee cautions, his eyes fixed on the screen. I follow his fingers as they roll a ball at the bottom of the keyboard, bringing the cone-shaped image to life.

The curser on the screen stops at several points on the screen, a series of numbers line up at the bottom. I'm not completely ignorant in working with an ultrasound machine, but my experience is limited to examining the contents of explosives and bunkers underground.

"Dr. Lee?" Elli's broken voice pulls me from my fixation with the ultrasound. "Is everything okay with my baby?"

The worry in her voice has me slipping an arm under her, tucking her against my chest as I hold her tight.

"While I agree with Dr. Baker on the due date he gave you, and everything looks great, there is one thing I'm concerned with."

CHAPTER TWENTY-TWO

ELLI

Disbelief renders me silent as Ryan holds me tight, his emotion-filled voice repeats over and over how happy I've made him, throwing in how he will never let anything hurt his family.

"I want you to take it easy for a few days, keep the stitches clean and dry until they fall out. Call Dr. Baker if you have any vaginal bleeding. Any questions?"

Only a million I think to myself, but I'm too stunned by Dr. Lee's news to verbalize any of them.

"Is it okay for her to travel? After what happened, I'd like to take her out of town for a while."

"The babies look good, so as long as there is no bleeding, I don't have any restrictions except for lots of rest."

Babies. Even after the multiple times I've heard it leave Dr. Lee's lips, my mind is still having an issue wrapping around the news I'm carrying twins.

"She will get tons of rest. You have my word on it."

Dr. Lee squeezes my sheet covered foot, bringing me out of my haze. "Congratulations you two, and good luck."

I wait until the door closes behind him before rounding on Ryan. "Tell me you're okay with this."

The same brilliant smile which split his face when he learned of my pregnancy returns with full force.

"Okay?" He asks incredulously. "Okay isn't even a choice in the drop-down box of how I feel right now."

Ryan tucks the paperwork the nurse left behind in his back pocket. "I was over the moon with the knowledge of having one with you, but now..." He fades off, swallowing hard as he helps me from the bed. "Now, I don't think my life can get any more perfect."

Tucking me safely under his arm, "Come on, we need to get the glass out of your hair, pack our bags and get the fuck away from DC for a few days."

"Wait, what about my job? I can't just take off."

"You have one job, Elli, growing those two babies inside you. Everything else in on me."

"But Mr. Cane."

"Judson won't say shit, especially not after what I have planned for his ass."

Pulling back on his hand, "You're not going to hit him, are you?"

"You want an honest answer?"

Half an hour later Ryan holds the detachable shower head over my scalp as he rinses the shampoo and, hopefully, all of the glass shards down the drain. He doesn't want to chance me getting a piece embedded into my foot in the shower. My clothes from earlier are at the bottom of the trash, Ryan assured me he will buy me a whole new wardrobe if I want. I declined, knowing it would be a waste of money, considering the impending expansion of my waistline.

"There, I think I got it all." Kissing my bare shoulder, his lips linger for several seconds. I love the feel of him against me, the warmth of his skin chases away the chill I hadn't realized plagued me until he came around.

"I have a few phone calls to make while you get dressed, and then we can get out of here."

Wrapping a towel around my head, "Where are we going exactly?"

Coming to stand behind me in front of the mirror, he wraps his massive body around mine, his hands coming to rest on my lower abdomen. "I sold the condo today and I have my eye on another property. One I want your opinion on."

Watching his reflection, a joy like I've never seen dances in his eyes. "Where?"

Placing a sloppy kiss to my neck, "It's a surprise. Now get dressed before I change my mind and bend you over this counter."

After towel drying my hair and changing into the spare set of clothes I'd packed the other night, I open the bathroom door to find Ryan sitting in the center of his king size bed, a laptop open on his legs.

"*I want you to leak every piece of video you guys have on her. Hell, get the shit Stavros has from his club if he's willing. I want her to regret the day she woke up and tried to take my family from me.*"

My heart swells at the conviction in his voice and when his eyes land on mine, I'm helpless to fight the pull to join him on the bed.

"*Thank fuck,*" came a voice from his laptop and I have to cover my mouth to keep from laughing. *"Give me twenty minutes and that bitch's naked ass will be all over the news."*

"Thanks, Zach. I'll see ya soon."

Ryan closes his laptop, "How the fuck do you get more beautiful every time I see you?" Tossing it to the side before pinning me to the mattress under him. Heated lips caress the skin of my neck as urgent fingers slide under my shirt and past the lace of my bra, kneading the flesh of my breast.

"Ryan," I moan, the hormone overload combined with the gallantry he's shown me has me purring like a cat in heat.

"I want you so much, Elli." Pressing his erection into my hip, he nips at the tender flesh of my collar.

"I want you, too," I confess, raising my arm up to pull him down closer. In my lust-filled haze, I forget about the seventeen stitches in my arm, and fire shoots down my arm as a quick reminder.

"Ouch," I yell, pulling my arm back as Ryan lifts himself as if doing a pushup.

"You okay?"

"Yeah, the numbing stuff is wearing off, and I forgot I can't use it."

Lowering himself, he kisses my lips and then my gauze covered arm, "We should get going."

WE ARE a few miles outside of the North Carolina border when my work phone begins to ring. Ryan shoots me a look but remains silent as I take the call.

"Elli York, how can I help you?"

"Elli, it's Olivia, I just heard about your attack. Are you okay?"

Turning my attention to the passing scenery outside my window, a sign for Asheville, North Carolina catches my interest.

"I will be, Olivia. The doctor wants me to get plenty of rest." Ryan squeezes our clasped hands, making the warm-buzzing feeling ignite once again.

"Oh, I'm so relieved. Capitol police are fluttering around the building like a swarm of bees. Rumors are spreading like wildfire as to who is responsible. They have your supervisor, Mr. Cane, in their office questioning him. From what I can gather, he's claiming your injuries are self-inflicted."

Sitting up straight in my seat, dropping Ryan's hand to place my phone on speaker.

"I'm sorry, Ms. Wesson, can you repeat that. I have my boyfriend in the car and want him to hear what you said."

"Of course. Hello, Ryan, congratulations on the baby, by the way. As I was telling Elli, the Capitol police are thick as thieves here in the office. Judson is claiming Elli's injuries are self-inflicted and not at the hands of Lindsey Jennings."

Ryan keeps his eyes trained on the road ahead, "Check her fingernails, they should be able to obtain a sample of Elli's DNA."

"Afraid it's not that simple…"

"I know, she has an alibi for her whereabouts since last night."

"Her producer, yes."

"That's okay, Olivia. Make sure you tune into the evening news tonight. Elli's coworkers are going to be busy checking a shit-ton of facts in the morning."

"Always do," she chuckles. "And Elli, you take all the time you need to recover. Send Judson to me if he gives you any trouble."

When Ryan pulls the car off the interstate a little after five, I assume we need fuel. When he drives past several gas stations, and further into town, I'm tempted to ask him if this is where he plans to buy a house. As he pulls into the parking lot of a chain hotel, I know this is just a stop.

Ryan helps me from the car, tossing his keys to the valet who hurries over to greet us. My arm is beginning to throb and my stomach churns, my body stiff from sitting in the car and the beating Lindsey handed me this morning. Inside the lobby of the hotel, Ryan walks up to the desk as if he's done it a thousand times, pulling his wallet from his back pocket, slipping out his credit card and ID before being asked for it.

"Mr. Biggs," The lady behind the desk speaks, her bright blue eyes a near-perfect match for Ryan's. "We have you staying one night, king bed in one of our garden suites."

"Yes."

The lady whose name tag reads Frances, types away on her keyboard, her smile attached to her lips like the polyester uniform she wore; required and something she tosses the second she exited the door.

"If you will sign here, and initial here for me?"

Ryan does as she asks, remaining polite, but not overly, laying her pen across the sheet of paper before sliding it back in her direction.

"Thank you, Mr. Biggs. We will have your bags delivered to your room shortly."

Ryan holds the door to the room open as I step inside, grateful my mouth is attached as I stand in awe in the center of the room. When I heard the term garden suite, I assumed it was the name of a floor, but it's not. As if inspired by a French garden, the suite opens up into a solarium, plants of every size and color bring the room just beyond the bed to life. Tall trees, planted in each corner, struggle to reach the metal frame of the structure.

"Elli," Ryan speaks softly beside me, as I stand unwilling to look away from the beauty before me. "Take your medicine, I know your arm is bugging you."

Slowly pulling my eyes to him, finding a bottle of water in his outstretched hand. "Dinner will be here in a few," tipping his chin to the bed behind me. "I'm going to grab a shower, go ahead and sign for it if I'm not out, be generous with the tip."

Placing a kiss to my cheek, he lifts his bag from the bed, disappearing behind a door I assume is the bathroom. Looking around the room, I feel ridiculous for allowing myself to become so lost in the garden I missed the delivery of my bags.

Fishing the medicine bottle out of my purse, I place a tablet under my tongue and wait for it to devolve. It worked like magic yesterday, completely erasing the nausea, allowing me to feel a million times better. As I wait for churning to go away, I locate the remote and click the television on. Settling my back against the headboard, I point the remote and peruse the channels, hoping to find a movie to watch. As I scan past several commercials, I land on the fresh face of Sonia Marsh, a White House reporter whom I've come to appreciate for her honest journalism.

"At least three individuals have come forward since the release of these tapes earlier this afternoon."

I was about to move to the next channel when a still photo of Lindsey, standing on a table in what looks to be a night club, the screen blurred to cover what I assume is her naked body.

"Lindsey Jennings has refused to comment on the validity of these videos."

The scene changes to what appears to be a packed night club, the base thumping in the background as Lindsey dances on the lap of my boss, while Senator Green sits at the table beside them.

"As you can see, Ms. Jennings appears to be performing a striptease for a table full of men, including former Senator Green

and Judson Cane, the current supervisor for the Fact Checker who was attacked at the Capitol Building this morning."

The video pans out as Lindsey moves down the table until several men in suits approach. The tall one in the center offering her a hand and assisting her back to the floor.

"While her involvement in the attack is now being questioned, it is this reporter's opinion, Jennings credibility may come under fire due to this..." The view narrows, showing Lindsey practically straddling the man in the suit. *"Gentleman's identity."*

The scene switches again, this time to the mug shot of the man in the suit, causing my heart to dip, as I slide my body to the end of the bed.

"Stavros Nakos, leader of one of New York's crime Family's and owner of the club where this video was taken. Our investigative team is still trying to piece together if there is any relationship between Jennings and Stavros, however, at this time it appears she was only a patron at the time. However..."

Another shift, this time to what I recognize as a similar hotel room to the one Congressman Howard put me up in when I first arrived. Lindsey is on all fours in the center of the bed, the penis of one man in her mouth, while another takes her from behind.

"Our experts have been able to identify the man you see standing on the bed as Louis Manzo, a former Capitol Police officer who was arrested for possessing child pornography. It is also notable to mention; Manzo was the sited source Jennings used in a number of her exclusive reports over the past few years. The man behind her, William Vale, who's recent plea agreement is now being investigated and may be revoked, sending him to prison for his involvement with former Senator Green."

My hand finds my mouth as photo after photo parades across

the screen, dozens of men she took to her bed, or in several instances—out in public.

"Oh, Lindsey. Why would you do this?" I think out loud, my heart breaking for Ryan.

"Because she's a soulless bitch."

Jolted, I jerk my head to find Ryan standing in a towel beside me, rivulets of water dancing over his tight muscles, caressing their way down, collecting in the fibers of the towel at his narrow waist.

I could see the hurt in his eyes, the years of believing the lies she told, holding on to the promise she made of never doing it again. How he ever found the courage to trust again was beyond me.

"I'm so sorry." Clearing the distance between us, I wrap myself around his middle as I kiss him with everything I have. "You incredibly, wonderful man," kissing him harder, pushing the towel away as I sink to my knees before him. "I swear, I will make you forget all the hurt she caused." Taking him in my mouth, his hand reaches down, spearing his digits into my hair. I moan around him as I take him in as far as I can, keeping our eyes locked while I bob my head.

"You already did," he murmurs before pulling his cock from my mouth, shifting our bodies so he was lying on top of me. "The second I laid eyes on you on the plane, I forgot all about her."

Placing a kiss to my lips, the sound of knocking on the door pulls a groan from his throat. "Do not fucking move, Elli." Punctuating each word as he lifts himself off the bed, wrapping the towel around his hips, which does nothing to hide his glorious erection. Less than a minute later, he returns with a tray full of food, setting it in on the table in the corner, before tossing the towel to the side and leaping back into bed.

"I have to feed you," he mumbles into my neck. "But first, I want to love you, if you'll let me?"

He's proven himself worthy a million times over. Not with his money or sweet words, but with knowing he had to get things right in his head before starting something new with me. Our relationship has been far from conventional, but at this moment I don't care.

Pulling him down, I throw everything I have into my kiss, pouring out how bad I want him to love me and never stop.

"It's going to be fast," he pants as he breaks the kiss. Leaning back to remove my pants, my underwear along for the ride as he tosses them both to the floor behind him. Keeping my injured arm above my head, I bend my knees as he enters me, wrapping his muscled arm tightly around my waist as he pounds into me.

"That's it, Elli. Fuck you feel good."

I've missed this, the feel of him thick and hard inside me, each thrust brings me close to the edge. Not a single ounce of effort is lost as he switches angles, rubbing his pelvis against my most sensitive spot.

"Mine," he swears, as he increases his thrusts, throwing me over the edge. "Fucking mine." His movements became sloppy, lifting himself up on his elbows, his intense gaze locks me in place. "All fucking mine," he cries as I feel him swell inside me, his lips crashing to mine, swallowing the surprised cry from the second orgasm his possession pulls from me.

After we ate and Ryan watches as I took some pain relievers Dr. Lee said would be safe for the babies, Ryan wraps his body around mine as I drift off to sleep, somewhere on the edge of twilight sleep I could have sworn I heard him say, "I love you, Elliott."

CHAPTER TWENTY-THREE

RYAN

Tom Eubanks, the owner of the cabin, stands beside his vintage Jeep, plaid shirt and University of Georgia hat atop his head.

"This is where you want to live?"

The tone of her voice says it all. Elli may have moved hundreds of miles to the big city, but the backwoods would never leave her soul. Leaning across the seat, I lick the underside of her bottom lip, before stealing a kiss. "Wait until you see inside."

Tom made it known he is eager to sell as the cabin is in foreclosure. He admitted to getting caught up in property investments but chose the wrong management service, who took off with a year's worth of rent payments. I'm sold based on the photos, but I want to not only see it in person but see what Elli thinks of it.

"Mr. Biggs?"

"Yes, sir," I acknowledge, rounding the front of my car to collect Elli. I'll need to trade this in soon, not only due to the drive from the main highway but to something more accommodating for two car seats.

"You made good time, wasn't expecting you for another half hour." Tom leans over, offering his hand as I come to stand before him.

"Elli and I are early risers, and there was no traffic." I half lied. Elli could have slept for a few more hours, but once I got a taste of her last night, I wanted more this morning. From the way she straddled my hips, I'm sure she wanted it too.

"All right, then. Let me show you the property."

Three wooden steps lead to the front porch, reminding me of one of the things I love about Matt and Rayne's house. Inside, the living room feels even bigger than the photo with its exposed wood ceilings and walls, and stone fireplace that goes from floor to ceiling against the far wall.

"As I mentioned on the phone, it's a little over four thousand square feet, six bedrooms, and four baths. The kitchen has new appliances and the guy was here last week cleaning the chimney."

"What about sewer and water?" Elli questions, running her fingers along the granite of the countertop.

Turning from the view of the mountain through the two sets of French doors, I find her wide-eyed with her hand over her mouth.

"I'm so sorry, tha—"

"Is an excellent question." I interrupt, sending her a wink as I clear the distance between us. Elli shakes her head, those ruddy cheeks of hers I love so much making their appearance. Placing a kiss to her cheek, I wrap myself around her back, "Is your blush from imagining me eating your sweet little pussy on this counter?" I whisper in her ear as I pretend to listen to Mr. Eubanks. I know more about his cabin than he does, including how the property on each side is for sale.

"Water and sewer are connected to city supply, trash picked up every Friday."

The property totals three wooded acres, with six on each side for sale. If Elli likes it, I plan to build a second cabin on the adjoining property, with a bunker like Matt's dug into the side of the mountain underneath it.

Tom lead us up the steps, to the second floor, Elli pauses at the landing to look down over the open living room. A slight frown forming on her face.

"Something wrong?"

"No, just thinking."

"About," turning to mimic her, leaning my upper body against the wooden rail.

"Never mind," she shakes her head. "It's silly," her voice cracks despite her smile.

Stopping her from turning away, "Talk to me, Elli. Did I do something wrong?"

Dipping her head, picking at the fibers coming apart on the gauze covering her injured arm. "You didn't do anything. I misinterpreted something you said, is all." Stiffening her shoulders, "Come on, you have more house to see."

She made it to the first bedroom before I caught up to her. "Mr. Eubanks, can you excuse us for just a moment?" Not bothering to wait for his answer, I escort Elli into the ensuite bathroom at the back of the room.

Closing the door behind us, "What did you misunderstand?"

Elli is a strong woman, one of the toughest I've ever met, so when her eyes fill with tears, I know the other shoe is about to fall.

"You said you were happy about these babies. How it was my job to grow them and you would take care of everything else."

Nodding my head, but remaining silent, I watch as she pushes past whatever is bothering her, refusing to give in to the sadness that begs to come forward.

"I just didn't think you would be doing it from six hundred miles away."

Confusion renders me silent. How did she come up with being apart?

"It's a beautiful cabin, Ryan, room for plenty of guests. Personally, I'd have a hard time leaving this and driving back to DC."

And just like Rayne slapping the shit out of me, her meaning hits me square in the chest, knocking the breath from me.

"Hold on, babe." Taking her face between my palms, tipping her chin up so I can see her eyes. "You didn't misinterpret anything. What I said about taking care of you and our babies, I meant doing it by your side."

"How, Ryan? When you're here and I'm back in DC where my job is?"

"Tell me something, Elli. Is DC everything you thought it would be?"

"Well, no. But—"

"Do you enjoy living there; the traffic, the expense?"

"Not exactly, but—"

"And do you really want to raise our babies in the little apartment you have? What happens when they get bigger and need fresh air?"

"No, but—"

"What about when it's time for them to go to school? Are you prepared to place them on a waiting list in hopes they get into somewhere safe?"

"No, Ryan." Raising her voice over mine. "I don't want to deal with any of that, but I will because I have to. I'm not in a position to buy a fancy condo like yours, or a luxury weekend gets away like this." Motioning with her hands around the room. "I'll work every day to provide what they need and sacrifice anything I have to, including the tiny apartment I have, in order to keep my children safe and happy."

"Our children," I correct her, my soul rejoicing in pride at her passion with her role as the mother of our children.

"What?"

"You said 'my children', those little peanuts in your womb are ours."

The skin between her brows furrows and as she opens her mouth to let me have it, I place my thumb over her lips.

"Listen, I want you to spend the next few days here with me. Explore the property and, before we leave for Matt and Rayne's wedding, I want your honest opinion about living here, with me."

CHAPTER TWENTY-FOUR

ELLI

Ryan follows Mr. Eubanks out to his truck while I stand staring out the window over the kitchen sink, the view of the mountain robbing my attention. It's easy to see why he wants to make the move from DC to here, and admittedly, something settles inside me the second I heard the familiar call of a whippoor-will when I climbed out of the car.

My life back in Virginia wasn't ideal, okay…it was downright shitty, but something is different about the hills and valleys of North Georgia.

The slamming of the screen door pulls me from the mountain's seduction, Ryan stands just inside the door, his cellphone in his hand.

"I'm sorry," crossing the room. "I'm ready to go whenever you are."

Keeping his head down, he looks up at me through his lashes. "We're staying here, remember?"

The sound of Mr. Eubanks' truck backfiring causes me to jump, but Ryan stands still as a statue, his eyes locked with mine.

"You mean here—here." Pointing to the floor with my index finger.

"Where else would I mean?"

Tipping my head back, catching the beauty of the honey-stained ceiling panels. "I assumed we would stay in a hotel, not this cabin."

Placing his hand on my left shoulder, "I'm sorry, Elli, I should have been clearer. Mr. Eubanks and I came to an agreement, two nights in the cabin and if we like it, I'll give him the full price he's asking."

The 'we' in his statement didn't escape me. On the contrary, it thrills me more than I can explain.

"We have a pantry and fridge full of food, a hot tub I can't wait to get you in and several acres of land I want to hold your hand while we explore."

His excitement is contagious, and I find myself smiling like a lunatic. Grabbing a bottle of water out of the refrigerator, I join him as we begin to explore.

"I THOUGHT Mr. Eubanks said it was three acres," I question as we sit on a rock overlooking the lake at the bottom of the hollow.

"It is," Ryan returns, his Adam's apple bobbing as he drains the bottle of water. "But I have plans to buy the land on either side, which is why I brought you this far."

Returning my gaze to the ripples in the water, evidence of the fish living well in the lake. I can't imagine what a piece of property like this cost, but from what I know of DC property prices, he could buy two of these with the profits from his condo.

Taking a deep breath, closing my eyes as I point my face to the sky. "God, I love the sweet smell of the mountains."

"Know what I love?"

Opening one eye, glancing at him from the side, a coy smile on my lips. "Waking me up to have sex."

Leaning forward, shaking his head slowly, his eyes serious and seductive. "No," he hesitates as his face grows closer to mine, the smell of his cologne enchants me. "You."

Cupping my neck with his hand, he covers my mouth with his, slipping his tongue past my lips, driving me crazy with the talented way he searches my mouth. Nipping at my bottom lip, something he discovered this morning makes me moan, before diving once again into the deep kiss which leaves me breathless.

"I love you, too. Ryan." I profess, unable to keep it hidden inside a second longer. "I wanted to hate you after what Lindsey said, but when Logan explained what a horrid creature she was to you, I couldn't fault you for being gun shy."

His blue eyes search mine. "I've loved you from the minute I saw you sitting on the plane. Your ankles crossed all prim and proper, taunting me with the mystery of what secrets you held between them."

I'd been taught from an early age to cross my legs at the ankle, to sit in any other fashion was considered sinful.

"When you stood up to Doug, I was about to run to the bathroom and jack off, you made me so hard."

My eyes dropped to his crotch, my thoughts at the time were of anger. I felt remorse not long after the insult left my mouth.

"When you didn't fall apart when the Congressman was shot, I knew you were the girl I need to be with. The one who could handle all the crazy shit my life has in it."

Funny, how differently I recall the moment, full of uncertainty and guesswork. Doing everything I could to ignore the man waving a gun around.

Taking my hand in his, he drops from his seat on the rock beside me, to his knee directly in front of me. "I love you, Elliott York. I don't know what I did to deserve having a family with you, but I'll gladly do it twelve more times if it gets me one more minute with you."

The giggle that leaves my throat competes with the sob which begs to be released. I'm the lucky one to have him, and I'll do everything to keep him.

"I want to wake up with you every morning and love you every night before you close your eyes to sleep. I want to be the star in all of your dreams like you are mine. I want to fight with you, laugh with you, and celebrate all the moments that make life worth living."

Reaching inside his shirt, he lifts his dog tags over his head, wadding them up in the palm of his hand.

"I didn't plan on asking you like this," the confidence he wore every day disappears, replaced by a humbling nervousness. "Hell, I don't even have a ring." His blue eyes flash to mine, "But, the moment is perfect, and I don't want to waste it. So, Elliot York, will you marry me?"

Time seems to stand still as his question fills my head. My throat feels thick with all of the doubt I've swallowed over the past few months. By far is the reason he stuck beside me, and I have to question if these little peanuts he speaks of are the reason behind his question.

"Ryan, I'm honored you would ask me, but I have to tell you something."

Worry colors his beautiful eyes, the skin puckering between his blue orbs.

"I've worked hard these last few years in order to separate myself from the girls I grew up with, like Lottie and Norma Jean. Girls who are perfectly willing to lay beside a man every night who may or may not be there because of a lapse in judgment resulting in the birth of a child. When I get married, I want it to be because the man who asks me is so in love with me, he can't imagine life without me."

Taking a deep breath, not entirely certain I want to know the answer to this. "Now tell me the truth," placing my hand on his cheek. "If I wasn't pregnant, would you still be on your knee, asking me to marry you?"

* * *

THE SUN DIPS below the tops of the trees, the chill of the evening beginning to roll in. Ryan holds my hand as we climb the steps, the cabin dark as we neglected to leave a light on.

"Surprise." A chorus rings out as Ryan flips on the living room lights. The room is filled with flowers and balloons, a happy birthday sign swaying over the center of the room.

"Happy birthday, Elli," Ryan whispers in my ear, my heart pounding against my chest so hard I'm worried it might come out.

Harper bounces in place until Ryan steps to the side to shake Aiden hand.

"Oh my god, look at you." She praises, swaying me back and forth as she holds me tight. "When Ryan told Logan it was your birthday and he was bringing you here, I couldn't stand you being so close and not coming to see you."

"Which turned into an event when she phoned me." The gentle voice of one of the women I don't know speaks from beside us, her dark hair pulled to the side, a strand of pearls around her neck.

"Elli, I'd like you to meet Kennedy, Zach's wife."

Shaking her hand, I notice the other ladies line up behind her. Each with a welcoming smile and not a hint of deceit among them.

"I'm Rayne, the one who is getting married in a few days." The next girl introduces herself, her hug just as crushing as Kennedy's. Her hair is not as dark as Kennedy's but still beautiful.

"Oh," I pull back. "Are we keeping you from last minute details?"

Shaking her head. "No, darlin'. The only thing left to do is slap on my dress and take his last name."

A collective laugh sounds in the room, my attention shifting to Matt lining up champagne glasses along the center island.

"Hey, I'm Jordan. Eleni wishes she could be here, but you'll meet her at the wedding." Jordan is dark-haired as well, big smile with perfect teeth, with the biggest set of diamond earrings in her ears I've ever seen.

"I love your earrings," I say as she pulls me in for a hug, the conversations hanging around the room going silent as all eyes turn to Ryan.

Tossing up his arms up in surrender. "She has my Saint Christopher, ladies."

And just like in the movies, once the awkward moment is over, the music comes back on and conversations resume.

Kennedy moves around the island where the men are standing, wrapping her arms around Ryan's neck. "I'm just so thankful

Lindsey is out of your system and you have finally found the happiness you deserve."

Three sparklers glow from the top of a double-decker cake, their flickering light reminds me of the Fourth of July celebrations back home. My brothers would have firecracker wars, tossing a lit bundle inside anything they could find in order to scare the daylights out of my mother and myself.

Ryan stands behind me, his protective arms surrounding me, singing happy birthday along with everyone else. The feel of his breath along my neck sends shivers down my spine, making me want my wish to be alone with him so he can take care of the fire he's creating between my thighs.

"Make a wish, Elli."

Closing my eyes, I pretend to do as he asks, I have so much and I don't dare hope for anything more. Instead, I say a prayer of thanks before leaning over and blowing out the sparkling candles. This is my life, one I never imagined I'd want, but so thankful I have.

CHAPTER TWENTY-FIVE

RYAN

"I propose a toast."

Matt held his champagne glass high in the air as he handed out the remaining glasses to the room. Logan sent me a text this morning, asking if I minded having the team and their wives invade our time alone in the cabin. Insisting it was time to introduce her to the other wives if I was serious about Elli.

"Here ya go, Daddy." Matt winks as he hands me mine. Elli moves to stand beside me, her glass, like Harper and Kennedy's full of sparkling apple juice.

Pulling her close, I place a kiss to her temple, running my fingers along the back of her neck, the chain holding my dog tags slides under my fingertips.

Elli's concerns over my reasoning behind my proposal are valid. I hope the sparkle in her eye and the dog tags around her neck are a positive sign she accepted my rationale. Elliott York is an exceptional young woman, one who captivated and bewitched me long before she blessed me with the title of father.

"To Elli," Matt's voice carries. "May she have the strength of Hercules, the wisdom of King Solomon, and the compassion of Florence Nightingale as she joins this motley crew."

* * *

SITTING AROUND THE FIRE PIT, beers in hand and steaks on the grill. The ladies safely on the screened in porch, the sweet sound of their laughter fills the air. Aiden sits to the right of me, his boots propped against the rocks of the pit, his eyes trained on Jordan.

"Your friend Judson has quite the colorful past."

Keeping my attention on the ladies, tipping my beer to my lips. "So I've heard."

"He's a bit of a professional job-hopper, although his application for Presidential detail has been turned down more than a hotel sheet."

There is no love lost between Judson and myself, and if I find out he had anything to do with Elli's attack, he's as good as dead.

"Not sure why he expects them to choose him, given the amount of debt he was carrying around until recently."

Logan throws another log on the fire, the air leavening the dead wood cracking, sending dozens of embers sparkling into the air.

"Two days ago, he applied again for the position. This time his credit is as clean as the air around here. Nearly fifty grand paid off in less than a few months."

"Must have sold a kidney," I deadpan, catching the eye of Elli, sending her an air kiss which makes her blush.

"Close," Aiden retorts. "Judson got his foot in the proverbial door by accepting a job at Andrews as a contractor. He started as a groundskeeper, worked in the department for three years before being chosen for an apprenticeship. He spent the next four years, his longest at anything other than playing with his own dick, going to school on the taxpayer's dime and learned the ins and outs of helicopter maintenance. After graduation, he went to work changing oil and gear grease, until several of the men above him were forced into retirement and he sailed up the channel like a fucking pirate ship."

Draining his beer, Aiden rises from his chair to flip the steaks. "He was granted access to schedules, new hire processing, and schematics of all the planes housed at Andrews."

The log Logan tossed on the fire rolls to the side as the ones underneath split from their centers turning to ash.

"I hacked into the system, Ryan," looking over his shoulder. "Less than ten minutes after Congressman Howard contacted you to come to Andrews, Judson logged into the program, checked the maintenance log of 747's, before making a call to Green. Fifteen minutes after the plane was in the air, two deposits were made in his account, fifty grand each."

"Let me guess," I huff, leaning over to grab a fresh beer from the bucket of ice. "My best friend, Senator Green?"

"Vale, actually, but from what I understand, they're like Russian dolls. Open one and the other is there to greet you."

"Who is the second?" Zach chimes in, his face hard and I swear he's about to jump into leader mode. "And don't you dare fucking say, Lindsey."

Aiden turns back to the steaks, the asshole keeping us waiting in suspense. "No, Viper, it's not Lindsey," turning to look at me over his shoulder. "She's broke, by the way. Her car is scheduled to be repossessed this week."

"Not my concern." I toss back and mean it. Lindsey will forever be known to me as the girl who showed me what not to do. "Now tell me who gave that motherfucker money?"

"Douglas Hayes."

Standing to my feet, "Are you serious?"

Aiden slowly nods his head as he pulls the cooked meat from the grill. "Yes, Doug was a trust fund baby who has a social media page filled with what he considered thrill-seeking moments. He made a post a few minutes before how he was going to go live on Facebook from Air Force One. Some girl made a comment about how he was full of it."

Tipping my head back in laughter. "That motherfucker was pissed off due to no Wi-Fi. He made fun of Elli's name, said Elliott was a strange name for a chick."

"Did you punch the fucker?"

"Nah, she took care of it herself, said she wasn't aware Doug was short for douche bag."

Aiden sets the tongs he used to flip the steaks to the side, hooking his hands on his hips. "It's your call what I do with this information, Ryan."

I ponder for a tenth of a second, shoving the evil I'd like to have rain down on her to the side. Knowing the bitch as I do, there is one way to get her and make it hurt. "Lindsey needs to watch her career tank. Send everything you have to Sonia Marsh, she's the one person who hates Lindsey more than I do."

THE SOUND of someone getting sick has me out of bed and bursting through the bathroom door, finding Elli on her knees, her head buried in the toilet.

Turning on the water, I wet a washcloth in cold water, draping it over the back of her neck, placing a kiss to her head before heading downstairs to grab her purse.

Rounding the last step, I find Aiden and Matt sitting at the bar, an open laptop between them. "Well, aren't we a bunch of over-achievers this morning?" I tease as I grab Elli's purse off the side table where I left it last night.

"Morning." Matt mumbles, his brows furrowed in deep concentration, eyes scanning the screen rapidly as I pass. Aiden reminds silent, which isn't unusual for him, however, my curiosity is peaked as to what they are so engrossed in.

"Something brewing?"

"Possibly a mission. Checking the validity now."

The sound of Elli retching stops Aiden's typing, his eyes flash to the ceiling above, spurring me into action. Rounding the banis-ter, "Let me know about the mission, I'm in if it pans out."

Elli's sitting on the end of the bed, the washcloth I gave her in her hands wiping her face. Setting the purse on the bed beside her, I kneel down in front of her, laying my open palms on her thighs. "This is a good sign you know. All those pregnancy hormones floating around making you sick."

Sniffing, she lowers the washcloth. "I know, and I'm trying not to complain," she snickers, reaching for the zipper of her purse. "But seriously, Ryan, this shit sucks."

I can't help the smile on my face. Elli isn't a big curser, her religious upbringing instrumental in her dislike for the slang, so to hear her drop one every now and then is comical.

"Hey, if I could do this part for you…"

Sliding the pill under her tongue, "I wouldn't let you, Ryan. Having your stomach betray you like this is straight from hell."

Wrapping my arms around her. "I love you, sweetness."

"I love you, too." She breathes into my chest, burrowing her face like a bunny.

"Aiden and Matt are downstairs. How about you lay back

down for a little while, I'll go down and start breakfast before everyone has to leave?"

"I'm fine, Ryan. I can cook."

"I know you can, but this is part of me taking care of you. The sun isn't even out yet until it is, I'll feel better if you got some more rest."

Elli nods her head, not bothering to argue as she crawls on all fours to my side of the bed, wrapping her body around my pillow. I spread the blankets over her shoulder, placing a kiss to her head before closing the door and heading back downstairs.

"You get her squared away?" Logan questions over the rim of a coffee cup, his running shoes dangling from his empty hand.

Reaching behind him, I pull a cup from the cabinet. "Yeah, the nausea is killing her, but she's incredible, tackling it head on and pushing forward."

"I know it's hard to watch the woman you love suffering, but I swear it's not forever."

Draping my leg over the barstool, wrapping my fingers around my steaming cup of coffee, "I know, Logan, it all seems so surreal to me. One minute I'm walking around, feeling like a zombie and the next I'm holding the hand of the girl who waved her magic wand and made everything better."

Matt stands from the stool beside me, "Don't kid yourself, it's you that has the magic wand. That girl up there," pointing to the ceiling. "Knows the meaning of commitment, and can spot bullshit from a mile away."

"Speaking of commitment," Aiden shuts his laptop, slapping Matt on the back as he fills his cup. "You have t-minus forty-seven hours until you tether your life to the lovely Rayne. Any last requests?"

A slow, devious smile takes over Matt's face, one I know will lead us to a night in jail, or Logan doing minor surgery by lamplight.

"Just one, fuckers."

CHAPTER TWENTY-SIX

ELLI

"Officials have opened an investigation after receiving evidence implicating a member of the Secret Service, Judson Cane."

When the smell of breakfast pulled me out of bed and downstairs, the guys were coming through the door, covered in sweat and dirt. Ryan ignored my squeals, wrapping me in his filthy arms and attacking my neck, whispering how I looked much better than before he left.

Logan asked how my arm was and when I admitted it was still burning, he wanted to have a look. Which is why I'm sitting at the bar sipping on a glass of ginger ale, watching Sonia Marsh as Logan pulls more glass out of my arm.

"FBI director, Ted Durant..." The scene switches from Sonia's face to the man I recognize as Sheriff Durant walking down a set of steps, news reporters surrounding him. You could tell the footage is older as Mr. Durant is wearing a heavy coat with snow falling all around him. Given this time of year, you'd be hard pressed to find snow in New York. *"Gave a statement early this morning, where he advises his department has validated the evidence and will move to do everything in their power to see Cane receives the maximum sentence."*

"Ouch," I cry, jumping slightly, as pain shoots up my arm. My boss and his legal woes are momentarily forgotten.

"Sorry, 'bout that." Logan apologizes but keeps going, tossing the blue-tinged piece of glass onto a bed of cotton balls, returning the pointed tweezers to the now bleeding cut. "Can't believe they didn't do this the first time," he mumbles, the muscles in his arms flexing with each flick of his wrist.

"And in other news, CNN has fired Lindsey Jennings. In a statement released to this station, CNN states while they appreciate Ms. Jennings' dedication to journalism, they cannot condone her methods of exchanging sex for exclusive information. The statement went on to say, while they wish her luck in the future, recent photos of her snorting cocaine from a man's genitalia are not included in their vision statement."

Gasps were heard all around as the screen shifts from the highlighted letter from CNN to a photo of Lindsey bent over a glass table, a rolled-up bill held up to the tip of her nose. While the naked man's nether region is blurred, you can still tell what she is doing.

Looking over my shoulder in search of Ryan, worried if he sees this, it will have a negative effect on him. What I find, however, is a man oblivious to the reports on the media, so concerned with my well-being, he is wiping the escaping blood before it can run down my arm.

* * *

"I'm so glad he has you," Kennedy whispers in my ear as she and I hug goodbye. "I cannot begin to tell you the drastic change in him, all smiles like the rest of them finally."

With a final squeeze, she unravels herself, long enough for an emotional Harper to latch on.

"You're coming to the wedding, right?" Harper's sniffles echo loudly in my ear, causing me to cringe and pull away. She'd been like this all morning, where I throw my guts up, Harper is emotional.

Last night, as the guys cooked us dinner, we compared due dates, tender boobs, and increased libidos. Jordan and Rayne laughed right along with us, not seeming to be bothered by talk of babies. This was new territory for me, having girls who want to be my friend, and not stand in constant judgment of me

"Yes, ma'am. Wouldn't miss it."

"Good, because you're one of us now."

Rayne is next, her watery smile contagious as she tugs at the pendant dangling from my neck. "I'm glad you're with him too. We hated seeing him so unhappy, especially after the wedding."

After dinner, we encouraged the guys to go downstairs to the lowest level and play pool and relax while we cleaned up the kitchen. With the last dish loaded in the dishwasher, I turned around to find Rayne sitting on the kitchen island, her eyes fixed on my pendant. When I asked her, what was wrong, she suggested we head back out on the patio, where I got to hear how each of them had a special piece of jewelry Ryan had turbocharged, their words, not mine. I blushed as they awed at the romance of how Ryan gave the necklace to me, sacrificing himself for me.

"You're pretty cool...Elliott." I found a kinship with Jordan. Besides having non-traditional first names, she and I didn't conform to what our families expected of us. She is an up-and-coming metal sculptor, and I broke the yoke my father tried to tether me within by marrying a man I couldn't stand. "But I can't wait for you to meet Eleni."

According to my new friends, Eleni is Alex's brand new wife. They hadn't been able to make this impromptu trip as they live on the West Coast of Florida, which is several hours away. Apparently. Eleni and I shared the same conservative style, minimal makeup, and modest clothing. She is the mastermind behind the pendant I wear around my neck, something Aarash and Mr. Green had no knowledge of. Which, as it turned out, was a good thing.

Ryan and I stand on the front porch waving goodbye to our guests. His body behind mine, those massive arms of his wrapped securely around me.

"Come on," he suggests, taking a nip at my earlobe. "Let's go have a seat on the patio and have a talk."

Turning hesitantly, tipping my head to the side, "Uh oh, should I be worried?"

Ryan walks back toward the front door, my hands firmly grasped in his. "Baby, you never have to worry another day in your life."

Standing on the patio, listening to the rustling of the leaves on the trees, the gentle wind creates Mother Nature's song. "Tell me something, Elli. If you wake up tomorrow and can be anything you want to be, what would you chose?"

"Promise not to laugh?"

"Of course."

"Well," turning to face him, loving the way he looks at me as if I'm the most precious thing in the world. "Back in Virginia, my father agreed to let me teach Sunday school in the church we attended. One of my favorite things to do with the children was read to them. Mostly stories from the Bible, but when the lesson was over, and we had time left, I would gather them around and make up a story. I've always wanted to do that on a grander scale, have the ability to tell any child who wants to listen, a story."

"So you would write children's books?"

"Yes, and travel," I add, seeing the world is very much something I want to do.

"You know, if I were to buy this cabin for us, you could sit out here and write those children's books. I have a friend who is an excellent illustrator, he could draw anything you want."

"What would we do for money? Both our jobs are back in DC."

"Babe, you've met my team, saw firsthand how we make money, lots of money. Enough that if I want to sit on my ass and not work another day, I can." Ryan backs me against the rail of the patio, "I want to do everything in my power to make you happy, and if writing a book while flying off to some exotic place is what will keep a smile on your face, then let's pack a bag and get the fuck out of here."

His silliness makes me laugh, which in turn, makes him laugh. "If I've learned anything from what's happened over the last few years, it's that life is short, and you have to make every minute count. I want all my minutes I have left in this life to be spent with you," rubbing the back of his knuckles over my stomach. "And these little miracles in here."

Placing a chaste kiss to my lips, "What do you say, Elli? Will you let me buy you this cabin and leave DC and all it's bad memories behind?"

CHAPTER TWENTY-SEVEN

RYAN

"I really like her, Ryan." The sun bounces off Eleni's shiny locks, a gentle wind coming off the pond plays with a few strands around her face. "She makes you happy, which is all I ever wanted for you."

Wrapping an arm around her tiny shoulders, taking in the tranquility of surrounding view, "I never told anyone this, but after Harper and Logan's wedding, I sat under this very tree. I stared out at the water praying for the strength to cut the chains Lindsey had placed on me or send me someone who would bring me the kind of peace this place gives."

Eleni looks up at me, her eyes squinting due to the sun, "Sounds to me like you got both."

Nodding my head in silent agreement. "I never knew happiness like this existed."

"I know what you mean, Ryan." Leaning her head on my shoulder, "I know what you mean."

A clearing throat behind us reminds me I've hogged Eleni for too long. While Alex understands the connection I have with her, his patience will hold out only so long.

"I hate to interrupt," Zach's voice surprises me, as I expected someone else. As I turn to face him, I'm met with four concerned faces. "But we need a minute with Ryan before the ceremony starts."

Eleni pushes up on her tip-toes, placing a chaste kiss to my cheek. "Of course, gentlemen, I'll leave you to it."

Everyone remains silent as Eleni walks past us to join the other girls admiring the flower-covered gazebo.

"Listen, Ryan, the girls are concerned about Elli."

"How so?"

"According to my wife, Elli listened to a voice mail message from an adoption agency, confirming an appointment for next week. Since there isn't a ring on her finger, Kennedy is worried things may not be settled between the two of you and Elli may not have the means to support the child on her own."

"Children," I correct, deciding this is the perfect opportunity to share at least part of the secret Elli and I have chosen to keep.

"Children? As in more than one?"

Smiling like a goddamn loon. "Elli doesn't want to ruin Rayne's wedding, so we're keeping it under wraps until it's over. We found out after the attack, we're having twins. As far as the absence of a ring on her finger, well...that is not my story to tell."

Zach extends a hand, "No one more than you deserve to be happy." His usual firm grip pulls me forward as he wraps me in a back-slapping hug. "Just don't wait too long to put my wife out of her misery."

"I won't, sir."

Zach steps back far enough I catch the grim faces of Aiden and Alex. "Awe, fuck, do I even want to know?"

Aiden looks behind him to where the girls stand around Matt, Kennedy adjusting his tie while Jordan helps him with his boutonnière. Harper and Elli stand off to the side, admiring the garden Rayne put along the front of the house.

"Lindsey was arrested last night."

"So?" I scoff

"She was trying to get into your condo. When the guards wouldn't let her pass, she tried to run over one of them with her car. Apparently, her landlord served her with eviction papers for non-payment of rent, for the last eight months, and she wanted you to fix it. Her car was repossessed this morning, coincidentally by the tow company contacted to remove it by the police."

I'd lost count of how many times I received a frantic message from her, needing money for this utility or that utility. What I wouldn't give to see her face when she learns the Porsche she drove around in, with her nose in the air, is headed for auction.

"Let me guess, she called one of you to bail her out?"

"No, she called the producer to bail her out. With the network breathing down his neck, he refused her call."

"Why do I get the impression there's a but hiding in the shadows?"

"Remember the other morning when you came downstairs and Matt and I were on the computer?"

"Yes, the mission you were validating."

Nodding, "Cane was arrested not long after the evidence hit Durant's desk. He posted bail but failed to show up for his arraignment hearing. His bail's been revoked, but…"

He doesn't need to finish, Cane may have been stupid enough to get caught, but he is smart enough to keep his credentials and sell his skills to the highest bidder. Chances are he knows, or at least suspects, how Durant got the information on him.

"Let me get Elli back to DC, and I'll deal with the fucker myself."

* * *

RAYNE WALKS DOWN THE AISLE, her simple white dress glowing in the South Carolina sun. Her father Jack and brother Will, stand on either side of her as she makes her way to Matt. Less than thirty people sit in white chairs beside the pond, the simple ceremony something the couple wanted.

No bridesmaids or groomsmen, just Matt waiting not-so-patiently as the local preacher begins the ceremony.

Elli sits high in her chair, commenting on how beautiful everything is, expressing her gratitude for being included. Her bottom lip quivers when she learns Matt built the gazebo, especially for this day. He, like the rest of us, willing to do anything to make our women happy.

"And do you, Matthew Parrish take Rayne Winters to be your lawfully wedded wife?"

If I were a betting man, I'd wager it would be hard pressed to find a happier bunch of men than the six of us. We've each battled incredible odds, near-death experiences, and dealt with the ramifications of our actions. Still, each of us found someone who can look past the rough exteriors and find the heart of a warrior inside. While the road hasn't been easy, the steps which brought us here have taught each of us valuable lessons.

"To have and to hold."

For Zach, it was knowing the difference between protecting and preventing.

"From this day forward."

For Logan, it's not allowing the past to rule his future.

"For better or worse."

For Matt, it's learning to forgive himself.

"Richer or for poorer."

For Aiden, it's age doesn't necessarily equal wisdom.

"In sickness and in health."

For Alex, it's learning from your mistakes and not repeating them.

"Till death do you part."

For me, it's learning to love myself, before I can expect anyone else to.

CHAPTER TWENTY-EIGHT

ELLI

"You sure I can't change your mind?" Jennifer stands outside my cubical, a box of donuts in her hands, doing her best Vanna White with the box.

Ryan and I spoke in detail on the drive back to DC on which direction to go regarding our future. He insisted I move out of my apartment and into his condo until I reminded him the property had been sold and it was silly for me to move twice. In the end, we compromised, he'll move into my apartment and I'll quit my job, allowing him to take care of me.

"Afraid not," standing to my full height. "But it doesn't mean we can't still be friends."

After Mr. Cane was arrested and the truth came out about his involvement in the plane crash, his employment with the government was terminated. Jennifer was moved into his position, quickly tossing out all his ridiculous rules, making this a more pleasant working environment.

Tossing the box to the desk, she wraps me in her arms. "We will always be friends, Elli. No job or stupid boy will change that."

When I handed in my letter of resignation, Jennifer laughed and said if she had a boyfriend who looked like Ryan, she'd willingly stay home too—baby or no baby. Once the news of my pregnancy circulated around the office, Congressman Howard offered me a new position in his office. One I turned down right after I called and canceled my appointment with the adoption agency.

"Speaking of stupid boys…" It was super late when we pulled into my apartment from the wedding, or early depending on how you look at it. Either way, imagine our surprise when we found Jennifer doing the walk of shame from Namur's apartment.

"Oh, Elli. He's so wonderful, and the things he can do with his —" Silencing her with my hand over her mouth, even with as incredible my sex life was, I don't\ need to hear about someone else's.

"Stop, I so don't need to hear this," I say as I move my hand away from her mouth.

"Sorry, I forget Ryan has been out of town for the past week."

Ten days, actually. Almost immediately after we returned from South Carolina, he gave me a key to his Jaguar, a fist full of cash, and then boarded a plane for Montana. I assume it has something to do with his family, however, I didn't ask and he didn't offer an explanation.

"It's okay. He called this morning to say he would definitely be home tonight."

"In that case, I'm cashing in my rain check for lunch, so I can get a ride in that car of his before he whisks you away."

Driving Ryan's car around is an exercise in anxiety. I've never been a car enthusiast, but when grown men stop and stare at you as you drive by, you find yourself Googling the name, and then fainting at the price tag.

"Ugh, I can't wait to give the thing back to him. I'm terrified someone will scratch it every time I go out."

* * *

RYAN'S FLIGHT is scheduled to land in ten minutes. I anxiously watch the monitor in baggage claim as dozens of passengers make their way down the escalator. A ping of jealousy hits me as I see the list of cities the arriving planes originated, Stockholm, Geneva, Venice, Paris, London. All the places I long to see but doubt I ever will.

"Excuse me?" A tiny voice speaks as someone pulls at the hem of my skirt. Looking down I see the cherub face of a little girl, a red rose held carefully in her hand. "This is for you." She says proudly, shoving the flower toward me.

"Why, thank you." I smile as she skips off to join her waiting parents, a final wave from her tiny fingers as they made their way to the carousel.

"Ma'am," Glancing to my left, I'm met with two more roses being held by a man dressed in a military uniform, an anchor with two stars on each side rest in the center of his cap. "These are for you." Tipping his head as he hands them off, and then makes his way in the same direction.

"Young lady," A white-haired elderly woman held three more roses, her lipstick matching the color of the blossoms almost perfectly. "Add these to the ones you've got and make sure to put them in water when you get home." I stand gobsmacked as she thrusts the flowers in my hand, taking off in the same direction as the others.

Looking up, Ryan's flight has five more minutes, but as I look back toward the escalator, I find a line of people with flowers in hand, headed in my direction. Glancing around, I notice a small crowd has formed, several people, stand to the side, cellphones in hand recording.

One by one the people in line hand me the rose in their hand, and then join the rest by the carousel. Just when I'm about to bolt, go hide in the bathroom until Ryan's plane arrives, I look to the escalator and see a massive teddy bear coming down.

All the people who've given me flowers now make their way back, standing beside the folks with their cellphones. As the massive teddy bear descends further, it's suddenly moved to the side to reveal Ryan's handsome face.

Stepping from the escalator, the crowd begins to cheer as Ryan sets the teddy bear to the floor, its head bouncing about. Dropping to his knees, he places his hands on my stomach, kissing the fabric covering my still flat belly. "Hello, babies, daddy brought you a present."

Looking up at me, he smiles as he pulls his left hand back, his pinky curled, the lights from overhead reflecting on the diamond ring sitting there. "Elliott York, you make me want to be a better man, see the world differently through your eyes. You give me a reason to wake up every morning and celebrate each day. I want to spend the rest of my life returning the love you've shown me. Please, say you will marry me?"

Hours later, as I collapse on top of him, slick with sweat and comfortably sated, I take the opportunity to admire the engagement ring he placed on my finger.

"If you don't like it, we can go find you something else."

"Ryan, no," I argue, my ringed hand against my chest. "I absolutely love this."

Flipping on top of me, "Good, because I love you, and I haven't nearly finished with you yet."

Ryan plants a searing kiss to my lips, his tongue dancing with mine, reigniting the fire inside me.

"I spoke with your father yesterday," he whispers in my ear, his teeth nipping at my earlobe.

As if a bucket of freezing water has been dumped on me, I push him back, scrambling for something to cover my naked body with.

"You what?"

Ryan rolls to the side, a devilish grin on his face. "Don't worry, I spoke with mine too, both of them congratulated us, and your father agreed to forgive me for hurting you when I left."

"Did he mention if he and Momma would be able to come?"

Ryan looks down at my hands, bringing the one closest to him up to his lips, gently kissing the ring he placed there.

"He said he would see."

I knew exactly what that meant, I'd heard it all my life. My father may have forgiven Ryan, but he hadn't forgiven me.

CHAPTER TWENTY-NINE

RYAN

I hate the gym at Elli's apartment. Namur tried to warn me about it when I paid him for keeping watch on her when I went to Montana, but I assumed he was being facetious. Half the equipment either doesn't work or is missing parts. I'm half tempted to drive across town and use mine at the condo, as the final sale isn't for another week.

Finally, setting a rhythm on the treadmill, my frustration gets the best of me when I don't bother to look at the caller ID as my music stops.

"Hello?"

"Ryan?" The frail voice of Lindsey echoes through my earphones, shooting my frustration to immeasurable levels. "Please don't hang up, I need your help."

Not bothering to acknowledge her, "I have no place to live, they-they took my car..." she drifts off, sobs cracking her words. "Are you there, Ryan?"

I can hear her crying, something Lindsey never did unless it benefited her. "I'm listening."

"I know you're getting married, I saw the ring on the news, but they want to send me to a woman's shelter."

And finally, the reason for the call. For as long as I've known Lindsey, she's had this sense of superiority over everyone. Her car had to be the current year, where she lived the trendiest. Her clothes, jewelry, all had to be better than everyone around her. About a year ago, she did a segment on women in crisis, where she visited several shelters reporting on their services and conditions. She came home that night and spoke of how she couldn't wait to get out of there, that it smelled poor.

"Please say you will help me, Ryan. I can make it worth your while, Elli doesn't have to know."

Bile fills my throat at the thought of touching her. "Unlike you, I don't keep shit from the woman I love. I could help you, Ms. Jennings—"

"Oh thank God, Ryan. I will need you to get my—"

"Hold on," I shout into the phone. "Don't fucking interrupt me. I said I could help you, but I'm not. You've got everything you've wanted, and now it's time you live with the consequences."

Ending the call feels like closing the final door with her. Lindsey Jennings would forever be the girl who taught me the most about myself, giving me examples to share with my children of how not to treat others.

Walking into the apartment, I'm surprised to see Elli sitting on the couch, the phone I gave her clenched between her fingers and a tear rolling down her face.

"Elli?" Crossing the room, dropping to my knees in front of her. "What's wrong, baby?"

Shoving her phone into my hands, "They aren't coming. I knew he wouldn't, stubborn asshole."

Elli rarely cussed, this was maybe the second time I've ever heard a foul word fall from her lips. Turning the phone, I snuggle in behind her as I read the email on the screen.

Elliott,
Your father came by the church this evening, asking if I could send a message to you. As I'm certain you are aware, the young man you are engaged to came to him and asked his forgiveness and his permission to marry you. And while he found it easy to forgive a stranger, he cannot find it in his heart to forgive you for abandoning the teachings he gave to you, by running away without asking his permission. He and your mother will not be attending your wedding.
I'm sorry, Elliot. I will try my best to remind him of God's commandments of forgiveness and how he loves us despite our sins.
In Christ,
Pastor Joe

I'M at a loss for words as to what to say to her, my throat grows thick at the thought she might give my ring back, ending our relationship.

"I'm sorry, sweetheart," I admit, holding her tight as I breathe in her delicate scent.

"Why are you sorry? I'm the one who has to walk down the aisle alone, plan this thing on my own..." she drifts off, as her body begins to shake. "I haven't even chosen a date." Her final revelation sends her into hysterics, forcing her to crawl into my lap and hug me tight.

"Babe," keeping my voice soft as to not upset her further. "I can have my mother here before dinner if you want. I know she isn't your real mother, but she's dying to meet you."

"I don't want to uproot anyone's life because of my personal tragedy."

"Hope Biggs isn't just anyone, Elli. She's my mom and the grandmother of those little ones inside you. She would love to come, trust me."

Pulling herself from my lap, she wipes her face on the edge of her sleeve, "No, I'll figure it out." Before running into the bathroom and closing the door.

I'm still trying to find my way around her apartment, but I remember a basket of laundry in the bedroom. Slipping down the hall, I hear her vomiting in the toilet, which quickens my pace. Grabbing the first washcloth I come to, and the bottle of medicine from her purse.

Placing the wet cloth to the back of her neck, I shake out one of the pills and wait patiently until she's finished. I learned the hard way it's best to leave her alone while she's getting sick. I made the mistake of rubbing her back, which made the nausea worse according to her.

"I don't know why I'm so upset about this," blowing her nose as she flushes the toilet, taking the offered pill from my hand. "When I was six or seven, my middle brother, Ethan, cut his foot so bad the doctor in town sent him to the hospital in Norfolk. They worked for three days trying to save his foot, but all my father could think about were the chores Ethan was missing. When he got out of the hospital, Ethan had to go stay with our pastor, as my dad wanted to put him back to feeding the pigs."

Placing the pill under her tongue, she sniffed as she stared at the ceiling. "Then, when Emmitt and his wife Sadie wanted to see a specialist because they couldn't get pregnant, my father said it was because he spoiled her too much, letting her have too many liberties. He made Emmitt lock her up in the barn for three days, with nothing to eat or drink."

Moving the shower curtain to the side, she turns on the water, holding her hand under the faucet as she waits for the water to warm. "Two years ago, a bunch of worms tore up our vegetable garden overnight. He blamed my mother because she planted the seeds while on her period."

Tugging her nightgown over her head. "Eight sons, he would brag to the men of our church. Eight sons to fill my table with grandsons." Deepening her voice to mock her father, as she steps from her panties and into the spray of the shower.

"But the jokes on him, Ryan. Eight sons and eight daughters-in-law, every damn one of them baron as a brick. My brother, Elijah, married five years and not once has his wife Nancy missed a period. She cooks and cleans, does everything my father tells her to, and still nothing. Emmitt, Ethan, Ezekiel, Everett, Eugene and Earl, all married for years and not a single grandchild to surround my father's precious table."

Slipping off my gym clothes, I climb in behind her, wrapping myself around her back, my hands immediately finding her stomach. She stands silent for several moments, letting the hot spray wash away the hurt she's bottled up inside.

"He tried to pawn me off on a man he wouldn't even sell a chicken to, assuming I was like the rest of his offspring, useless as tits on a boar. I've been punished my entire life for being a girl, tied with a name he chose before I was born." Spinning in my arms, determination clear in my eyes, placing her hands on my chest. "I pray our children never know a cruel word in their life, never feel the pain of hunger when their parents are too prideful to ask for help. I never want our children to question how much they are loved and wanted. Even if their parents did put the cart before the horse."

Her ability to turn a negative into a positive is hot as fuck to me. Dipping down, I take a single nipple between my lips, swirling my tongue around the taut peak. Running my fingers down her still flat stomach, until I feel the soft curls at the apex of her thighs. A brazen moan flows from her throat as her fingers bury themselves to my scalp. Using the trail forged by my fingers, I lap at her skin with my lips and tongue, the water from the shower diluting her rich scent.

Raising her leg to the edge of the tub, I dive between her folds, circling her clit with my tongue and fingers. Nipping at the thick flesh, gripping it between my teeth and shaking my head back and forth.

"Ryan," she moans, her voice deep with need.

"Wear it the fuck out, baby." Oh, how I love hearing my name fall from her lips. Whether it is to ask me a question or show me how well I'm eating her pussy. Speeding up my movements, knowing how much she loves it when I do.

"Yes," placing her hand at the back of my head, pushing my face closer to where she wants me most. "Right t-there, Ryan." Another thing I love about her, she isn't afraid to tell me what she wants, how she needs to be touched.

Slipping two fingers into her entrance, I feel her legs begin shaking, the first sign of her impending orgasm. I'm never satisfied with just one, she can give herself a single orgasm anytime she wants, it's my job to give her a reason to wait for me to do it.

Burning my fingers to my knuckles, I run the tips over the

textured skin deep inside her, her sharp intake of breath tells me I've reached the magic spot. Her legs tremble as her walls clench with her orgasm, my name leaving her lips with such force I nearly stand and salute her.

Steadying her, I rise to my feet, kissing her perfect lips, she pants something unintelligible before opening those gorgeous eyes of her, blue orbs dark with need. When she drops to her knees, I'm about to argue. This had been about her, a not-so-subtle reminder of why she chose me.

"No, Elli—"

"Hush, Ryan. I won't always be in a position to get on my knees for you, better enjoy this while you still can."

* * *

IT WAS NEARING lunchtime before I found a minute to take a break from packing up my condo. I left Elli on the sofa with strict instructions to eat the sandwich I made her and not move a muscle until the movie she'd stumbled upon was over.

Closing my office door completely, I grab my phone to check on a text message I'd sent while Elli got dressed this morning. Pleased with the answer, I sit down at my desk and contact the team.

"How was Montana?" Aiden is the first face to pop on the screen, his signature backward cap in place.

"Not as productive as Utah." I shoot back, keeping my voice low so Elli won't hear me.

Zach's face pops up next, a smudge of paint on his cheek. "You said he'd go hide at his grandmas' place."

Leaning back in my chair, "Bastard was hiding in the shed of her house. The poor lady had no idea he was there."

"You guys should have been there," Alex starts, heavy metal playing in the background. I'd taken him along for protection for Judson, as I wanted to beat the fuck out of him. "Ghost pulls his ass out of the shed, dirt and shit flying everywhere, when this little old lady comes out of the back door, broom in hand screaming for us to hold him for her."

Cane hopped on a bus the second he was released on bond; I had used the city's security cameras to track him. He zig-zagged across the country, assuming he was fooling somebody with his tactics, all it did was make it easier to find him. Once he changed buses in Oklahoma, I knew exactly where he was going. His rejected security clearance listed a grandmother in Utah.

"Ghost flips him around, ties him to the clothesline pole, and handed granny his expandable baton."

Shrugging my shoulders, "The broom in her hand was counter-productive for her weight. I gave her an equalizer."

Judson's grandma was all of four-feet tall, ninety pounds soaking wet and used a walker to get around. From the little I gathered, not caring to look further, she was the step-grandparent, whose husband, Judson's grandfather, left his life insurance to and not the grandchildren. Judson contested the will and lost, creating a huge rift in the family.

"Now that you're all here, I'm going to assume everyone saw the proposal on the news last night. If not, check your email as I sent a copy to everyone early this morning. Kennedy and the other ladies can rest tonight knowing Elli said yes and by the size of the diamond, my financial stability should be clear."

Leaning forward, my arms crossed on my desk. "Unfortunately, not everyone is happy with this proposal as Elli received an email from back in Virginia. Her father has basically written her off."

"Are you fucking kidding?"

"Sadly, Alex, I am not. However, I do have a plan, one I'll need each of you in order to pull off.

Zach, like the true leader he is, "We're in."

ELLI IS fast asleep on the couch by the time I have my office packed, the plate that held her sandwich now contains a few crumbs and her wadded up napkin. Crossing the room, I sit on the loveseat across from her, basking in delicate features of her face. This exquisitely beautiful woman is mine, the children she carries, tangible proof of the love we share.

The sound of the doorbell chimes, pulling Elli from her slumber, stretching like a cat enjoying the afternoon sun.

"Evening, sweetheart." Bending over her warm and soft body, placing a kiss to her pouty lips. "I thought you'd be hungry when you woke up. Come on, I have a surprise for you."

Elli stubbles as she takes the first step, her nap still holding onto her. Bending down, I scoop her up bridal style as I cross the room to the foyer.

"Ryan," she playfully chastises.

"Just practicing." I tease back, mostly serious.

Placing her back on her feet as we reach the door, the sound of her stomach grumbles as I reach for the handle. "Remember, I love you."

Elli's mouth drops open, her hand reaching out to stop me, but it's too late. If her mother isn't allowed to be here, I will lend her mine for a while.

"Hey, Mom, thanks for coming."

My mom gives me a half-hearted hug, her attention on Elli.

Seeing how broken my fiancée was after hearing the news from her father, I couldn't sit back and do nothing. My mother is one of the strongest, kindest people I know, and when I told her what happened, she insisted on flying to DC and helping Elli. I booked her a flight and had Namur and Jennifer pick her up from the airport. If anyone can fix the hole in Elli's heart, Hope Biggs can.

"You are more beautiful than my son described." Mom holds her arms open, clearing the distance between the pair, surrounding Elli in the kind of embrace I remember.

"Elli, this my mom, Hope Biggs. Mom, this is my Elli."

Mom loosens her hold on Elli, but doesn't let go, "Oh and how glad I am to meet you."

Mom moves to place her hands on Elli's cheeks, giving her the once over as a watery smile comes over my mother's face.

"Ryan Oliver, tell me you have tea in this house?"

"Yes, ma'am."

"Then go and put the kettle on, only the best conversations are held over a cup of tea. I have a new daughter to get to know." Wrapping an arm around Elli, the two push past me as my mother begins inquiring on how Elli's been feeling.

Delighted in my decision to contact my mother, I take a step toward the kitchen when the doorbell chimes again. I'm not expecting anyone else, so when I look through the peephole, a laugh breaks from my throat as I pull the door open.

"Hello, Ryan. We understand there's a wedding to plan."

CHAPTER THIRTY

ELLI

"You're more than I could have hoped for in a daughter."

Hope's words run on repeat inside my head. Her unique smell of sugar and cinnamon fills me with a warmth I haven't felt since my grandmother passed away.

Looking into her kind face, I can see where Ryan gets his vibrant eyes and long lashes. Hope is a classic beauty, her smooth, tan complexion, with the tiniest of wisdom lines around her features. Kindness flows off her in waves, from the genuine smile on her face to the words dripping from her lips.

"Hello," a familiar sing-song voice calls down the hall. Ryan appears at the threshold, his hand behind his neck, and surprise written across his face. It's the group of women who come to stand behind him that have my heart so full of joy my body can't contain it. Tears stream down my cheeks as I make my way to where Harper stands beside Meredith.

The same pregnancy hormones which rule my every emotion, also turn Harper into a sniffling mess.

"When Ryan told the guys about your father, we couldn't sit back and not do something to make your day special."

Shifting my attention to Ryan, "You told them?"

"Oh, don't be cross with him, Elli." Meredith steps around, laying her handbag on the glass table. "There are no secrets between him and his team, given the sensitivity of their work." Meredith Forbes is grace personified, which is clearly demonstrated as she sits straight as a pin on the leather sofa.

"You have a problem, and it's Ryan's job as your husband to help fix it."

"It's what he's always been good at," Hope adds, pride in her voice as she joins Meredith on the sofa.

"Now tell me, Elli. Is there a chance your mother will stand against your father and contact you?"

"I highly doubt it," sitting with a huff in my spot from earlier. "She doesn't know any different. She was raised to serve her husband, just as her mother before her and her's before her."

"If you don't mind me asking, how are you not back there serving a man?"

Hope wasn't the first to ask me. When Jennifer inquired as to why I wore a dress every day, I let it slip it was part of my upbringing. When she dived further, I gave her a small slice of what my life was like. "I wasn't supposed to be a girl. My father believed, as did the other men in his family, that only males would come to York men. I believe he didn't know how to handle having a daughter, so he ignored me for the most part, putting my rearing into the hands of my mother."

Ryan returns with a tray of cups and the makings for tea in one hand, a pot of steaming water in the other. Hope jumps to her feet at the same time Meredith encourages Harper to take a seat.

"Love you," Ryan places a soft kiss to my lips. "I have a few errands to run. Will you be okay here?" My stomach rumbles before I can answer, gaining another kiss from Ryan. "Dinner is on its way. I'll be back."

"Love you, too."

I watch as Ryan makes the rounds, kissing each lady's cheek before sending a final wave as he heads out the door.

"You were saying, Elli?" Hope prods as she pours hot water in the cups, Meredith adding the tea bag to steep.

"Oh?" My mind draws a blank.

Meredith and Hope share a look before breaking out into laughter. "Pregnancy brain," they say in unison before turning back to the cups of tea. "You were telling us how you came to be here, instead of serving a husband in Virginia."

"Oh, right." I pause, feeling the heat of my bush coloring my cheeks. "By the time I was born, my mother had the care of the house down to fine art, which enabled her to do more with the ladies of the church. She would bring me along, allowing me to play with the other children as they canned vegetables or made blankets and such. Which is where I got my first taste of reading."

Patsy Tripp, the youngest daughter of my former boss, owned a small bookstore, or at least it looked like one to my four-year-old self. In reality, it was a couple of bookcases in her playroom, but it was still more than I had. Their home was across the street from the church, and the usual meeting spot for lady's activities.

"The first time I opened a book, I was instantly in love. I remember staring at the words written under the pictures, trying to guess what they meant. My mother saw the light in my eyes and did everything she could to keep it there. We hid books in the woods and the chicken coop and would sneak out there after our chores were done. She would look at old magazines while I read. As I grew, the books grew with me, until one afternoon, my mother was asked to look in on Mrs. Tripp who'd given birth to her fourth child, I went along to help. As I was putting food in their refrigerator, I came across a National Geographic magazine on their table. When Mr. Tripp came in to get something to eat, he noticed me looking and gave me the magazine. I wore the pages thin by the time I had to toss it out. I loved learning about the lives of people on the other side of the world, imagining what it would be to travel to where they live, seeing the incredible beauty they saw every day."

The downside of daydreaming was getting in my father's way on occasion, or being caught not paying attention to what he was trying to show me. I'd had a switch taken to the backs of my legs a fair amount of times for aggravating him.

"When I turned fifteen, Mr. Tripp offered to let me work after school for him in his factory. Which is where I discovered the glorious world of the internet."

"And thus a glance at the free world." Meredith finishes, handing me a cup of tea.

"Well, I for one am glad things happened the way they did," Hope admits proudly as she sits back in her chair, smoothing out the fabric of her pants. "Granted, I wish my son would never have met Lindsey."

"Just be glad he was smart enough never to have gotten her pregnant."

Raising the cup to my lips in order to keep from spouting the truth. What happened between Lindsey and Ryan is their business, and not my story to tell.

"So tell us, Elli?" Harper wiggles from side to side in her chair, her eyes bright with mischief. "What does your dream wedding dress look like?"

Sadness falls over me, recalling the words my mother spoke

when my father first gave permission for Wesley to pursue me. "Don't let him do anything to keep you from wearing white to the courthouse."

"I-I know I can't exactly wear white—"

The chime of the doorbell interrupts me, earning me time to get my emotions under control. Like most girls, I imagined my perfect wedding day, complete with a long white dress and handsome groom.

Harper jumps from her chair faster than I can, "Let me get that."

Meredith and Hope refill their cups, exchanging opinions on the view of Pennsylvania Avenue behind them.

Hushed voices in the entry have me setting my cup on the end table, ready to stand and see who has arrived. Harper rounds the corner, her hands full of bags from the Irish restaurant down the street, the smile of some familiar faces immediately behind her.

"Oh thank god, you made it," Meredith replaced the pot of water back on the tray, rising from her chair, taking Kennedy in a tight hug. "Look at you, just as beautiful as Harper and Elli with your pregnancy."

Rayne steps around the hugging pair, "Hey, girl. Congratulations." Bending over, she wraps me in a side hug to avoid hitting me with the bag of food she's carrying with the other.

"Thank you. What are you doing here?"

"Meredith put out the word you needed help planning your wedding. I'm here to help you chose flowers, Eleni..." Rayne moves her body to the side, giving me a clear view of everyone. "Is here to help you pick your dress."

Meredith moves behind Eleni, gripping her shoulders in a hug. "Which is perfect, as Elli was about to tell us about her dream dress."

Eleni moves to sit beside me, placing a kiss to my cheek. "Since you and I share a more conservative look, everyone agreed I'd be the best one to help, in case you can't decide."

Meredith resumes her seat, crossing her legs, "Go ahead, Elli. You were saying something about white."

Taking a deep breath, "Since wearing white is out of the question, I could look for something in a pale yellow or cream."

A deep line forms in the center of Hope's forehead, her squinting eyes making the lines around her face deepen. "Why is white out of the question?"

Confused, "Um…I'm pregnant. White is for virgins."

Meredith clears her throat, then raises her right hand, "By a show of hands, how many of you wore white on your wedding day?"

Kennedy, Rayne, Harper, Eleni, and Hope all raise their hands in the air.

"Now how many of you were virgins?" Every single hand goes down.

"Pfft, Matt and I had sex the morning of our ceremony," Rayne admits, gaining a few giggles.

"The tradition of wearing a white dress wasn't even popular until Queen Victoria wore one in the eighteen-hundreds. Later, it became a sign of wealth to be able to afford a dress worn only once. Somewhere along the line, virginity was tagged to it." Kennedy reasons, spinning her engagement ring around her finger.

"So again, Elli. Do you have a dream dress in mind?"

"Yes," my voice quivers with joy. "I want a long dress, covered in lace, with a veil to match. I picture it fluttering down the aisle behind me."

"And where will this aisle be?" Hope quizzes, leaning over to take her cup.

"Well," I begin, the image of the church coming to life inside my head. "Our church choir was invited to sing at a revival in Arkansas. Three of my brothers sang every Sunday and our Pastor came to my father requesting for them and my mother to attend. Now my father would never dream of telling Pastor Joe no. So, he made my mother take me along since he didn't want to have to look after me."

My mom worked late into the night making food for the rest of the boys and my father to eat. While she was excited to see her three youngest sings on stage, she wasn't looking forward to the mess we would come home to.

"The church they sang in was huge and hotels were booked up for miles. Pastor Joe was able to find host families for us to stay with. The couple who welcomed us lived not far from Thorncrown Chapel. When it was time to leave, they took us by and the minute I saw it, I knew I wanted to get married there."

Meredith held her phone in her hand, a pair of reading glasses resting on her nose. "Oh, Elli, this is beautiful."

Hope mimics her stance, minus the reading glasses. "And Eureka Springs is beautiful this time of year." Putting her phone face down on her lap, "Meredith, they have this incredible spa that offers sugar scrubs. Have you ever had one?"

I let their conversation fade into the background, going all the way to Arkansas for a wedding was a pipe dream.

"Hey, I know that look," Eleni whispers beside me, bumping her shoulder against mine.

"Sorry, it's nothing." I try to argue, shifting away from her.

"It is something," erasing the distance I placed between us. "You know, we're more alike than just taste in clothing."

"How do you figure?"

"We both chose education over boys, for one. Two, the men we fell in love with came with more baggage than Louis Vuitton."

Tipping my head back, filling my cheeks with air before blowing it out. "Weddings cost money." I surmise, "And I don't have a job anymore. I have a little saved, but not the thousands it will cost to rent the Chapel. Then there's the dress, the flowers, and photographer, the list goes on and on. While Ryan says he'll take care of me, I don't think he means he'll open his wallet for me to spend as I like."

Laying her left hand over the top of mine, her olive complexion such a contrast to my pale one. Her engagement ring sparkles beautifully in the lamplight. "Listen, I understand where you're coming from. I also know how much Ryan adores you and would want you to have your heart's desire." Picking up my hand, turning it until my palm faces the ceiling, "Which is why he asked me to give you this."

Nestled in the middle of my hand is a shiny black credit card, my name scrolled across the bottom.

"Elli?" Meredith calls from her spot on the sofa, her phone tucked between her shoulder and ear. "We need the date for the wedding, Josh has the chapel on the phone."

"Josh?"

"Her personal attorney," Harper clarifies. "Take it from me, don't question it, just give him what he asks for."

CHAPTER THIRTY-ONE

RYAN

I've always enjoyed the crisp air of early morning in the mountains. Watching the fog as it clings to the vegetation, holding on to the last second before the rays of the sun chase it into thin air. Catching the deer as they make their way across the ridge, in search of a place to lay low for the day.

Today is my last full day as a single man, and the first day of opening statements in Green's trial, something I'm not sorry to be missing. I washed my hands of the situation the moment I passed Judson over to authorities, collecting the bounty and sending it to someone I felt could use it.

Lifting my coffee to my lips, I hear my brother, Miles, attempting to sneak up on me, something he has never succeeded in doing.

"A herd of elephants running from a pride of lions are quieter than you."

Miles, never one to give up, remains in his hiding place behind the door. I can practically hear the gears in his brain convincing him to remain still to try and confuse me.

Leaping over the rail, I maneuver down the side of the cabin, behind the house and through the side door into the kitchen. My father stands beside the coffee pot, his face full of sleep. Holding my finger to my lips, I point to Miles across the room, hunkered down behind the slightly open door.

Approaching, I keep my eyes trained on Miles's mischievous grin, his hand on the doorknob waiting for the perfect moment to pounce.

"Who are we waiting for?" I whisper in his direction, jolting him, forcing the most girlish scream to leave his throat. "How the—?"

Just like when we were kids, once the fear has left, the need for revenge takes over as he hurls himself into my midsection, the pair of us tumbling over an ottoman in the center of the room.

"Goddamn it, Ry," Miles shouts, his back to the floor with my booted foot in his chest. "How the hell can you still do that?"

Hollis, my next eldest brother, drops down onto the leather sofa, reaching down and messing Miles's hair. "He's a SEAL, you dumbass."

Lifting my boot off his chest, I reach down and help him to his feet. "Even if I wasn't a SEAL, you are much too loud to sneak up on anybody."

Cooper snickers from his spot against the kitchen counter, as my father sits a carafe of juice on the table.

"Good morning, sweet boy." Mom kisses my cheek as she walks in from behind me, the fresh smell of the mountain air in her wake. "I come bearing gifts."

The smell of cooked bacon hits me long before the caterers step through the door. When Mom and Meredith reserved the six cabins just a few miles from the church, they arranged to have each meal prepared and delivered, affording everyone the ability to enjoy the amenities and not worry about cooking or cleaning up.

I'll never forget the look on Elli's face when I came back to the condo the night she chose the date, worried beyond belief on how much this wedding was costing me. Even when I showed her my bank balance, she sat in disbelief. I understood her apprehension, going from struggling for every dime to being comfortable in the blink of an eye. While I never had to worry about money growing up, my family owning one of the top producing horse ranches in the country, I saw others who weren't as fortunate.

"Get your hands out of there," Mom warns Cooper, a split-second before slapping his hand when he reaches into the pan of bacon. "Just because we aren't at home doesn't mean you can forget your manners."

The catering crew goes to work, setting the food up buffet style as my two remaining brothers, Zeke and Cade come stumbling out of their room. They attempted to take me and my team on in drinking last night and, long story short, Matt and I had to carry them to bed just before midnight.

"Morning," Cade croaks, taking a cup of coffee from Dad, then collapsing into a chair. Zeke follows suit, the pair looking like hammered dog shit.

Pulling my phone from my back pocket, I type out a text to Elli, telling her good morning and how much I love her.

"Ryan, honey. Grab a plate before your brothers eat everything."

Looking up from my phone, "I'm waiting for Elli." The room is now filled with familiar chaos, Cooper and Miles piling food on their plates, while Zeke tries to con Mom into bringing him food.

"Smart man," Cooper tosses out, shoveling a strip of bacon into his mouth, pointing a second at me. "Cause Elli is hot."

Slipping my phone back in my pocket, "First off, baby brother, I learned from the best how to treat my wife." Nodding at our father. Reaching across the table, snatching the piece of bacon out of his hand, twisting his fingers backward and slamming them on the table. "Two, don't talk about my fucking wife like that." Releasing with his finger with a shove, sending him teetering backward in his chair, "And third, hell yeah, she is."

A BLUE HAZE of campfire smoke hangs in the air, hugging the edges of the trees and lantern posts. Keeping with the woodsy theme of the wedding, my mom and Meredith hired a party planner to transform the area between the cabins into what they described as rustic, with a modern twist.

Lanterns hang from temporary posts strategically placed around the grounds, guiding guests to the massive tent constructed to blend in with the cabins. Faux stone steps were laid out like carpets creating paths to the center tent from each cabin.

Wildflowers mixed with pine branches, wrapped in raffia adorned nearly every surface. Thousands of candles flicker inside lanterns and votives, while burlap dresses up the rented chairs and tables inside. Walking around the tent, I bid the men manning the fire a hello as I make my way to the furthest cabin from mine.

Once I handed the keys to the condo I never wanted, over to a couple who couldn't wait to move in, I drove Elli back to the cabin in north Georgia I purchased for us. My brothers flew out a few days after we settled in, helping me clear the spot of land I used to build my office. Cooper fell instantly in love with my girl and was pissed as hell when she denied having a sister he could inquire after.

Passing the smaller of the six rented cabins, it's windows still dark as when we arrived. I'd sent word through Pastor Joe of this wedding, directions on how to get here and even sent money to him for the journey. All without telling Elli. She'd been the happiest I'd ever seen her in the past three months. Between planning the wedding and writing children's books, she didn't have time to be sad about her parents.

Her severe morning sickness had passed, replaced with an insatiable need for me. For the first time in my entire life, I said no to sex one morning not even a month ago. She'd woken me four times in the night, and I had nothing left to give. I ended up feasting between her thighs to release the pressure for her, because well, it's my job to take care of her.

Climbing the steps to what had been labeled as the bridal suite, my presence beyond the threshold strictly prohibited. Despite my fiancée's need for nearly constant sex, she'd placed a moratorium on sleeping together once we arrived here. Which was fine, except when a guy is used to getting laid several times a day and then nothing, things start to hurt.

As my foot lands on the top step, the cabin door opens wide, revealing my beautiful girl with a smile just for me. Dressed in a white eyelet dress that went below her knees, cowboy boots and a denim jacket. Her red hair is pulled half up, adorned with the same flowers from the tent behind me.

"Elliott Lavinia York, you look..." I drift off, the word to describe how beautiful she is escaping me. When I discovered her middle name, I asked why her father chose something so feminine. Lavinia was her grandmother's name, who'd pitched a fit of outrage with the news of Elli being a girl, instead of a boy as everyone assumed. She demanded the child be named after her.

"Ready to get married," she finishes, a gleam in her eye I'd become well aquatinted with since entering her second trimester.

Holding my hand out for her, "Come on, beautiful. We don't want to be late for rehearsal."

Josh was able to pull several strings in getting the chapel Elli wanted for the entire day of the wedding. However, there was a ceremony tonight Elli refused to interfere with. A couple from Oklahoma, the bride had been diagnosed with inoperable cancer, the groom, home on leave from the military long enough to marry the woman before heading back. When I learned of the couple, I placed a call to Logan's dad. Weston arranged a second opinion for the woman if she so chose to do so.

A little over an hour later, I held her hand as we walk under the awning of the tent as a chorus of cheers rings out, echoing off the trees. Elli looks around the interior of the tent in awe, hugging my mother tight when we pass her, whispering something into her ear I will leave between them.

The buffet table is covered in cooked meats, a variety of prepared salads, and all the trimmings for a southern barbecue. It's rustic and casual and absolutely perfect for the occasion.

I selected my eldest brother, Cade, to be my best man, reserving my teammates for something special I planned for the beautiful girl beside me.

"Good evening everyone. For those of you who don't know me, my name is Danny Biggs. This is my wife, Hope, and we are the parents of the groom."

Applause breaks out, making it impossible for him to continue. My brother, Cooper, puts his fingers to his lips, producing his signature ear-numbing whistle.

"We'd like to take this opportunity to thank each of you for coming and celebrating with us on the eve of Ryan and Elliott's wedding. Being a father of six boys, over the years I've grown accustomed to the various giggling young ladies who would appear at our dinner table, believing she'd managed to corral whichever one of my sons she had beside her, only to be replaced by a new face the next week."

Cringing, I pull Elli close, "I should have warned you, my father has a horrible sense of humor."

Cupping my cheek with her hand, "It's okay, your mother told me." Unable to resist, I place a kiss to her lips, the clearing of a throat preventing me from going too far.

"But as I look at Ryan's face, I see myself at his age, completely and undeniably in love with the woman beside him. I must admit, when I was first introduced to Elliott, I wasn't certain she would fit into the rough group that is our family. But after she warmed up to us, I knew this was the woman for my son. Elli, in a few short hours, you will become a Biggs. We love you and can't wait to see what the future holds for you and Ryan." Holding his glass high in the air, "To Ryan and Elli."

My father crosses the room, leans over and places a kiss to Elli's cheek, whispering something in her ear which brings a tear to her eye. She waves me off when my possessive side kicks in, looking instead to the front of the tent where my team stands in a unified line.

"My name is Logan Forbes and I've had the honor to serve beside Ryan for the past several years. From the first jump out of the back of a cargo plane over dense jungle, Ryan has put this team's safety first, constantly looking and listening for any possible threats to us. While I can't share specific stories of missions, I can tell you the moment where I watched a miracle happen right before my very eyes. Many of you have seen the footage of Ryan and Elli as they exited the plane, delivering an injured Congressman to safety. The press showed Ryan as a hero, endangering his own life while ensuring Elli and Congressman Howard survived the plane crash and days in the desert with no resources. But I'm here to tell you, Ryan wasn't the hero that day...Elli was."

Logan reaches inside his dress pants, as he begins to cross the tent slowly.

"As a SEAL, Ryan has not only trained for survival in situations such as a plane crash, he's done it, as have each of us. Knowing how to find water and food in the middle of the desert is second nature to Ryan. And while most would argue he still deserves the label of hero, I'd beg to differ, because I know the real Ryan. The real man made of flesh and blood, with hopes and dreams, and fears and nightmares of the demons who take pride in reminding him of the decisions he's made in order to survive. And while Ryan did his job keeping them alive, it was Elli who gave selfishly of herself to save Ryan. She gave him hope when he had none, showed him joy when he couldn't laugh, gave him a vision of what life could be when he couldn't see. She gave him love when all he could feel was hate."

One by one my teammates follow Logan across the room, remaining in a singular line as he comes to stand before Elli.

"I've sewn hundreds of wounded men back together, but I've never made a single one of them as whole as you've made my friend." Logan's voice cracks as he places his trident on the table before her. Stepping to the side, Zach approaches.

"You led him out of the darkness." Laying his medal for bravery beside the trident, then steps behind Logan.

"Showed him forgiveness, when he didn't deserve it." Matt let one of his medals for marksmanship join the trident.

"Showed him a love he never knew." Aiden tosses his challenge coin to the table, spinning round and round beside the trident.

"Reminded him what the word family means." Alex laid his Purple Heart across the trident.

Standing from my chair, I reach into the pocket of my pants, removing the black box I'd been keeping for months. "For giving me a reason to trust again."

CHAPTER THIRTY-TWO

ELLI

L ight dances off the diamond dangling from the chain around my neck. Tears threaten in the background at the memory of how Ryan placed the box on the table, shifting my hair to the side as he placed the chain around my neck.

"Don't you do it, Elli." My eyes shift to Harper's reflection in the mirror, her eyes just as glassy as mine. "I cried enough last night to tied me over for a lifetime, today is a happy day."

Last night had indeed been a festival of emotions, leaving me both emotionally and physically drained, enabling me to slip off into a restful sleep despite not having Ryan beside me.

"She's right," Hope agrees, skimming her fingers over the fabric of my veil. "Today, I gain a daughter and we are one day closer to meeting my grandchildren."

Her mention of the twins has me looking at my stomach in the mirror. Surrendering to the notion Ryan is more than able to take care of me has not come easy. Conflicted between the under-standing of what the salary a member of the Secret Service makes and Ryan's ability to afford the luxuries surrounding him, has me questioning everything.

The devil is in the details, something my grandmother once said helped clear my mind and allow me to understand not everything is at it appears. Ryan's source of income isn't from his job with the government, but with the money he earns performing as part of the mercenary team.

Meredith didn't blink an eye when I said I wanted the wedding to take place in three months. She hired a dress designer, whose name I'd read about in the tabloids, who dropped everything and came to Ryan's condo the next day. We traveled three times to New York for fittings, each time Ryan showed me something new about the city, piquing my interest in the places he plans to take me on our honeymoon.

My dress is everything I envisioned. Delicate lace over lush satin, a full shirt, and long train, with a veil so thin it appears to glide behind me.

"Here," Kennedy grabbed my left hand, placing a penny in the center of my palm. "Your something borrowed. I had this in my shoe the day Zach and I were married, I found it on the ground when I was out riding. Zach and I weren't talking at the time, but it gave him an opportunity to approach me and work it out."

Clearing the emotion from my throat, "Thank you. I'll make sure I give it to you before we leave."

"It's okay, Elli. You're a part of us, we will see a lot of each other in the future."

"My turn, my turn," Harper shimmies between us, lifting my wrist and wrapping a gorgeous diamond bracelet around it. "Your Ryan is the mastermind behind placing trackers inside the everyday items of the men we love. Each of us, as those men chose to devote their lives to us, gave us a piece of jewelry he added a tracking device to. When we learned, he didn't give one to Lindsey, we knew his heart was still waiting for its perfect match...you."

My hand trembles as she fastens the clasp, a few sniffles echo behind me. "Please don't be mad, we asked him to do this. The icon you've worn since Afghanistan was given to him by Eleni and, while we love you to death, we want him to have it back so we can continue to know where he is if there's trouble."

Nodding my head in silent agreement. "I feel bad now, all I gave him was a dumb radio."

When Ryan moved us to Georgia, he arranged to have the contents of his storage unit in Montana transported. I was introduced to a new side of him, the geeky guy who enjoys fixing old radios. One night, I ventured out to the cabin he made his office to find him looking at a vintage radio on eBay that he'd been outbid on. After a lengthy search, I found another and purchased it for him. This morning when I woke up, I gave a photo of the radio to Danny to give to him when they were getting ready.

"Here is something blue," Eleni hands me what looked like an eye circled in dark blue. "It's called the all-seeing eye. Greeks believe it will ward off any evil spirits as you walk down the aisle."

The florist, who was standing to the side handing out bouquets, motions for Eleni to hand it to her. Taking it, she attaches it to the ribbon of my flowers.

"You have something new, so you need something old." Hope reaches up, taking the pearl earrings from her lobes. "These belonged to Ryan's grandmother. I wore them on my wedding day and I'd love it if you did as well."

"Are you sure?" The tears which I've held off until now won't surrender, flowing down my cheeks faster than the makeup artist Meredith hired can catch them.

"You're my only daughter, at least until Cooper gets over his heartbreak of you not having any sisters." We both laugh as she helps put the earrings in my ears, smoothing my veil back in place.

"It's time, Elli."

With a final dusting of powder from the makeup artist, the florist hands me my bouquet, the trident pin Logan gave me standing proudly in the center. Descending the stairs, it takes all hands to get my dress into the back of the SUV which would take us down the road to the chapel.

Memories hit me of being a young girl sitting in the back of a station wagon, the world around me going by in reverse. I assumed the church would look different, but as I stand here outside the doors, the opposite is true. I feel so tiny beneath the pine trees, just as I did all those years ago.

As I wait for the doors to open, I can't help but feel sad none of the guests inside will be a member of my family. I'd declined Danny's offer to walk me down the aisle, assuring him I would do fine walking alone. Even with everything my father has done, I can't help but miss him.

One by one, the girls disappear inside, I feel closest to Harper, so I asked her to stand with me. The other wives agreeing whole-heartedly with the choice.

"Ms. Elliott," Aiden stands with his elbow crooked in my direction, his black tux fitting him just right. "Are you ready?"

Confused, I take his offered arm as the doors open and the wedding march plays softly overhead. Everyone stands as I take my first step, finding Alex not ten feet in front of me.

As I approach, Alex extends his arm as Aiden hands me off, kissing me on the cheek before letting me go. Taking Alex's arm,

Aiden walks behind us as we grow closer to Logan, standing in a similar tuxedo to the other two.

Taking slow steps, I focus on every detail of the church; the wooden pews stained the color of good sweet tea, the lines of the church, the windows reaching high in the sky, allowing Mother Nature to show off her beauty.

Logan is next to extend his arm, allowing Alex to kiss me before taking over. When Logan steps to my side, I get my first glance at Ryan. My emotions hit me so hard I have to stop and catch my breath. He's always been the most handsome man I've ever seen, but now...I have no words.

When Ryan takes notice, he mouths the words he loves me, my body spurring into action. My feet carry me closer to the man I love and can't wait to rid him of the tux covering those delicious muscles of his.

Zach stands not five feet from the end of the aisle, his hands crossed in front of him, patiently waiting for me to arrive. He bows as Logan lifts my hand from his arm, taking my offered hand in his, "Ryan couldn't stand the thought of you doing this alone, so he asked the team to bring you to him." With a kiss to the back of my hand, Zach keeps our hands raised as the minister Meredith flew from New York, encourages the guests to take a seat.

"Who gives this woman to this man?"

"We do, Sir." Their collective voices echo off the metal rafters, sounding more like the military men they are and less like the position they fill.

Ryan hugs each man as they pass, each giving me one last kiss to the cheek before he takes my hand and leads me up the step to the altar.

The vows we exchange aren't original, spoken at least a million times by couples throughout the ages. But it doesn't matter, because the second I feel Ryan take my hand, everything disappears around me. His gentleness as he places the ring on my finger, helping me slide his over his knuckle when it got stuck and wiping the errant tear as I say I do.

"By the power vested in me, I now pronounce you husband and wife."

Ryan doesn't wait for the minister to finish, dipping me low and kissing me within an inch of my life. Picking me up bridal style and rushing back down the aisle, not stopping until we burst through the door where he kisses me hard once again.

Ryan suddenly pulls away, twisting our bodies as if protecting me from something.

"Bettie?"

"I'm sorry," the frail voice of my mother sounds. "I know I'm not welcome, but I had to see for myself my little girl is happy."

My mother stands at the edge of the woods, her Sunday hat securely in place, falling in line with the gray color of her suit. She was never allowed to wear anything bright or pretty, my father believing gray and black are the colors of a married woman.

"Mom, of course, you're welcome." Closing the distance between us, wrapping her tight in a hug. "How did you get here? Does Daddy know you're gone?"

Mom steps away, her arms falling to her sides as they always do. "He doesn't know I'm here. I took the money from selling your car and hid it in the chicken coop. A few days ago, I overheard him talking about your wedding and the money Mr. Biggs sent, telling your brother Ezekiel he could afford to buy a new tractor to plow the field. Yesterday, he got hurt real bad when the tractor backed over him. They have him in the same hospital as Ethan when he got hurt. He won't let me visit, so I took the money and came here instead."

Gripping her hand in mine, "I'm so glad you came. Please say you can stay for the reception?"

My mother glances around, and I can feel the tension in the grip of her fingers. "I don't know, Elliott. This isn't..."

"It's okay, Mrs. York, you have nothing to worry about. Besides, Elli's right, we're glad you're here."

Hope and Danny hold hands as they come out of the church, their joy-filled smiles drop slightly as they take in the sight of my mom.

"Mrs. York—"

"Please," Mom begins, her head dipped slightly. "Call me Bettie, we're family after all." She tries so hard to hold a smile, something my father discourages.

Ryan motions for his parents to join us. "Mom, Dad, this is Bettie York, Elli's mother. Bettie, these are my parents, Hope and Danny Biggs."

Danny slides an arm around Hope, extending the other to my mother. "Pleasure to meet you, Bettie. And may I say, what a beautiful woman you've raised. We couldn't be prouder of our son's choice in a wife."

I'm not sure how my father-in-law knew, but he'd managed to say the exact phrase that would set my mom at ease. Where my father believed, pride was a sin, my mother strived to be perfect in his eyes.

"Your son is a good man," Mom gestures toward Ryan. "Came and visited with my husband before he married my daughter. Fixed my radio while he did it."

Gasping, I turn to Ryan, the coy grin he has when he knows he did something right on his lips. "You fixed the radio in the dining room?"

Bending down, Ryan places a kiss to the shell of my ear, "I

wanted to make things right between us, and I needed your family to know how important you are to me."

Snuggling into him, the significance of what he's done is huge. The radio originally belonged to my maternal grandmother, who received it as a gift from my grandfather. When my parents were married, the radio was passed down to Mom. When it abruptly quit working one evening, I found her out in the garden, crying. When I asked what was wrong, she confessed the one and only time my father ever danced with her was while listening to music on that radio the day they were married.

"Would you like to ride with us to the reception? Give these kids a moment to themselves?" Hope has such a kindness about her, something my mom picks up as she silently agrees to follow them to their waiting car.

Ryan wastes no time in picking me up and tossing both of us into the back seat of the waiting SUV, my giggles silenced by his commanding lips. His tongue caresses mine, hands everywhere, labored breaths against the skin of my neck as he tells me how much he loves and wants me.

All too soon, we pull up to the reception hall, the car idling, but Ryan not seeming to care until Kennedy pounds on the window, demanding Ryan get off me so they can fix my bustle. Chastising him for keeping a pregnant woman waiting to eat.

"Ladies and gentlemen, it is my pleasure to introduce for the first time, Mr. and Mrs. Ryan Biggs. Put your hands together and make some noise."

Hope and Meredith spared no expense for this party, hiring both a DJ and a six-piece band to play through the night. The rustic feel of the rehearsal dinner was carried through, with chairs covered in burlap and the same flowers on the tables.

An enormous cake stands in the center of the dance floor as we walk in, our initials gracing the top of the multi-layered tiers. Ryan picks up the cake cutter from the small display table, twisting it around a few times in his hand before shaking his head, tossing it back to the table. Zach emerges from the crowd, a beautiful sword in his hands, which Ryan takes and slices through the cake with ease before handing the sword back to Zach. Feeding me the tiniest of bites from a fork, before allowing me to smash his piece on his chin and nose.

Once dinner is cleared away and the band begins to play, the DJ calls us up to have our first dance as a married couple. However, Ryan being the incredible man he is, leads me to the edge of the dance floor where his team stands, handing me to Zach before crossing the room to where my mother sits between Hope and Meredith. Holding out his hand to her, my mother rises to her feet as Ryan glides her around the dance floor, the smile on her face something I haven't seen in years.

After a few turns around the floor, Cooper stands up, tapping Ryan on the shoulder before asking to cut in.

Ryan makes his way to me, spinning me around as if he's danced his whole life, handing me off to Zach once the song was over. One by one, I dance with each member of the team, every one of them telling me how they love me for bringing Ryan back and for making him the happy guy they knew from when they first met him.

Several hours into the night, the daughter of the minister Meredith flew in for the ceremony, asks Ryan to dance with her. As I stand on the edge of the dance floor, a glass of water in hand, Harper and the other wives surround me.

"Makes your ovaries want to combust, huh?" Kennedy points at Ryan and the little girl. He is practically bent in half so he can hold her the way she wanted, the smile on her face worth it all.

"They were toast the first time I saw him," I admit no longer caring if people heard me speak of such intimate things.

"They broke the mold when they made our guys," Eleni admits as she clinks her glass to mine.

"Which is a tragedy, as the world needs more alpha men like ours," I add, knowing how safe I feel with him by my side.

"You got that right. Ain't nothing in the world like being fucked hard against a wall, and by a man who knows how." Harper tucks her bottom lip between her teeth, her eyes locked on her husband talking with Ryan's dad across the way.

When the song ends, Ryan bows to the little girl, causing her to laugh, and then run off to her father. His eyes immediately find mine, crossing the floor in several deliberate strides. His gaze intense, creating a fire in my core.

"Are you ready to get out of here?"

"Will this be a smooth departure or should I pay attention to the safety briefing?"

"You might want to buckle in, Baby. This is about to be one hell of a ride."

EPILOGUE

FIVE MONTHS LATER...

I don't think I will ever grow tired of watching my wife sleep. *Wife...*

It's still incredible to me how a woman like Elli chose me, out of all the available men in the world to share her life with. So much has happened since the day we stood before our friends and family, promising to love and honor one another. Kennedy gave birth to a boy, Keegan. He's the spitting image of Zach, down to a birthmark on the back of his shoulder.

Not long after Keegan was born, Kennedy received a call her boss and mentor in Colorado had passed away in her sleep, leaving the rehab center to her in her will. Zach contacted me to see if it was something I would consider undertaking with my history of raising horses. While I have no desire to uproot and move to Colorado, my brother Cade did. He's running the center for now but has an option to buy if he chooses at the end of the year.

Harper and Logan have a boy as well, Grayson, and are ready to try for number two. Since Grayson's birth, Logan has been training hard for a fitness competition. We've all been giving him encouragement, although our wives beg to differ, labeling it as down-right hatefulness.

Aiden and Jordan have discussed marriage, but Jordan is of the belief it is just a piece of paper. She's perfectly content to remain the way they are, but Aiden is still working on her. His argument is if it's just a piece of paper, then sign it and take his name. I won't be surprised when the call comes in she has relented. Jordan loves Aiden as much as Elli loves me, willing to do anything to make the other happy.

Barely a month ago, word came through Roe was spotted in West Virginia, working on a prison detail picking up trash along the highway. Aiden did some digging, and sure enough, Monroe Parsons was convicted of aggravated assault on a police officer, sentenced to five years in a state correctional facility. There's been no word about Corey, it's as if he's disappeared into thin air. I have a suspicion, Angel may have collected a debt, but only time will tell.

While there are no children on the horizon for Alex and Eleni, her parents announced their retirement and are handing the business over to her. Eleni is actively looking for a seasoned accountant to join her but hasn't found anyone who meets her criteria.

Alex's parents remodeled the area above the restaurant, turning it into three apartments they rent out for extra income. Christos finally came clean about his involvement with Stavros, but they refuse to sell the diner, believing in having a backup plan for their children. Nick has moved up in the rank with Stavros, he's now part of his inner circle.

Stavros officially declared war on Abernathy after proving his involvement with the Romanians and theft of his guns and the drugs Aaron was pushing through the strip club.

Velvet Touch remains closed. A forensic accountant linked Green as the financial backer and tied him to the container ship full of the kidnapped women Aaron sold to him. Green was sentenced a few months ago for the murder of Selena Ramirez. His attorney is appealing the ruling, but with positive DNA and her blood and skin tissue found in his ring, it doesn't look good. Not that it will matter, as he still has to stand trial for conspiring with a known terrorist.

Steele's daughter, Catarina, gave compelling testimony against Green and Vale, making the prosecution regret making a deal with Vale.

Judson is still in jail, charged with multiple counts of conspiracy to deceive the government, and facilitating a crime due to his role in Elli's attack.

CNN hired Sonia Marsh as Lindsey's replacement. Her style is different and well received by the viewing public, no more tits hanging out, just an honest face and news from around the globe.

The couple who purchased my condo called me not long after Elli and I got back from our honeymoon. They found a box I'd left in a closet and wanted to know if I needed it or not. Elli had a craving for the Irish restaurant not far from the condo, so we jumped on a plane and headed to DC. The next morning, I was out running, when I passed by a chain coffee shop. Thinking my new wife might enjoy a hot chocolate, I reached for the door handle, only to come up short as I noticed Lindsey working behind the counter. I'd followed her arrest and subsequent conviction for aggravated assault, earning her three years probation and community service. Gone were her layers of makeup and perfect hair, in their place, were dark circles under her eyes and the signature ball cap the rest of her co-workers wore atop her head. The blonde hair she spent thousands to maintain, brassy and showing her dark roots. I turned away from the door and headed back to the hotel, to my wife and my future.

Elli and her mother have re-established communication. They speak on the phone when Bettie goes to church for her lady's meetings, keeping a cellphone Elli gave her tucked away in a locked cabinet away from prying eyes. Wesley and Norma Jean lasted two months before she found him with her sister Lottie in a back bedroom of the trailer she bought for him.

Elli's father recovered from his accident, none the wiser to his wife attending our wedding. Logan and Zach made sure she arrived back at her home safely, the radio I'd fixed for her playing softly in the background. Ironically, after he left the hospital, I received a call from him, admitting he'd used the money I sent to purchase a new tractor. Due to the accident, he felt it was god way of punishing him for stealing and has been working hard to gain repentance and play an active role in his daughter's life.

As for Elli, I made sure she had at least five pins on the map she'd hung in the lower level of the cabin. We spend the first two months of our married life traveling between London, Rome, Scotland, Ireland and Greece. She worried I would be bored as I'd seen those cities previously. I assured her it wouldn't be a problem, as this was the first time I was seeing them with her. We walked and talked, discovering the rich culture of each city we visited. I loved her late into each night and she woke me just the same each morning.

The biggest, and perhaps most overwhelming, change is the two babies sleeping in my arms. Elli woke me early yesterday morning when her water broke in our bed. After a frantic two-hour drive to Atlanta, followed by sixteen grueling hours of labor, Ashton and Parker Biggs were born.

Elli was adamant on not having matching names, nothing even

close to the names she and I had. She wanted our children to discover their individuality, grow in the knowledge they were the most important things in our lives, and live every day knowing how much they are loved.

I couldn't agree more and as I look at their tiny faces, I can't wait to teach them how to fix things, ride a bike, write a computer program, and share them with the incredible extended family who is waiting not-so-patiently in the visitor's room.

What began as a mission to take down a mad-man, turned the lives of six men into something worth fighting for.

Zach got his dream of owning a tattoo shop.

Logan kept his promise to a dying man.

Matt found forgiveness.

Aiden learned age is just a number.

Alex found the meaning of commitment.

And I was the luckiest of them all. Not only did I learn to trust again, I also got the honor of being a father and husband. The greatest gift I could ever hope for.

The End.

OTHER BOOKS IN THIS SERIES

TRIDENT BROTHERHOOD

Signed, SEALed, Delivered

Operation SEAL

A SEAL's Regret

SEAL the Deal

A SEAL's Heart

A SEAL's Honor

CODE OF SILENCE SERIES

THE BAD BOYS OF THE MAFIA.

Shamrocks & Secrets

Claddagh & Chaos

Stolen Secrets

Secret Sin

Secret Atonement

Buried Secrets Coming Fall 2019

Secrets & Lies Coming Winter 2019

SOUTHERN JUSTICE TRILOGY

WHEN THE GOOD GUYS FOLLOW THE BAD
BOYS RULES. KU EXCLUSIVE.

Absolute Power

Absolute Corruption

Absolute Valor

STICKY-SWEET ROMANCE

Crain's Landing

JUSTICE

REVENGE REALLY IS BEST SERVED COLD.

Justice

ABOUT THE AUTHOR

Cayce Poponea is the bestselling author of Absolute Power.

A true romantic at heart, she writes the type of fiction she loves to read. With strong female characters who are not easily swayed by the devilishly good looks and charisma of the male leads. All served with a twist you may never see coming. While Cayce believes falling in love is a hearts desire, she also feels men should capture our souls as well as turn our heads.

From the Mafia men who take charge, to the military men who are there to save the damsel in distress, her characters capture your heart and imagination. She encourages you to place your real life on hold and escape to a world where the laundry is all done, the bills are all paid and the men are a perfect as you allow them to be.

Cayce lives her own love story in Georgia with her husband of eighteen years and her three dogs. Leave your cares behind and settle in with the stories she creates just for you.

CPSIA information can be obtained
at www.ICGtesting.com
Printed in the USA
BVHW032114291019
562449BV00001B/31/P